CW00481200

THE WINTER WAIF

LYNETTE REES

Boldwood

First published in Great Britain in 2023 by Boldwood Books Ltd.

Copyright © Lynette Rees, 2023

Cover Design by Colin Thomas

Cover Photography: Colin Thomas

The moral right of Lynette Rees to be identified as the author of this work has been asserted in accordance with the Copyright, Designs and Patents Act 1988.

All rights reserved. No part of this book may be reproduced in any form or by any electronic or mechanical means, including information storage and retrieval systems, without written permission from the author, except for the use of brief quotations in a book review.

This book is a work of fiction and, except in the case of historical fact, any resemblance to actual persons, living or dead, is purely coincidental.

Every effort has been made to obtain the necessary permissions with reference to copyright material, both illustrative and quoted. We apologise for any omissions in this respect and will be pleased to make the appropriate acknowledgements in any future edition.

A CIP catalogue record for this book is available from the British Library.

Paperback ISBN 978-1-80549-013-5

Large Print ISBN978-1-83751-998-9

Hardback ISBN 978-1-83751-997-2

Ebook ISBN 978-1-83751-995-8

Kindle ISBN 978-1-83751-996-5

Audio CD ISBN 978-1-80549-010-4

MP3 CD ISBN 978-1-80549-011-1

Digital audio download ISBN 978-1-83751-993-4

Boldwood Books Ltd
23 Bowerdean Street
London SW6 3TN
www.boldwoodbooks.com

For Leyna and Nathan. You've been with me over the years on my writing journey. I'm so proud of the adults you've both become. Love as always.

PART I

1

MERTHYR TYDFIL, SOUTH WALES, 1884

From the corner of the living room, twelve-year-old Betsan Morgan watched her mam working away on her sewing machine. The whirring of the machine and Mam's rhythmic tapping of her foot on the treadle as she fed the material through were a comfort to her. The jabbering of the needle as it moved up and down was quite mesmerising at times.

Betsan made a little sketch with her notepad and pencil of the partially finished gown her mother was creating, which was displayed on a wooden mannequin against the wall. Mam had made such a fine job of it so far. It was being created for a schoolmistress called Cynthia Eastwood who lived in a large house in the Pontmorlais area of the town. Whenever Mam created a new garment, Betsan enjoyed sketching it to keep as a memento of her mother's handiwork.

This particular dress had a fine vertical blue stripe running through its white heavy cotton, and soon it would have a lace insert added to the bodice, collar and cuffs.

The whirring ceased for a moment and Mam turned around

in her chair. 'Will you please pass me a piece of that lace from my work basket, *cariad*?'

Betsan nodded, laying down her pencil and notebook, immediately knowing which piece of lace her mother meant. It was Belgian and she'd purchased it from a stall at Merthyr Market just last week. People came from far and wide to their modest home in Plymouth Street for her mother to make garments for them. Sometimes it was several girls' petticoats she needed to run up or a man's work shirt, usually items her mother could complete quite quickly, though on occasions she had made a bridal gown, a party dress or a day gown like she was making today. Often, people arrived at the house with clothes that needed repairing that they couldn't afford to throw away, so it wasn't unusual for customers to stay and wait while she hemmed a pair of trousers or shortened a skirt.

Earlier, a lady from Abercanaid had arrived and Betsan was despatched to make a cup of tea for her while they waited until Mam had finished taking up the sleeves on a jacket for her. The kettle was on the hob all day long at home and Betsan liked that. She'd often perch on a little stool in the corner of the room listening to the adults gossiping away, though sometimes she hardly understood what they meant.

'Have you heard about Mrs Prosser from down the road?' one such customer had said to her mother recently.

'No?' Mam had said, shaking her head.

'She's having trouble with you-know-who.' The woman had pursed her lips and crossed her hands one over the other in a disapproving fashion. Her mother had nodded sympathetically. Mam wasn't one for gossip. She'd listen all right but she wasn't the sort who would spread malicious tales around the area.

Betsan scrabbled about in her mother's wicker work basket

until she located the beautiful white Belgian lace, which was wound around a small piece of card, and she handed it to her.

Her mother smiled. 'Once I've done this, we'll have some tea and crumpets, shall we?'

Betsan nodded eagerly. She loved these times with her mother. Her three-year-old twin siblings, Aled and Alys, were being cared for next door by a good friend and neighbour to them all, the elderly Bronwen Jenkins. Dad was at work at the Star Inn again. He worked all hours there: if he wasn't manning the bar or dealing with unruly customers then he was supervising deliveries of barrels of ale or helping to clean up the place ready for opening time. Though that establishment hardly ever seemed to close. She'd been in there a couple of times and the strong smell of beer fumes and smoke made her feel like throwing up, though she guessed Dad was used to it.

The sewing machine sprang into action again and it wasn't a minute or two before her mam coughed. One of her 'winter coughs' she'd called it, but she seemed to be coughing more than usual today.

A knock on the living room door caused them to turn their heads. It was Bronwen Jenkins. Her salt-and-pepper-coloured hair was visible as she peered around the doorway before she simply walked in, as she was prone to do.

'Hello, both,' she said in her strong West Walian accent. 'I've just left the twins with Bert a moment, as I wondered if...' She didn't get to finish what she was saying as Mam interrupted with another cough. Bronwen stared at her. 'Gwendolyn, now there's a nasty cough you have there.'

Mam nodded. 'Oh, I'll be all right.'

'Why don't you get yourself off to bed for a spell? I can mind the children a little while longer. Betsan can come next door as well.'

Mam shook her head and smiled weakly. 'If only I were able to – the rest would do me good – but I have a gown that needs completing today.'

'I wish I could help you with that.' Mrs Jenkins chuckled. 'I'm that cack-handed though I'd mess it up for you. Always had fingers like sausages!' She winked at Betsan, who smiled in amusement as the woman wriggled her fingers.

'Thank you. I appreciate the thought.'

'I'll tell you what, I'll pop back next door to fetch that bottle of cough medicine I had from Doctor Llewellyn last month when Bert was ill. That'll do the trick for you. There's enough left in the bottle until you can buy some yourself.' Betsan's mother nodded gratefully. 'And I'll stop for a few minutes to brew up some tea.'

'We were going to toast some crumpets on the fork in front of the fire,' said Betsan, hoping her mother hadn't forgotten that.

'Well, if that's what you want to do then I shall help you.' Mrs Jenkins smiled and then she turned and left the room, closing the door behind her to keep the heat in.

'Isn't that kind of her?' said Mam, looking at Betsan. 'I really need to get back to my work now but it will be a help if Mrs Jenkins brews up and toasts those crumpets for us.'

Betsan stared hard at her mother. She really didn't look at all well this morning and Betsan wondered if her father realised just how sick she was becoming lately.

Mam placed the flat of her hand on her chest and coughed again. Without even being told to do so, Betsan lifted the metal tongs from the fireplace and placed an extra couple of lumps of coal from the brass scuttle onto the fire. It was the least she could do. She felt a sense of relief when Mrs Jenkins returned with a brown bottle of medicine, the cork making a plopping sound as she opened it to pour a spoonful for her mother. That should make her mam better, surely?

By teatime, when her father was due home from work for a couple of hours before his evening shift, Betsan had expected her mother to be a little better, but in fact, her condition had worsened. Thankfully, she'd managed to complete the day gown for Miss Eastwood who'd arrived to collect it. Pleased with the result, she'd paid what was owed and went on her way. Hadn't she even noticed how pale Mam looked? The woman must have had other things on her mind as she seemed in a rush and had left shortly afterwards.

The oil lamp was lit on the windowsill while her mother lay on the couch beneath. The lamp reflected a yellowy glow, which highlighted the gaunt shadows beneath her mother's eyes. Mam hadn't managed to complete all her work after all, as there were some petticoats she'd promised to a customer. She'd instructed Betsan to send any callers around to Bronwen's house where their neighbour would explain what had happened and tell them that when Gwendolyn was better in a day or two, the work would be completed.

When Dad returned home, he walked into the living room as he always did, usually with something cheerful to say to them all, but Betsan realised there was something up when the twins were kept next door instead of returning home.

'What's going on here?' he asked, blinking, his large dark eyes looking full of concern.

'Mam's not been at all well today...' Betsan shook her head sadly.

'Oh, Gwen, what's the matter, my sweet?' He was now on his

knees at his wife's side, where she still lay reclining on the sofa, her eyes closing. She seemed unable to keep them open even for Betsan's father.

He held her hand and touched her brow.

'Fetch a cold, wet flannel!' He looked at Betsan. 'She's burning up. Your mother's got some sort of fever.'

Betsan did as told. She couldn't find the flannel her mam used to wipe the twins' faces so she dipped a spare tray cloth in a bowl of water, rinsed it out and passed it to her father, who proceeded to gently wipe her mother's brow. Frowning, he looked at Betsan.

'Now listen carefully,' he said with some concern. 'I need to fetch the doctor. Stay with your mother and try to keep her awake. If that cloth gets warm then soak it in cold water again and put it straight back on her forehead. Do you understand me?'

Betsan nodded. Suddenly everything seemed so urgent. Why hadn't Mrs Jenkins's cough medicine worked? The woman had assured Mam that it would. It had done the trick for Mr Jenkins when he had a cough. She chewed on her bottom lip, worrying whether she ought to tell her father about it just in case.

Swallowing, she said, 'Mrs Jenkins gave Mam some cough medicine this morning. Might that have caused this?'

Smiling, but with tears in his eyes that he blinked away, Dad ruffled her hair. 'No, poppet. I know the medicine you mean. Bert was taking it – is that the one?'

'Yes.'

'It's just a normal cough medicine that wouldn't harm her. At any rate, it might make Mam a little drowsy but to be truthful with you, she hasn't been right for days now. Be a big girl and look after your mam while I'm gone. I won't be long. Doctor

Llewellyn should have finished his surgery by now – with any luck I can persuade him to come to the house.'

During the time her father was gone in search of the doctor, Betsan's heart raced as she tried to keep her mam awake.

'Come on, Mam,' she urged as she wiped her mother's brow. 'Please wake up. We need you.'

Her mother stirred and said something unintelligible that sounded like: 'Tell them I'm coming soon...' but she couldn't be quite sure that was what she'd said at all. Should she run next door and get Mrs Jenkins? She'd know what to do but then maybe her father would be cross with her for leaving Mam alone.

Still undecided about what to do next, she heard the front door open and voices advancing along the passageway until she saw her father emerge through the living room door with Doctor Llewellyn shadowing him.

'She's over here, doctor,' her father was saying, his eyes large and fearful. 'She won't seem to come around...'

'Here, let me see.' The doctor removed his top hat and cape, which he placed on the table, and then he was kneeling at her mother's side. Betsan watched him touch her brow and then he asked her father to loosen his wife's clothing so he might examine her. Glancing at Betsan, then back at her father, he added, 'Perhaps it might be best to send the girl out of the room?'

Her father nodded and, laying a gentle hand on her shoulder, he whispered, 'Go in next door to Mrs Jenkins. You can return later when the doctor has gone. Try not to worry too much.'

Betsan felt rooted to the spot, unable to say anything, but instead she nodded and reluctantly left.

'Whatever's the matter, dear?' Mrs Jenkins asked when she

arrived. 'You look like you've seen a bloomin' ghost or something.'

'It's Mam. The doctor's with her now. Dad had to go out and fetch him.'

Glancing at the twins who were seated at the table eating a bowl of cawl each – a lamb stew – Mrs Jenkins said, 'Keep an eye on your brother and sister.'

Betsan watched as Mrs Jenkins drew back the curtain to peer out. It was dark outside save for the golden glow of a street lamp at the end of the road.

'Aye, I can see the doctor's carriage outside. Now don't fret, I'll go around while you stay here.'

While Mrs Jenkins left the house, Betsan sat with her brother and sister. Aled looked up at her and smiled. He had a runny nose and he wiped it on the back of his shirtsleeve.

'Mam's always telling you not to do that!' Betsan chided but then she smiled, as her brother and sister had no idea what on earth was going on and she didn't want to worry them.

'Me finished soup,' said Alys. 'Want to play now.'

'No, both of you stay by the table in case Mrs Jenkins wants you to eat something else.'

Betsan scanned the room and she wondered for a moment where Mr Jenkins was, then she recalled he was on night shifts this week at the pit. He worked at the Gethin Pit in Abercanaid run by the Crawshay family. The Crawshays also ran the iron-works at Cyfarthfa, which lit up the skies at night. One thing about living in Merthyr: the people had to work hard for a living and often at dangerous occupations.

It seemed an age until Mrs Jenkins returned and when she did she had a concerned look on her face.

'Tell me now then, Betsan,' she said in barely a whisper, 'your mother's sister – your Aunt Maggie – where is she these days? I know she and your mam were very close but I don't see her any more.'

'No, she doesn't call at our house any longer. I heard Mam and Dad say something about her "hitting the bottle" but I don't understand what that meant.'

Mrs Jenkins huffed out a little breath. 'Aw, maybe your father will explain it to you one day. I know what it means but it's not my place to explain what's happened to your aunt. So I'm guessing she's not likely to call to see your mother now, then?'

Why did Mrs Jenkins make it sound as if it was important for Aunt Maggie to call to the house to see Mam?

'Is Mam all right, Mrs Jenkins? What has the doctor said?'

'Well, he said she needs some rest and he's giving her some strong medicine. Your father is going to carry her to their bedroom. Now, this pair' – she smiled at the twins – 'will be all right here until your mam gets better, so when the doctor leaves, go back next door, as I'm sure your father would appreciate some company.' Betsan nodded. 'Meanwhile, I was just about to give the twins some sponge pudding and custard. Would you like some, Betsan?'

The twins remained seated at the table with big, bright eyes, spoons still in hand.

Betsan shook her head, realising she couldn't eat at a time like this – at least not until she'd spoken to her father.

'No thank you, Mrs Jenkins,' she said in barely a whisper.

'I guess you're not hungry then.' Mrs Jenkins had a note of sympathy to her voice. 'I'll send some around for you and your father later when this pair are snuggled up in bed.' She moved over to the window and peered out from behind the curtain again. 'The doctor's carriage is just leaving. You return next door now, Betsan. Be a big, brave girl for your father.'

With a lump in her throat, Betsan walked towards the door.

A nervous, swirling sensation gripped her stomach, which she'd only ever remembered happening once before and that's when she'd been told Aunt Maggie wouldn't be calling to their house any longer.

* * *

Betsan's father had to return to the Star Inn for his shift and so, somehow, between them, Betsan and Bronwen cared for her mother and the twins. It wasn't an easy task and, although initially Gwendolyn appeared to make some improvement, gradually as the days wore on her condition deteriorated and the doctor was summoned once again. By now she had begun to cough up blood.

That night after the twins had been put to bed, Betsan's father sat her down to explain something to her.

'Betsan,' he said softly. 'Doctor Llewellyn has said your mother's condition will not improve and soon she will go to join the other angels in heaven.'

Betsan's eyes filled with tears and she blinked and took a deep breath. She had no intention of breaking down in front of her father. Somehow, something wouldn't allow her to lose control and cry. She had to be strong for everyone right now, particularly Mam.

'Does that mean Mam will be with Grandma Jones in heaven?'

'Yes,' said her father stoically. 'Grandma and Grandpa Jones will be waiting for their precious daughter to join them again.'

'That's all right then.' Betsan sniffed and then she turned her head away from her father to compose herself. When she turned back to face him, he had tears in his eyes too.

Two days later, Gwendolyn Morgan passed away in her own

bed at home and what a sad day that was. Doctor Llewellyn had been summoned to pronounce her mother dead. She'd been sent out of the bedroom at that point but when he'd appeared on the landing with his stethoscope strung around his neck and he'd nodded grimly at her father, she just knew.

For the following few days, all the curtains were drawn. Bronwen Jenkins lit candles in the bedroom and there was a small stream of folk coming back and forth to the house to pay their condolences, some of whom Betsan recognised as customers and neighbours. The callers were dressed in black, including Mrs Jenkins. No one asked Betsan or Aled and Alys to wear black, but Betsan felt like she should. She had a dark grey serviceable dress so she chose to wear that.

It was almost as though the lifeblood had disappeared from the house and, when everyone finally departed, Betsan found herself staring at her mother's sewing machine, now silent in the corner.

2

The day of the funeral was miserable, dark and dismal. Gunmetal-grey storm clouds had gathered overhead and threatened to burst at any moment. Betsan had wanted to go to the cemetery to her mother's graveside for the burial but Mrs Jenkins had insisted that it wasn't the done thing. The women in the Welsh valleys attended services either at home or at church but they did not attend burials at the graveside itself. It was more commonplace to remain at home and prepare food for the return of the menfolk. Betsan didn't agree with this. She'd once attended a neighbour's funeral where she helped to prepare the food at the house and, as the women waited and waited for the men to return, the clock had ticked away. They'd all sat there looking at one another until finally, Mrs Owen – sister of the widow – had declared, 'Well, that's it then. They've obviously gone on to the pub instead!'

Betsan had been mortified for those women – all the trouble they'd gone to. In the event, some of the more elderly men had returned, the ones who weren't used to frequenting pubs as they were very religious sorts. The others turned up later worse for wear. Betsan wished they hadn't returned at all as they'd made right shows of themselves, speaking in loud voices, and one of them kept hiccupping and asking if there was any whisky in the house, while another dropped a plate of sandwiches.

Oh no, she didn't want that sort at her mother's funeral, so she'd told her father about her fears. He'd just smiled, laid a hand on her shoulder and said, 'I'm used to dealing with that sort at the Star Inn. They won't mess with me! And if they turn up here inebriated, then I shall shut the door in their faces. Please do not concern yourself, Betsan. It shan't be a problem.'

Her father was big and strong, and he made her feel protected. What he said went, so she knew he'd keep them all safe but she didn't understand what he meant by the word *inebriated*. She decided to ask Mrs Jenkins later – that's if she still remembered it by then.

After dressing the twins in their Sunday best, she stared out of the window, noticing a few drops of rain on the glass pane. It was raining after all, and as her mam's coffin was to be transported to the cemetery on the back of the horse and cart her father had paid for, she worried about it getting wet. How she'd have liked it if her father could have afforded one of those fancy horse-drawn funeral carriages where the horses wore blinkers and black feathered plumes. Sometimes they had a young boy in a top hat walking behind them. The one she'd seen was a nice-looking blonde lad with an angelic face. She didn't know if she could do that job though; it seemed so upsetting to her.

'Come on now, Betsan,' said Mrs Jenkins from behind her. 'I'm taking this pair to Gladys Williams's house down the road. They'll be all right there for a couple of hours. A funeral is no place for children as young as this. Then I want you to help me prepare the food.'

Betsan nodded. A rivulet of rain trickled down the window-pane and she turned to face Mrs Jenkins.

'What does the word *inerietated* mean?' She wrinkled her nose.

Mrs Jenkins frowned for a moment. 'Pardon?' Then she smiled as recognition dawned. 'Do you mean the word *inebriated*, Betsan?'

Betsan nodded enthusiastically. 'Yes, that's the word I meant.'

'Well, it means drunk. Why do you ask?'

'I was worried in case any of the men turn up drunk here after the funeral and Dad used that word.'

'Likely he thought he was talking to a little adult for a while there, Betsan. You are so grown up of late, I expect he forgot that there are words you don't understand.'

Betsan glanced at the ceiling in thought. 'Is that what Mam and Dad meant about Aunt Maggie hitting the bottle? That she was drunk?'

Mrs Jenkins nodded as she let out a little sigh. 'Yes. I think you're old enough to be told if you're old enough to be asking questions. I know it's not my place really – as I said before to you – but yes, Aunt Maggie was sent away from here by your father as she was turning up drunk in the small hours and upsetting your mother. He only told me that yesterday as he feels so remorseful: he can't find her now to attend her own sister's funeral.'

'She lives in that place called China.' Betsan blinked. 'It's not far away! I don't even understand why it's called that and I don't like the name.'

'Your father is aware of where she lives, Betsan. Some people think the area's named China because years ago it was ruled over by a man who was a bully. He terrorised the people who lived there and was given the nickname 'The Emperor of China'.

Though there are others who say it got its name due to the numerous tea shops set up in the area. A lot of tea comes from China. Who knows? Whichever is true, the name has well and truly stuck over the years and it's an area that most ordinary folk fear to tread. Even the police are wary of it.'

'But why's that?'

'It's full of pickpockets and women who, how shall I say, well, they're not nice women like me or your mother was.'

'How?' Betsan placed her index finger on her chin and pursed her lips in puzzlement.

'My, my, you do ask a lot of questions for a young lady!' Mrs Jenkins tutted in an amusing fashion as she shook her head. Betsan knew she wasn't being scornful or anything – the woman was just teasing her. Mrs Jenkins paused for a moment, then carried on, 'Well, the women there, not all of them of course, but there is a certain sort who sell themselves to men. They dress up in gaudy, gay frocks that no self-respecting woman would choose to wear, put thick rouge on their cheeks and lips, and they wear cheap perfume. You can tell them a mile off.'

Betsan still didn't really understand. Selling themselves to men? What on earth for? But she didn't push Mrs Jenkins any further as the woman wanted to crack on with preparing the food, so instead she said, 'So, Dad didn't find Aunt Maggie?'

'No, my love. Would you have liked her to be here today?'

Without hesitation, Betsan nodded. 'Yes, I would, even if she was *ineriated*, I mean inebriated. She wouldn't be as bad as any of the men, I'm sure.'

'You might have a good point there, *cariad*. Now if you take the twins to Gladys Williams's house I can crack on here – there's a good girl. Don't dawdle there, mind. Likely she'll want to keep you talking. She's a nosy old trout!'

Despite feeling upset, Betsan was amused and she stifled a

giggle as Mrs Jenkins carried on.

'She'll want to know the ins and outs of a duck's backside, that one!'

Betsan covered the twins in a shawl each and then she chose her best one to wear for when she'd be taking them to Mrs Williams's house, which was just down the road a few houses away. When she reached her front door, remembering what Mrs Jenkins had said, she quickly explained that she'd have to return as soon as possible to help prepare the food.

Surprisingly, the woman didn't try to keep her there so she pecked her brother and sister on the cheeks and told them to be good and she'd return later for them.

Back at the house, Mrs Jenkins had sliced a couple of fruit loaves.

'They were all right when you left them with her?'

Betsan nodded.

'Good, good. Now wash your hands and get a pinny on and butter those slices. Most people like their *bara brith* with a bit of butter on and your father has bought some nice salted butter from the market. Leave some slices unbuttered though, just in case. I'll put the kettle on to boil as there's to be a short service at the house first. There'll be another longer one at the chapel later for the men.'

Betsan thought it all very convenient that in the guise of going to a chapel service, the men could get away with slipping to the pub. It was a man's world all right – her mam had always told her that, but in her father's defence, he did put his wife and family first when he was able to.

Mrs Jenkins was just wiping her hands on a towel when there was a knock on the front door. Betsan heard her father's footsteps as he walked through the passageway and then she heard the voice of the Reverend Mr Glanmor Griffiths. He amused her a lot as his accent was more Welsh than most and occasionally, being a Welsh speaker, he spoke a hybrid of both languages. He also had a very loud, booming voice – which she guessed was because he preached from the pulpit every Sunday.

'Sad to be here on this solemn occasion...' she heard him say as he stepped into the house. 'The Lord gives and the Lord takes away. Save us o Lord our God... *Achub ni, O Arglwydd ein Duw...*'

David Morgan opened the living room door to allow the man access. 'Mr Griffiths is here!' he announced.

Glanmor Griffiths removed his top hat and nodded his head at them. Then he stepped towards Betsan and, laying a hand on her shoulder, said, 'How are you bearing up, my dear child?'

'I'm all right thank you, Mr Griffiths.' Betsan was wary of the man. He preached fire and brimstone from the pulpit in chapel, although her father maintained that his bark was worse than his bite. He, too, had known him since he was a child.

'Good to hear, dear girl. *Da iawn*. It would be a very poor day if you and your family did not have the great faith in God you all have, as there are many heathens in this town who have fallen under the influence of Beelzebub! They drink alcohol until it is coming out of their ears!'

As if sensing Mr Griffiths was about to go off on a long rant, David Morgan directed him into the scullery. 'Take a seat here, Mr Griffiths, and Bronwen shall pour you a cup of tea. You're quite early so there's plenty of time before they all arrive.'

It was a good quarter of an hour before people started to arrive. The funeral director's horse and cart waited outside. At the end of the service at the house, it would transport the coffin to the chapel, which was only a couple of streets away.

While Mr Griffiths was taking his second cup of tea, Bronwen Jenkins whispered to Betsan, 'Pay no heed to him. As you know, he's all fire and brimstone and as loud as loud can be.

I think maybe he's partially deaf; he's getting on in years. I don't think he realises he scares the life out of most folk.'

'I don't know who he meant by the Beelze something or other,' Betsan said.

'Beelzebub?'

'Yes.'

'That's the Devil himself – just another word.'

'Oh, I thought he meant a man from Merthyr.'

Mrs Jenkins chuckled. 'Well, he probably visits Merthyr people quite a lot, *cariad*!'

So that's who the man had meant! Why hadn't he just said so?

'Shall I butter this bread now?' she asked as she eyed up the fresh plates of bread Mrs Jenkins had just sliced. The woman was a dab hand at slicing thinly without it falling apart even though she reckoned she had sausage fingers.

'Yes, thank you. But first could you ask if anyone would like a cup of tea before the service begins?'

Betsan nodded and did as she was told. There were now quite a few people her father had let in through the front door and she noticed some more, whom she recognised as neighbours, standing outside in the street. At least it had stopped raining for a while.

Then she saw it: the funeral director's cart. Her stomach flipped over to think her mam was inside that coffin. It had been in the parlour for a few days as people had called to the house as a mark of respect but it had been removed last night and taken to what the funeral director called 'The Chapel of Rest'. Her father had explained this was because it would give them more room at home for the short service.

'Well, hello there, Betsan!' a soft feminine voice said.

She glanced across to the open living room door, seeing her Aunt Eira enter. Aunt Eira was her father's elder sister and had been a tower of strength to him. She was accompanied by her husband, Uncle Wyn, a quiet and diminutive man who always appeared to be in his wife's shadow. Mam had said they were like chalk and cheese.

'Hello,' Betsan greeted.

'Come here, *cariad*.'

The woman hugged her tightly to her bosom and she could feel her soft, powdery cheek against her own – slightly wet, but Betsan didn't know whether the woman had shed a tear or two or whether it was just spitting with rain again.

Eventually the woman pulled away. 'And how are you feeling today?'

Betsan swallowed a lump in her throat. As soon as anyone questioned how she was after her mother's death, she found it difficult to deal with it, but she was determined to put on a brave front. 'I'm all right, Auntie.'

'That's good – it will be a very emotional day for you.' She looked past her as if searching for someone. 'Your Aunt Maggie, has she arrived yet?'

'Er no... she's...'

Before she had time to answer, Mrs Jenkins intervened as if she realised it would be difficult to explain Maggie's absence.

'Betsan, can you ask if anyone would like a cup of tea, please?'

Betsan nodded and she went around the funeral crowd slowly, asking people if they'd like anything. All the women declined the cups of tea as they'd be remaining at the house anyhow while the men went to the chapel and the burial in the chapel grounds. Only two men asked for a cup of tea and Mrs Jenkins raised her brow when Betsan informed her that Glanmor Griffiths had requested a glass of brandy!

'Fire and brimstone and the perils of drink...' Betsan

muttered as she went to comply with his request. She shook her head with surprise. Beelzebub indeed! Maybe Mr Griffiths liked a drink himself.

Overhearing what had gone on, her father spoke in hushed tones. 'I don't think he's much of a drinker – probably needs a bit of a pick-me-up before preaching today from the pulpit.'

Adults did the strangest things at times. They often seemed to say one thing and then do another.

* * *

Betsan stood with her face pressed up against the glass, watching the funeral cortège leave the house. She'd said her goodbyes to her mam yesterday afternoon, back when the open coffin was still in the parlour. Mam had looked so serene, her face still pale, but she looked at peace and she reminded Betsan of a wax doll she'd once spotted at Mr Crowther's Toy Shop on Merthyr High Street.

Droplets of water splashed against the windowpane and the sea of black-suited and hatted men disappeared behind the funeral cart, but the tears still failed to arrive.

Oh, Mam, she silently said to herself, *why did you have to get sick and leave us all?*

But it wasn't her mother she was angry with, it was some God that could take her mother away from her like that. In frustration, she collected the empty crockery with such force it rattled on the tray, which caused Bronwen Jenkins to scurry out of the scullery.

'Good grief, what's going on here?'

'I feel... I feel...' Somehow the words wouldn't come. It seemed as though they were stuck in her throat and trying to choke her.

'I know,' said Mrs Jenkins in a sympathetic tone. 'It's a tough day for you. Look, leave those and come and take a seat in the scullery with me and the other women. The cups can wait to be washed for a little while longer. We shan't be needing them as only a couple were used and if we do, should anyone else show up, we can wash them quickly. I notice our good old minister, Griffiths, asked for another glass of brandy!' She chuckled, which caused Betsan to smile. Maybe her father was right and it was a difficult day for him too.

* * *

It was only later that night when the twins were in their bed and Betsan curled up in her own that she felt able to let go. The house was now silent. She lay down on her pillow and closed her eyes, almost drifting off to sleep.

Then she felt it: someone was stroking her hair. Mam! She wasn't dead at all, she'd returned to her, but when she opened her eyes all she saw was the flickering shadow on the bedroom wall of the almost extinguished candle. Mam had gone forever, she realised.

It was only then she was able to break down and cry.

* * *

The following weeks and months were difficult ones for the family. David Morgan had to take on extra shifts at the Star Inn, which brought him into contact with more nefarious sorts as he worked through until the early hours of the morning. Bronwen Jenkins agreed to help out but Betsan's father insisted on paying her back by doing odd jobs in return. He desperately needed to work those extra hours as now he'd no longer be able to rely on the extra earnings her mother had brought in with her dress-making business. They hadn't been rich by any means but they'd been better off than many in Merthyr. Now there was an old blanket strewn over the sewing machine, as it was a constant reminder to all that Mam was no longer with them.

Betsan's thoughts turned towards Aunt Maggie. If only she could see her. Betsan could picture her face so clearly: she looked so much like her mother. Mam's hair was as dark as Aunt Maggie's was blonde, but their facial features were very similar. She was a little younger and carried more weight. Betsan remembered her as having a big bosom and a hearty laugh. She'd also been more coarse than her mother, not ladylike as Mam had been, but she remembered she'd enjoyed Aunt Maggie's company; she was a fun sort of person to be around. Maybe she'd be able to bring that sewing machine back to life. She seemed to remember her helping Mam once or twice. But no one knew where Maggie was. Her father claimed he'd tried to find her before the funeral and she had no reason to disbelieve him. After all, why should he try to prevent the woman from attending her own sister's funeral? It would just be too cruel for words.

* * *

'Betsan,' Mrs Jenkins said one day, 'what's on your mind, *cariad*? You look like you have the weight of the world on those young shoulders of yours.'

'Oh, Mrs Jenkins.' Betsan felt her eyes brim with unshed tears. 'I miss Mam so very much and I was thinking...'

'You were thinking what?'

'That maybe I'd like to find Aunt Maggie.'

Mrs Jenkins rubbed a hand over her hair. 'I don't know if that would be a good idea. It sounds to me as if your aunt has gone... how shall I say this, a little wayward.'

'Wayward!' Betsan wrinkled her nose.

'Yes, well, from what your father has indicated, she's just doing as she likes around the China area. You see...' she let out a long slow breath of exasperation, '...he's been trying for all these months to locate her and finally he did.'

'He did?' Betsan stood up, her hands on her hips, head held high. 'Then why didn't he tell me? He knows how much I want to see her!'

Mrs Jenkins chewed on her bottom lip and laid a reassuring hand on Betsan's shoulder. 'Likely, he doesn't want to upset you. From what he was told by someone living there, your Aunt Maggie has taken to associating with Elgan Hughes, the dealer.' The woman shook her head. 'Sadly, they're running some sort of racket between them. In my opinion, he's only a jumped-up rag-and-bone man!'

Betsan frowned. 'Racket?'

The only racket she knew of was when folk said someone was causing a racket when they were making a loud noise but, then again, Aunt Maggie was a very loud woman compared to how quiet her mam had been.

'I don't think I should tell you any more than that,' said Mrs Jenkins, a look of concern in her eyes. 'Suffice to say, they've both been on the wrong side of the law, more than once. That's all you need to know, for the time being. But other than her getting up to some shenanigans to fuel her alcohol consumption, I should imagine, she appears to be in fine fettle from what your father learned. So I wouldn't go concerning yourself with the likes of her. She's a rum sort, make no mistake about it!' She pursed her lips in disapproval.

Betsan wanted to find out more – she'd heard of that Elgan

Hughes. He rode his horse and cart around the streets buying things from folk in the neighbourhood. She recalled how Gladys Williams, when her husband was out of work, had once sold him a fancy walnut cabinet to try to make ends meet. It had been part of the woman's wedding trousseau from many years before. That had upset her so, her mam had once told her. Mrs Williams had reckoned it was worth far more than she was given for it but as she couldn't find a better offer and desperately needed the money, there was little choice.

Before Betsan had a chance to say anything further, there was the sound of the front door being clicked open and shut and then approaching footsteps in the passageway. Dad was home.

Mrs Jenkins placed an index finger to her lips. 'Don't mention any of this conversation to your father, Betsan. Not to distress him. Let him tell you in his own good time. Promise me?'

Betsan nodded, not wishing to upset her father for all the world.

* * *

As the months wore on, the days took on a regular pattern of Mrs Jenkins taking care of the twins, sometimes with Betsan's help when she wasn't at school. Betsan loved going to school and was keen to learn new things. She had learned to read and write at a young age, which had given her the freedom to read books at the library and find out more about things in general. The schoolteachers were very strict and classes large to overflowing but she managed to keep herself out of any serious trouble and avoided the cane like some of her peers got.

It was a few months later when Betsan noticed that her father had changed. He had smartened himself up. Now, he no longer wore a black jacket and tie; instead, he wore a new twill jacket and brown striped shirt. His moustache was no longer big and bushy and his sideburns had all but disappeared. Now his moustache was neat and pencil-slim and he smoothed his hair down with pomade, which made it look sleek and shiny. Bronwen Jenkins thought it was because he was looking for a new job to improve his circumstances but Betsan wasn't so sure; there was just something different about him altogether and he rarely mentioned her mother these days.

One day she even caught him carrying the large portrait of her from the passageway. It was a painting Betsan loved to gaze at because it was of her mother as a young woman. The artist had painted it before Gwendolyn Jones had even set eyes on her husband-to-be. Her long dark hair fell in waves on her shoulders and her beautiful violet eyes seemed alive and full of life. She wore an emerald-coloured dress and matching jacket and in her hand were a bunch of dog daisies – her favourite flower.

'Where are you going with the painting, Dad?' Betsan asked.

Turning, a deep pink flush seeped over her father's face as though he were caught in the act. He must have assumed she was busy with her homework but she had finished that some time ago.

'I... er... I'm just putting it up in the attic for the time being.' He shot her a disarming smile, which made it hard to be mad at him.

'But why?' He seemed at a loss for words and so then she asked, 'Is it because Mam's death upsets you so much?'

He huffed out a breath and nodded. 'Yes, something like that.' She said no more about it and made to turn away, but as if thinking better of it, he whispered after her, 'But you can see it whenever you wish, Betsan. It's only going up in the attic for the time being. I won't get rid of it.'

Sometimes she was allowed to play up in the attic. It was

where she kept the doll's house Uncle Wyn had made for her one Christmas, so she supposed she could go there to spend time with Mam alone. That suited her for the time being.

* * *

A few weeks later, while Mrs Jenkins was babysitting them, David Morgan arrived home with a young lady on his arm. Mrs Jenkins had just given the twins their tea and Betsan was sitting on her favourite stool near the fireplace.

She glanced up when the pair entered. The woman wore a bright burgundy dress with black frills around the neckline displaying her ample bosom. It wasn't the way her mam would have chosen to dress at all and Betsan watched as Mrs Jenkins narrowed her gaze in the woman's direction. It was almost a year since Mam had passed away but it was still a shock to find some strange woman with her father.

Who on earth is she, she wondered.

'Good evening, all!' her father greeted in a voice that sounded quite refined for him. 'This is Miss Elinor Evans!'

The woman beside him giggled. She looked quite young compared to her father and Betsan wondered if this woman were to be employed by him, maybe to take some of the burden from Mrs Jenkins – after all, she wasn't getting any younger. Dad had once hinted that if he could afford it, he might employ someone as a part-time housekeeper. But this woman didn't look how Betsan expected a housekeeper to look at all. She had long dark hair that fell in coils on her shoulders and a brazen sort of demeanour. Her chocolate-brown eyes seemed to glint mischievously and, for some reason, it made Betsan's heart sink. She hadn't even spoken to the woman as yet, but there was something about her that warned she was not going to be good news.

'Hello,' said Mrs Jenkins, looking as surprised as Betsan was.

'Charmed, I'm sure!' Elinor glanced over at Betsan's father, who was smiling back as if she had just lit up the room for him.

'Say hello then, Betsan,' he chided.

'Hello,' said Betsan. Her mouth had dried up and she feared what her father would say next. The twins didn't seem to be bothered at all as they carried on eating their supper.

Her father took Elinor by the elbow and escorted her further into the room. 'And this is the living room,' he said.

Betsan and Mrs Jenkins exchanged worried glances with one another.

'I'll show you the rest of the house after we've had some tea. Betsan, go and put the kettle on to boil, will you? There's a good girl.' He handed her a package wrapped in a muslin cloth. 'I bought a fruit cake from the bakery for us to have with the tea, while Elinor makes your acquaintance.'

Mrs Jenkins nodded and then turned her attention back to the twins who were making a mess of their minced beef in gravy, trying to shovel too much into their mouths. She wiped Aled's face with her handkerchief as she gently scolded the pair with a smile on her face.

Betsan's father was now speaking to Elinor in barely a whisper and she was gazing up and smiling at him, the way her mother used to when he was teasing her. A pain hit Betsan in the gut. This wasn't right; it wasn't right at all. Angrily, she stomped off to the scullery to put the kettle on to boil.

Mrs Jenkins was hotfooting it behind.

'Oh, Betsan love,' she said in a whisper.

Betsan turned to face her with glazed eyes. 'I... I don't know what's happening.'

'Nor do I.' Mrs Jenkins hugged her closely and then released her. 'It seems to me he has some sort of designs on this young woman, bringing her here to meet the family and see where he lives.'

'I thought at first maybe she was going to be our new house-keeper.' Betsan sniffed.

'She's no housekeeper – the state of her. I know I shouldn't be nasty but it appears as if there is little work in her. Did you notice the length of her fingernails? And that make-up she's got on. It's not decent. Your mother would never have dressed like that either; a good woman she was. Let's hope your father doesn't get too serious about this woman.'

But as Mrs Jenkins said the words, Betsan realised, even at her tender age, her father had fallen for the young woman.

She brewed a pot of tea and Mrs Jenkins sliced the rich fruit cake, which would have set David Morgan back a pretty penny, for it was not the cheap sort people often baked at home – this was high quality; he was out to impress by the look of it.

They all sat around the table, Elinor laughing at the twins' antics from time to time. At least she seemed to like them.

Finally, Mrs Jenkins stood and announced, 'I'll put this pair to bed now as I have to get back next door to dish up food for Bert – he's on nights again this week.'

Betsan's father smiled. 'Thanks for your help once again, Mrs Jenkins.'

She returned the smile. 'Good as gold this pair are, aren't you, kids?' She directed her glance at the twins who smiled wide, toothy grins at her. It was obvious how much they loved her. Although not a replacement for their mother, she was the nearest thing.

Once Mrs Jenkins and the twins had disappeared upstairs, Betsan noticed Elinor becoming more affectionate with her father, leaning in to him from her chair and whispering into his ear while stroking his arm. It made Betsan feel like an unwelcome visitor in her own home.

So, she stood and began to clear the table, scraping the crumbs off the plates and stacking them ready to take to the scullery. There was no offer of help whatsoever from Elinor.

'Betsan!' her father called as she stood with the tray of used crockery in her hands.

She turned to face him.

'How about some more tea for me and Elinor?'

She gritted her teeth but found herself nodding in return.

When she brought the tea tray in, her father stood and headed over to the sideboard. What was he after? It was soon revealed to be a half-empty bottle of brandy left over from the funeral. He was pouring it in their cups of tea! Betsan could hardly believe her eyes. Why was Dad acting this way? Considering he worked in a pub, he barely drank at all. The odd pint now and again but she'd never seen her father drunk – quite the opposite. He had seemed thoroughly disgusted when Aunt Maggie went off the rails.

Feeling herself welling up with grief and upset, Betsan climbed the stairs to go to the attic, seeing Mrs Jenkins on the landing where she was closing the twins' bedroom door.

The woman smiled at her. 'Everything all right now, *cariad*?'

'No, not really,' whispered Betsan. 'I'm going up to the attic to see Mam...'

Mrs Jenkins frowned. 'What on earth do you mean by that?'

'Dad's put her portrait up there. I've been going up there to speak to her when I feel upset or lonely.' She now kept her sketch pad and pencil up there and sometimes scribbled away creating garments she imagined her mother would have made.

'Aw, Betsan. I'm sorry to hear that. Maybe your father finds it difficult having that painting facing him on the wall day by day. It's a reminder of what he's lost and he has mourned a decent amount of time. It appears to me that now he's getting on with his life...'

Betsan nodded sadly as she turned away to climb the ladder, wishing all the while she could just get on with her own life.

* * *

Following that evening, Elinor Evans became a regular visitor to the house, much to the disapproval of Bronwen Jenkins. She didn't say too much about the issue to Betsan, but she could see the way the woman shook her head or narrowed her gaze in Elinor's direction. It was clear that she was far from happy with the woman's presence at the house.

Elinor was now appearing at the house almost every day and making herself quite at home. Betsan even woke up one night thinking she could hear strange squeaking sounds and muffled voices coming from her parents' bedroom but by the next day she'd convinced herself she'd dreamt the whole thing because when she came downstairs for breakfast the following morning, there was no sign of the young woman, only Mrs Jenkins spooning out porridge for the twins.

'Maybe your father will tire of her soon,' Mrs Jenkins said as she spooned some oatmeal from a saucepan into a bowl for Betsan.

Betsan smiled weakly. Somehow she doubted it very much. She guessed Mrs Jenkins doubted it too but wanted to sound hopeful the situation would change.

Betsan had just finished her porridge and was about to set off for school when a bump sounded from upstairs. She glanced at the ceiling. Was there something ghostly going on as Mam's portrait was now in the attic? She exchanged a worried glance with Mrs Jenkins.

'It'll be something falling over in the bedroom I expect...'

But then there was the sound of footsteps and the door slowly opened. All eyes turned towards it, including those of the twins. And there, standing framed in the doorway, was Elinor Evans. She looked such a sight too. Her long dark hair was messed up and her rouge smudged over her cheeks, but worst of all she wasn't even dressed properly. She just wore a petticoat that exposed the top half of her bosom and she had a shawl around her shoulders, which Betsan recognised as her mother's. She gritted her teeth and balled her hands into fists at her sides – the flaming cheek of her!

'W... what are you still doing here?' Mrs Jenkins lifted her chin and glared at the woman.

'It was getting late last night so I stayed over,' Elinor replied. 'What's it to you anyhow? David asked me to stop.' She eyed the pan of porridge in the middle of the table. 'Any of that left?'

'Yes, but if you want some, you'll have to wear something decent at this table!' Mrs Jenkins pursed her lips then shook her head in disbelief.

'Oh, I had no idea you were so high and mighty!' Elinor said in a false refined voice and then she bobbed a curtsey, which caused the twins to giggle. But then, as if thinking better of it, she added, 'Brr... it's a bit cold in here, think I'll put my glad rags on anyhow and return.'

'Yes, you'd better do that!' Mrs Jenkins raised her voice and Betsan noticed the woman's neck was now flushed.

Once Elinor had departed, Mrs Jenkins looked at Betsan. 'I don't know how much longer I can put up with that sort of behaviour. I'm going to have to have a word with your father.'

Betsan frowned. 'It's happened before?'

'Yes, every morning this week. This is early for her to rise. I don't want to hurt you, *cariad*, but the woman's all but moved into this house – well, at night-time at least. I think she's trying to get her feet under the table.'

Betsan was baffled. 'But I've never seen her here before in the mornings.'

Mrs Jenkins's face scrunched into a scowled-up expression Betsan had not seen on her before. Elinor was obviously winding her up.

'No, you wouldn't have, she seems to wait until you leave for school before rising. One morning, the lazy so-and-so didn't arise until eleven o'clock! What sort of time is that? The day's half over.' She approached Betsan and spoke quietly so the twins wouldn't hear. 'I think I'm going to have to stop helping out if your father moves her in completely. I'm sorry about that, Betsan...'

Tears sprang to Betsan's eyes. 'Please don't leave us...'

She sniffed and her bottom lip trembled.

'I won't leave you completely; I'll only be next door, *cariad*. You can call whenever you wish. But if your father continues to have carnal knowledge, outside marriage, of that young woman then I can't be a party to it. It's indecent and not Christian!'

Betsan had no idea what carnal knowledge meant and she didn't like to ask either; the woman was upset enough as it was.

'Please don't concern yourself,' Mrs Jenkins continued. 'My door will always be open to you and the twins. Your father will have to get someone else to do what I've been doing.'

Betsan nodded dolefully. She needed to get to school and put this all out of her mind. Maybe by the time she returned home, her father would have come to his senses and got rid of that brazen Elinor Evans and then all would return to normal once again.

3

But when Betsan returned from school that day, all was not resolved. Elinor had remained at the house and, with Mrs Jenkins having returned next door, she was now caring for the twins. Betsan's heart sank to see her playing on the floor with her brother and sister. She was wearing one of her mother's day dresses. It was the blue floral one that had always looked so pretty on Mam. The one she'd worn for special shopping trips and afternoon tea at friends' houses. Not quite her Sunday best but almost. The dress made Elinor look frumpy and much older than her years, though she was obviously making some sort of an effort after what Mrs Jenkins had implied. And who knew what sort of words the women had had with one another while she was at school?

Elinor's head turned away from where she was playing with Alys's doll and she looked towards Betsan. 'And how are you, darling?' she asked in an artificially high voice.

Betsan forced a smile but deep down she was irked that the woman was taking over her mother's position in the home. She hadn't minded when Mrs Jenkins had done practically the same thing because she did not have any sort of designs on her father.

'Cat got your tongue?' Elinor continued, her chocolate eyes glinting.

'Yes, I'm all right, thank you.' Betsan thought she'd better reply even if she didn't feel like doing so. She didn't want her father to become cross with her.

'That's better, darling!' Elinor smiled and then stood. 'Now then, I thought I'd make us all our tea. How does stew and dumplings sound?' Betsan nodded eagerly, noticing how delicious it smelled, going by the aroma drifting towards her from the scullery. She thought Elinor had cooked it herself but then the woman spoiled the small inroads she had made by adding, 'That old battleaxe next door cooked it before she walked out. Says she'll never step a foot inside 'ere ever again. What do you make of that, eh? Thinks she's better than me but let me tell you...'

Elinor was about to go off on some sort of rant when there was the sound of the front door opening and closing.

'Who's that?' Betsan's eyes enlarged. Her father wasn't due home from work yet.

'That'll be my friend Florrie. She's been here all afternoon while you were in school. She's keeping me company. She just popped out to get some provisions for us all with the money your father left for me.'

Betsan gulped. It was bad enough having to put up with one new stranger in her home, never mind another. Her head turned as Florrie entered the room. The young woman was around the same age as Elinor. She was breathtakingly beautiful, as blonde as Elinor was dark. Her enormous blue eyes framed with long eyelashes were a stand-out feature of her face, though like Elinor, she wore too much rouge and painted her lips.

''Ello, ducks!' she greeted. The woman had a strange accent; it didn't sound as if she came from Merthyr Tydfil.

'Hello,' Betsan replied. For some reason she immediately took to Florrie and she didn't know why.

'Aren't you the pretty one?' Florrie made her way into the room with a wicker basket over the crook of her arm. 'So, you're Betsan, are you?'

'Yes.' She smiled.

'Come and help me put these away and we'll have a cup of tea, ducks.'

Betsan thought it strange the woman kept calling her 'ducks' so she looked at her and said, 'You're not from Merthyr, are you?'

'No. I'm from London. My folk came here to work in the iron-works a few years ago. I was young then, not much older than you, but I've never lost me accent. I hooked up with Elinor as we both worked as barmaids at the pub.'

'The Star Inn?' Betsan blinked in quick succession as realisation set in.

'Yes. I'm still working there but Elinor has now left so she can rest, what with her condition...' Florrie's hand flew to her face as though she'd let it slip out.

Betsan didn't get it at all. Why hadn't Dad told her he'd met Elinor as he worked with her at the pub? And what kind of condition did Elinor have? Was she sick like Mam had been? Was she going to die?

'Aw, don't fret so much,' Florrie continued in a cheerful tone of voice. 'Your father can explain it all to you later. Now be a good girl and put that kettle on to boil.'

Betsan needed that cup of tea but she doubted she'd be able to eat the stew, despite being ravenous earlier on. There were just too many shocks in store in one day for her.

* * *

It was only a few days later when Betsan's father called her to speak with him downstairs. The twins were already fast asleep in their beds and Betsan had been readying herself for bed. Even Elinor herself was taking a nap.

She seemed to be taking quite a lot of 'naps' lately, Betsan thought. Maybe Mrs Jenkins was correct, referring to her as a lazy so-and-so.

In her nightdress, with a shawl draped around her shoulders, Betsan padded barefoot down the wooden staircase. As she descended, she could see the flickering shadows the candle in her hand cast on the wall, and her image looked very strange indeed, almost as though she were twice her size.

She hesitated as she approached the bottom step and noticed the living room door was ajar. Her father was seated in his favourite wing-backed armchair by the fireplace. He glanced up as she entered and smiled with uncertainty. She'd seen that look before – the night he'd told her that Mam wasn't going to get any better. Was he about to tell her that Elinor was going to go the same way? As much as she disliked the young woman, she wouldn't wish that on her for all the world.

He beckoned her over. 'Put the candle down on the table and come over here, Betsan...'

She did as she was told and made her way over to him and then drew out her stool and sat on it to listen to what he had to say.

'You're getting to be so grown up lately so I need to tell you this – the twins are too young to understand the implication...' He bit his lower lip, looking up at the ceiling as if working out what he was to say to her.

Oh no, what was he about to tell her?

He brought his gaze back to her face. 'You've noticed that Elinor has been staying over here a lot lately?'

A lot? It was all the time now – day and night.

'Well, there's a reason for it, you see… She's going to have a baby!'

Her father looked at her, trying to gauge her response.

Suddenly, she wanted to run from the room and vomit. It felt as if she'd been kicked in the stomach by a mule. She fought to catch her breath for a moment before saying, 'I… d… didn't know.'

'Yes,' he continued. 'It's not what I had planned, believe me, so soon after your mother's death – it's only been a bare year or so – but Elinor makes me happy and so now I have to do the decent thing and marry her. How do you feel about that?'

Marry her? It was one thing Elinor being pregnant, and Betsan knew very well where babies came from as her mother had explained it to her, but it was another her father marrying the woman!

'Does that mean she's now going to be our mother?' She shook her head in disbelief. This couldn't be happening to her. It had to be a bad dream, surely?

'Yes. Elinor will be your stepmother. We're getting married as soon as possible but please don't tell anyone about the pregnancy. We will let people think the baby is premature when he or she is born.'

Betsan's eyes welled with tears. 'So, when are you getting married?'

'This Saturday. I've had a word with Glanmor Griffiths and he'll conduct the ceremony. There won't be many there though, just our family and one or two friends.'

'Mrs Jenkins next door?'

Her father shook his head. 'Sadly not. Elinor doesn't like the woman. Apparently they've had words with one another.'

Of course she knew of this but hadn't told her father, yet she did question what version of events Elinor had told him.

'Don't look so worried, Betsan!' her father said cheerfully. 'You'll get to pick a nice new dress and can help choose something new for the twins too. Elinor and Florrie will take you all shopping in Merthyr tomorrow.'

That was some consolation, she supposed: she badly needed new clothes as the sleeves on her dresses were now riding up over her wrists and her hemlines were looking shorter than usual. When Mam was alive she'd have done something about that, either run up some new clothing for her or let down her skirt hems and the cuffs of her blouses.

Elinor couldn't do anything like that; she wasn't as clever as Mam.

Oh, Mam, why did you have to die and leave me?

* * *

'Ouch!' Betsan grimaced as the owner of the gown shop accidentally pricked her leg with a sewing pin. She was stood on a stool as the lady hemmed up her gown. It hadn't been her choice. It was far too bright for her liking. Loud, Mrs Jenkins would have called it, but as the bridesmaid gown was Elinor's choice what could she expect? A bright canary-yellow might have been all right for some but Betsan thought she'd look a right show in the dress.

What disappointed her the most was the fact she would never, ever wish to wear it again, not even to a party or Sunday school. And Elinor had not just insisted on the colour, but she wanted the woman to make it as frilly and ribbony as possible. It was going to look more like something Alys would wear than a girl of her age. She was now thirteen years old! The twins' outfits were quite smart. For Aled, a matching waistcoat and trousers, white shirt and bow tie; and for Alys, a similar dress to Betsan's, which of course suited *her*, but at least the little girl's was white.

Elinor and Florrie had both beamed at all three children dressed in their bridal wear.

Can't you both tell how silly I look, thought Betsan as she secretly scowled behind their backs. With the white frilly pantaloons that showed just beneath the dress, she felt more like Little Bo-Peep than a bridesmaid.

When she told Mrs Jenkins about it later that day, saying how she'd wished she could have had a dress more like Alys had in white, Mrs Jenkins had smiled, her head angled to one side. 'But it wouldn't be seemly for you to wear white now, would it, Betsan? As that's reserved as a bride's prerogative!'

'She's not going to wear white anyhow...' Betsan shook her head, realising she'd almost let the cat out of the bag.

'Yes, she probably feels ashamed to wear white with her reputation, though not all brides do, of course.'

'I'm sorry you're not invited to the wedding...' Betsan lowered her head.

'Aw, *cariad*, I wasn't expecting to be – not with how things are between me and Elinor. I don't think we'd ever get on anyhow as we have different morals and principles.'

Morals and principles aside, Betsan realised it was far more than that. Elinor Evans was what her mam would have termed a 'liberty taker'. She was out for what she could get – that much was evident – and she was taking her liberty from her father. He was spending money right, left and centre on fine blooming fripperies. Those bridal outfits had cost a lot of money, and had been charged to an account Dad had made at the shop, and heaven knew how much the bridal gown would cost. If he'd spent that sort of money while Mam was alive, she'd have shaken her head and looked on in disapproval.

'I'm going to miss having you there though, Mrs Jenkins. I don't really want to go. I don't want to see Dad marrying another woman, especially one like her!' Betsan's chin jutted out and her bottom lip trembled.

'Never fear, *bach*,' said Mrs Jenkins, drawing near to her and lifting her chin to gaze into her eyes. 'The day will be over soon enough...'

'But what about afterwards?' Betsan whimpered.

Unfortunately, Bronwen Jenkins had no answer to that particular question.

* * *

The wedding day was in stark contrast to the day of Mam's funeral. Now after a couple of weeks of grey skies and dismal-looking rain clouds, the sun had made an appearance and blue skies were starting to show. The gods were really shining on Elinor Evans today. The night before the wedding David Morgan had spent sleeping at the Star Inn so the pair were parted as tradition warranted. Betsan thought it was silly as up until now they had been living practically as man and wife, and though it wasn't talked about, Betsan could tell by the whispers behind gloved hands of the women in the street that Dad had turned his humble abode into a hotbed of gossip and intrigue. Mrs Jenkins had described it all as 'Nine Days' News' and she said that people would soon forget all about it when her father and Elinor wed, but Betsan wasn't so sure. She guessed that everyone would work out that the baby would arrive a little sooner than expected.

But, still, nothing could dampen Elinor's spirits today. She sang as she got herself ready and it was Florrie who looked after the kids, making breakfast for everyone and organising the twins into their wedding outfits. Betsan sat on the edge of her bed staring at hers, which was hanging on the wardrobe door. A vision of herself rushing downstairs to grab those large dress-making scissors from her mother's sewing basket and shredding the offending outfit to smithereens came to mind. What a show that would be! She'd love to wipe that smug smile off Elinor's face, especially on today of all days.

But it wasn't in her nature to be that cruel and she knew she was going to have to wear the ruddy dress and paste a smile on her face for the sake of her father. She couldn't work out if he was really happy about marrying Elinor or not. He still gave Elinor money whenever she asked and was compliant in other ways, but sometimes Betsan felt that maybe the shine of the relationship had tarnished when he'd realised she was pregnant.

After staring at the gaudy, awful dress a little while longer, Betsan slowly rose from the bed to put it on. Slipping it over her head, she remembered those blooming pantaloons. What a palaver! Now she'd have to slip those on too. She could always pretend she was wearing something else, just for one day. And like Mrs Jenkins had said, it would soon be over.

The wedding party was to be transported to the small chapel by a cart her father had borrowed from one of the draymen who delivered to the pub. It had been decked out with flowers and ribbons, and two white, black-blinkered shire horses were in place to power it along. Oh, this was going to be a showy affair for Elinor. There might not be that many attending the wedding but people would see them passing through the streets. Most in Plymouth Street wouldn't have seen such a sight for many a year.

At least no one could see Betsan's pantaloons while she sat on the back of the dray cart. She grabbed on tightly to her brother and sister's hands. They were all seated on a small bench, while Elinor and Florrie rode up the front with the driver.

There was a strong stench of ale emanating around them and Betsan wrinkled her nose. She didn't want to feel like she needed to throw up. It smelled so much like the pub but at least they were out in the open air. She glanced across at Mrs Jenkins's house, glimpsing the woman stood behind the curtain, frantically waving at her. Betsan smiled and returned the wave. Bronwen had been a good friend and neighbour to her mam so surely she must be upset too. That must be why she had chosen not to stand on her doorstep like some of the neighbours were now doing. Of course, she realised that some were doing so to have a right old nosy. They wouldn't have liked Elinor Evans any more than Mrs Jenkins did; her brash appearance was enough to put off most decent folk.

One or two neighbours waved at them but most of the womenfolk were standing around and appeared to be whispering. She thought she heard one of the neighbours saying, 'Those poor children...' but then the woman was shushed by the lady beside her.

Tears sprang to Betsan's eyes. They were leaving this house and by the time they returned to it, everything would have changed. Dad would have a new wife instead of their mam.

She looked down at Alys who was merrily kicking her feet back and forth. She seemed to love her new dress and kept calling it her 'party frock'. Aled, although quiet, seemed content enough. The twins were too young to realise what was happening and maybe that was a good thing. They no longer cried themselves to sleep or called out for their mother during the night. It had been a good couple of months since they'd even asked about her as there was no longer a portrait in the passageway entrance to the house. Their memory of Mam was fading maybe forever, but Betsan would never forget.

There was a sudden jolt as the drayman flicked his whip and the horses propelled the cart forward. Aled smiled broadly. This was a big adventure for him and Alys too had a smile on her face, but Betsan felt they were moving into the unknown. A topsy-turvy world where nothing and no one made sense any more.

4

Betsan's father was gazing at his wife-to-be at the altar with a look in his eyes that previously she'd only seen for her mother.

'I, David John Morgan, take thee, Elinor Mildred Evans, to be my wedded wife, to have and to hold from this day forward, for better, for worse, for richer, for poorer, in sickness and in health, to love and to cherish, till death do us part, according to God's holy ordinance; and thereto I pledge thee my faith...'

Betsan glanced at the other wedding guests, of which there were few, and they all seemed to have smiling faces, including Aled and Alys. Why was she the only one who had any misgivings about this marriage? The only other person who shared Betsan's sentiment was Mrs Jenkins, who was not present, and even she was doing her best to remain tight-lipped, being supportive to the children.

Elinor had a sickly-sweet expression on her face and Betsan guessed this was the day she'd always dreamed of. The dress suited her well, though if they had the wedding a week later, she probably wouldn't have been able to fit into it, with the advancing pregnancy. Pretty white lace covered the bodice and leg-of-mutton sleeves gave the gown a sense of elegance. The skirt looked like a satin material. It wasn't white but a pale pink, which suited Elinor's features, and she wore a matching-coloured wide-brimmed hat trimmed with pink and white silk roses and a large feather. Betsan had to admit that she looked quite beautiful, and in that moment she could see the woman through her father's eyes.

But as young as she was, even Betsan knew that although she was beautiful on the outside, she was not so beautiful inside. Why couldn't Dad see that?

Reverend Glanmor Griffiths conducted the service properly – there was no sign of him partaking of any alcohol this time – and she wondered if he'd been invited to the party back at their house later that day. Aunt Eira and Uncle Wyn were invited but although they showed up at the chapel they were not returning to the house afterwards. Betsan wondered why.

A thought suddenly occurred to her: maybe they weren't as pleased about the wedding as she'd imagined they were.

* * *

'Get out of bed, you lazy little wretch!' Someone was shrieking at her and it wasn't her mother.

Betsan fought to open her eyes and as she did so the figure came into focus. Elinor was looming over her bed with the yellow bridesmaid dress in her hand, shaking it roughly as though she were shaking out a feather quilt.

'Why have you treated your brand-new dress this way?' she demanded as she continued to shake it over Betsan's head.

Betsan fought to think. What had she possibly done that was so wrong? She'd undressed for bed as usual and hung the offending dress up in her wardrobe – she knew she had. Rubbing her eyes, she began to speak. 'W... what time is it?'

'Never mind the ruddy time, you upstart! Why did I find your dress all crumpled up at the back of the wardrobe?'

'I'm sorry, I don't know.' Betsan was genuinely puzzled. 'All I can think is that maybe I didn't hang it properly on the hanger and it slipped off.'

Elinor gritted her teeth. It was a plausible excuse, Betsan thought. Then she remembered the twins had been running around the bedrooms. The party had gone on for hours, but Betsan had taken herself off to bed early to escape it all. As the wedding party were still eating and drinking downstairs, the twins had been playing hide-and-seek with one another. Most probably Aled had hidden in the wardrobe. It seemed to be his favourite hiding place of late.

Not wanting to incur their new stepmother's wrath, she looked Elinor in the eyes and said, 'I am sorry. I was probably tired and I should have hung the *beautiful* dress up properly. It shan't happen again.'

Elinor's features relaxed and she nodded. Really, there wasn't much more that could be said.

'Well, make sure you iron it today and hang it up properly afterwards. There's an Irish woman who has set up a stall in the marketplace and she buys second-hand goods. Might get a pretty penny for it and the twins' outfits and all.'

Betsan had thought her father had paid for those outfits with a view to them being used afterwards as their 'Sunday best', and she guessed that Elinor would keep any money made from their sale. But in truth, she would be glad to see the back of her Little Bo-Peep dress.

After Elinor stormed out of the room, Betsan breathed out a sigh of relief.

Phew! That had been a close one. If she hadn't calmed Elinor down who knew what might have happened to her and the twins. Elinor had a temper on her – that was for sure.

* * *

Over the following weeks, Betsan noticed Elinor becoming increasingly irritated by her presence. It had all begun with that bridesmaid dress incident and now everything appeared to be escalating like a snowball rolling down a hill. If it wasn't something about her appearance – 'You need to brush those rats' tails of yours!' or 'You'll always be a plain Jane, Betsan! Nothing much you can do about it though!' – it was gripes about the tasks she carried out – 'Get back and scrub those plates, girl! There's still bits of food on them,' or 'This tea tastes like gnat's pee!' or 'You can't do anything right, you're hopeless!'

It was all beginning to get Betsan down. How she wished Mrs Jenkins was still taking care of them and her father had never set eyes on Elinor Evans! The trouble was she felt it unfair to offload on Mrs Jenkins as she had troubles of her own.

As if the name-calling wasn't enough, Elinor then became more physical in her attacks. There was the constant jabbing of a finger in Betsan's chest when she told her off, and once, when Betsan had dared to answer back, Elinor had slapped her across her face. It had stung too and when she'd looked at her reflection in the wardrobe mirror afterwards, her cheek looked red raw. But that wasn't the worst of it – a slap she felt she could handle. It was when Elinor insisted on brushing her 'rats' tails' that Betsan began to fear the woman. Betsan's hair was thick and unruly at times and it went frizzy when it got damp, and her stepmother seemed to relish dragging the comb through it. Each time she felt every little tug on her scalp, so much so that it brought tears to her eyes on many occasions.

How much more of this could she withstand? She'd tried talking about it to her father one evening but he'd just grinned and said, 'You always did have wiry hair, our Betsan. Your mam had trouble with it too!'

Betsan felt like blurting out, 'But Mam never intentionally hurt me,' but thought better of it as her father was absolutely besotted – or bewitched – by her stepmother. She'd simply turned away with tears in her eyes as he returned to reading the newspaper. What was the use? He'd never believe her account against Elinor's. Even if she told him that the woman had sold their bridal outfits to Mrs O'Connell on the market and pocketed the money for herself, her dad would find some excuse for his wife's behaviour.

As she made to leave the room, her father glanced up from his newspaper.

'Goodnight, poppet,' he said, smiling. 'Where's my kiss then?'

Betsan stooped to kiss his proffered cheek and then he carried on reading his newspaper. As she left the room, Elinor brushed past her roughly, causing Betsan to stumble. This time the woman didn't yell, 'Out of my way, you wretched article!' as she might have done if her father was not watching with a gleam in his eyes. Instead, she smiled and said, 'Oops-a-daisy, darlin'! Aren't I the clumsy one!'

Even though Elinor's tone was bright and friendly, that bump against her was no accident. But how could that possibly be proven?

With a heavy heart, Betsan climbed the stairs to bed. She was beginning to see how she was indeed a wretched article, living a wretched life. Her only consolation was that the twins seemed happy enough; they loved Elinor as she played games on the floor with them and from what Betsan could see she appeared to adore them too. So why did the woman dislike her so much? Was it right what Mrs Jenkins had said about her looking like her mam? And was it at Elinor's request that her father had removed that painting from the passageway?

If only she were able to see her Aunt Maggie, even if only for a short while. Seeing the woman would be a tonic and a reminder of the happy days with her mother. The days before her illness had taken hold and ravaged her body. The days before Aunt Maggie had been banished from their house.

Back then, the home had been full of love and laughter and she had many a happy memory of her mother and Aunt Maggie in the scullery giggling like two schoolgirls. They had once been very close as sisters but something had gone badly wrong. Betsan hadn't always remembered Aunt Maggie as a drinker, no. Although a little coarse and loud at times and what some might have described as a 'diamond in the rough', the woman had been sober, solid and reliable back then. Betsan even had memories from before the twins were born, of Aunt Maggie holding her hand and taking her to and from school.

In fact, as she came to recall her memories of her beloved aunt, she wondered if things had somehow soured around the time of the twins' birth. She seemed to call around the house a lot less after Aled and Alys were born, maybe once a month instead of on a daily basis. Perhaps Mrs Jenkins could shed some light on that particular issue if she asked her?

* * *

Betsan had sneaked out of the house without her stepmother's knowledge to visit Mrs Jenkins. As far as Elinor was concerned, Betsan was in the attic with her mother's portrait. Surprisingly, that was one thing that Elinor seemed to respect: Betsan going to the attic to 'spend time with Mam', as she referred to it. But then again, she had to question whether Elinor was afraid of the attic itself. She'd once heard her speak of it, saying how she swore it was haunted as footsteps could sometimes be overheard upstairs.

When Betsan left, Elinor was playing with Aled and Alys on the living room floor and her father was reading his newspaper. It seemed a contented scene. It was almost as though she didn't belong to this family any longer. It felt as if she were on the other side of a window – alone and unloved – stood in the freezing cold air as she watched them all at a distance.

As Betsan spoke to Mrs Jenkins, who had given her a cup of cocoa, she felt at peace for the first time in a long while. It was a bitterly cold day and Betsan was pleased of its warmth as she wrapped her fingers around the cup and tasted the velvety-smooth, sweet texture of the cocoa.

'So, you're wondering if something happened around the time of the twins' birth that caused your aunt to be banished from the house?' Bronwen Jenkins arched an eyebrow as if surprised.

'Yes.' Betsan blinked.

'But you've already been told that it was because of her drinking habit.'

Betsan bit her bottom lip and shook her head. 'I think it's also something else.'

Mrs Jenkins sighed and replaced her own cup in its saucer. 'It's really not for me to tell you, *cariad*. Your dad needs to but you are on the right track...'

What on earth did she mean by that?

Betsan frowned. 'Please tell me?'

'I can't, Betsan. You'll just have to ask your father. It's not my business and if I told you I'd get in trouble for it.' She heaved her large frame out of the chair.

'But Dad won't tell me anything these days. Whatever I say to him he doesn't believe any more.'

'Elinor's probably poisoned his mind – that's why,' said Mrs Jenkins with a sympathetic tone. She resat herself at the table and sighed even louder than before. 'Very well then, but you have to swear you won't tell a soul that I told you, all right?'

Betsan nodded and licked her finger to make the sign of a cross over her heart. 'I promise.'

'Well,' said Mrs Jenkins, drawing near, 'it's not common knowledge, but Aled and Alys are your Aunt Maggie's children.'

Betsan gasped. 'But how?'

'From what your mother told me, Maggie got involved with a married man who didn't want to know when she got pregnant, though if you ask me, I think they're Elgan Hughes's offspring. He was married but since then his wife has passed away and I think he's taken up with your aunt again since she's hit the bottle.'

For a moment, Betsan's lip quivered. 'So, they're not really my brother and sister?'

She fought to keep the tears from forming in her eyes.

'No, they're not. Now you asked me to tell you and I'm saying the truth here but even though they're not your brother and sister, they would be your first cousins so it's almost the same, closer even as they were brought up as your siblings, so you mustn't think that way. As far as those two little ones are concerned, they are your brother and sister. Understood?'

She nodded and then gulped. 'But how come Mam and Dad have brought them up as their own?'

'Do you remember your mother going away for a spell and I took care of you, sweetheart? It was some time ago, mind you.'

Betsan pondered for a moment. 'Yes, I think I do. Was it that time when I stayed at your house?'

Mrs Jenkins nodded. 'That was the time. You'd have been about nine years old back then, *cariad*.'

She recalled a time when she had pined for her mother but had been informed she'd gone to stay with Grandma and Grandpa Jones in Brecon. Her grandparents had still been alive at that time but sadly both had passed away two years ago, one shortly after the other. Grandpa had died of a broken heart, her mam had said. Was that all a lie then about Mam going to stay with them?

'But why did I stop with you and Mr Jenkins?'

'Your mother had gone to help your Aunt Maggie following the twins' birth but she, your auntie, I mean, turned a little bit strange afterwards, so your mam had to stay with her to care for her. She'd been renting a room but the twins' birth did odd things to her mind. Your mam did the best she could under the circumstances but, as it was told to me, your mother awoke one morning to discover your aunt had disappeared. Your father did his best to search for her, but when she hadn't returned after a couple of days, he enquired at the police station and discovered your Aunt Maggie locked up in one of their cells.'

Betsan frowned. 'But what did she do that was so wrong?'

'You have to understand, she wasn't well, love. Not in her right mind. She'd taken to the streets and somehow managed to get hold of some alcohol. It's almost as though she'd forgotten she had any children at all...'

Mrs Jenkins seemed to go off in a bit of a trance, prompting Betsan to ask, 'So, what happened after that then?'

'Your mother and father, not wanting Aled and Alys to end up in the workhouse, took them back home. They even paid Maggie's rent for her as that's the sort they were. They were residing in rented rooms themselves back then. They decided to look for somewhere else to live and I knew next door to me was up for rent, so I told them about it.'

Betsan wrinkled her nose. 'I'd forgotten we lived in those rooms.'

'Yes, you did, my love.'

'But how did you know Mam and Dad back then?'

'I was working at the Star Inn with your father in those days as I cleaned the place. Your parents were looking to move as they intended bringing up Aled and Alys as their own children. They didn't want folk knowing the truth – it's a big disgrace for any child to be born out of wedlock. I expect they wanted to save your aunt from the shame of it all as well – but in the end, she made a good job of shaming herself anyhow.'

Betsan nodded, all the while wondering how her parents had managed to keep the twins' birth a secret all that time. No doubt, it was to protect both them and their mother's reputation. Sometimes she felt she just couldn't figure out adults at all.

* * *

On the run-up to Christmas that year, the weather was bitterly cold with a threat of snow on the horizon, going by the grey ominous clouds gathered overhead. Even the geese hanging from the eaves of the poulterer's shop on Merthyr High Street looked frozen to death.

When Betsan questioned Mrs Jenkins about whether it would actually snow or not, she laughed and threw her head back, declaring, 'It's far too cold to snow, my love!'

How could it be too cold to snow? That was ridiculous but she'd heard people say that many a time and often it proved to be true. The clouds, although grey, had a slight pink tinge to them. It was going to snow this time for sure. The pavements outside were covered in a layer of frosting and her father had warned Elinor to take care walking outside as he didn't want her to hurt herself or, of course, miscarry the baby.

Elinor's mood had improved of late. The advancing pregnancy seemed to be sitting well with her. During the past week, she had developed a glow and almost a sense of mischief ensued, as though she were up to something or other – or maybe she had some sort of plans that no one was privy to. Betsan put it down to the approaching festive season. She'd noticed this time of the year often put a smile on folks' faces even if they didn't have two ha'pennies to rub together.

Betsan had overheard a conversation that week in which Elinor had boasted to Florrie that Christmas was going to be good because extra cash was on the way to her. It was odd though, as Betsan hadn't noticed her father taking on any more shifts at the pub. So where was all this cash going to come from?

Shrugging her shoulders, she nipped into Mrs Jenkins's scullery to tell her about it. The woman was equally baffled.

'Only thing I can think of is someone has left her a little something in their will, maybe? Or something like that.'

Betsan could tell by the way the woman rolled her eyes that she thought it unlikely.

Thinking no more of it, she put the idea out of her mind, but a few days later she'd soon discover where the money was to come from.

* * *

Betsan was excited as it was the last day of school before they broke up for the Christmas holiday. That morning, she'd rushed off in excitement as there was to be a small party held at the school. Pupils were asked to contribute something so Mrs Jenkins had helped her to bake some sausage rolls to take in. Betsan had been barely able to contain her excitement and wondered how she'd manage to keep her hands off them on the way there. Her mouth watered just at the thought of them on the plate in her wicker basket, covered with a tray cloth.

Even Elinor had been nice to her that morning, smiling at her sweetly and preparing porridge for her beforehand. Maybe the woman wasn't as bad as she'd initially thought. And soon, she and the twins would have a new baby brother or sister that would bring the whole family together.

She'd enjoyed her day at school as they'd played games such as musical chairs, with Mrs Roberts playing songs on the piano like 'Here we go around the Mulberry Bush' and 'Ring O' Roses'. As soon as the music stopped, they all had to find a chair, with only one having been removed. Betsan was the fastest out of all the girls and, in the end, it was left to one remaining chair, which she just made it to in time before Rebecca Masters got there. Betsan's prize was an embroidered bookmark that someone from the sewing class had made and the book *Mary Jones and Her Bible*, the story of a young girl who longed to have her own Bible. She loved reading and she'd heard all about that particular book last year as Mrs Harris, who taught English, had read out several pages each lesson to the class.

Oh, she was so excited. Wait until she told Mrs Jenkins later!

The party itself had gone well and there was such delicious food to be consumed by all, as well as the sausage rolls and other savouries others had brought along. There were a variety of sandwiches: ham, cheese, corned beef; and there was strawberry jelly, blancmange and homemade cordials of ginger beer and lemonade. It was the best time ever.

At the end, the tables and chairs were cleared from the hall and the children sat on the floor as Mrs Roberts played carols on the piano. They all sang along as they faced the giant Christmas tree beside her. It was illuminated by miniature red candles that appeared to flicker with every note they sang. It had been such a lovely day.

Then Mr Winstone, the headmaster, wished them all a happy Christmas and a peaceful new year and they were free to go home – an hour earlier than usual. Betsan practically floated all the way home with her book and bookmark in her basket, as well as the empty plate covered in crumbs. She couldn't wait to read *Mary Jones and Her Bible* in bed later that evening.

As she approached Plymouth Street, she admired the windows decked for Christmas. Some of the shops had windows adorned with holly and ivy, and some even had lit candles in the window. She decided to go inside her own house first before calling to see Mrs Jenkins to tell her how well the sausage rolls had gone down.

She opened her front door, expecting the usual noises, the twins running around pretending to be choo-choo trains and Elinor laughing at them, but the house was silent. It felt as though it were empty. No one home.

Feeling puzzled, Betsan placed her wicker basket on the scullery table and then entered the living room, gasping as she noticed something wasn't quite right.

There against the wall was a smart, new-looking Welsh dresser adorned with blue and white crockery. Her mam had always wanted one of those and Dad had always promised her one when the time was right. Where had this come from? Then she remembered how Elinor had spoken about the money she was coming into. But hang on, there was something else different about the room. Yes, there was a small pine Christmas tree near the window, decorated with all kinds of ornaments.

Why hadn't Elinor waited for her to return home so she could help dress the tree? Mam had always allowed her to help and she'd enjoyed it as they sang Christmas carols together and drank cups of hot chocolate as they went along.

But no, those two new items weren't what made Betsan gasp. It wasn't that there was a new Welsh dresser and a Christmas tree up in the room; there was something *missing*.

Mam's sewing machine!

It had gone. Had Dad moved it upstairs maybe? Or into the scullery?

Running from room to room in a blind panic, feeling as though she could barely breathe, Betsan searched for the machine but it was nowhere to be seen.

There had to be some kind of an explanation, surely? Dad would never get rid of that.

In a last-ditch attempt at finding it, she climbed the ladder to the attic but it wasn't there – only Mam's portrait staring back at her. Feeling thoroughly defeated, Betsan fell to her knees looking up at her mother. Her shoulders began to heave as she cried her heart out. The sewing machine was gone and maybe for good.

Hearing voices downstairs, she wiped her eyes on the sleeves of her dress, descended the ladder, and then made her way down there.

Elinor and Florrie were bringing baskets of provisions into the scullery and setting them down on the table.

''Ere, you did well there, gal,' Florrie was saying. 'Knocking that stallholder down like that. You managed to get that goose for half the price!'

Elinor laughed. 'Yes, done well today. Got a fair price for that old crock of a sewing machine too – used it in part exchange for that dresser I told you about. I'll show you in a minute.'

Betsan could hardly believe her ears. Standing with her hands on her hips in the doorway, with her chin jutting out, she said, 'You did what?'

Both the women's heads turned in Betsan's direction.

'Hello there, luvvy,' said Florrie almost nervously.

'I didn't hear you there.' Elinor smiled, but Betsan could tell she was nervous too. 'You know you mustn't creep up on folk like that. You almost gave me a heart attack and that won't do in my cond—'

But before she had a chance to finish, Betsan was up right next to her, gritting her teeth and clenching her fists with anger.

'How dare you!' she yelled in her face.

Florrie's mouth popped open, shocked. 'Hey, luvvy, don't speak to your stepma like that! It's so rude!'

'No, what I find rude is my stepmother selling my mother's sewing machine to buy that ruddy dresser in the room next door. It wasn't hers to sell. My mother wanted me to inherit that. Does Dad know?'

A flush crept up on Elinor's face. 'Er, no. I was going to tell him about it tonight. What are you worried about? It were only an old crock; it wasn't being used. Elgan Hughes gave me a good price for it. I still have some money left over after he exchanged it for the dresser.'

She dipped her hand into her basket and offered her open palm with some coins to Betsan.

This was all too much and Betsan knocked her hand out of the way, scattering the coins onto the floor.

'Well, really!' shouted Florrie. 'That ain't no way to speak to your elders. Get to your room at once!' She pointed to the open door.

'I'm not taking any orders from you or anyone!' Betsan felt

her anger justified in the circumstances. The last connection to her mother had been removed and maybe forever.

Elinor looked at her with tears in her eyes.

'I'm sorry. I didn't know it meant so much to you. It was just sitting in the corner with a blanket over it; I thought it was causing more grief than happiness.' She burst into tears.

'Save your crocodile tears for someone who cares!' Betsan smarted.

Florrie glared at her, while Elinor let out a gasp.

Only, she didn't *stop* gasping, and she was holding her stomach as she puffed loudly.

''Ere, take a seat,' Florrie said soothingly. Elinor did as told, gingerly easing herself into a chair beside the table.

As Elinor sat, Betsan noticed how flushed the woman's face had become and beads of perspiration had broken out on her forehead.

She was going into labour and it was all Betsan's fault.

'Now look what yer've gone and done!' yelled Florrie.

Betsan fled from the house, bumping into the corner of the table in her haste and almost tripping over the doormat. She'd call next door to Mrs Jenkins – that's what she'd do. But when she got there, the house was in darkness. It was then she remembered Mrs Jenkins telling her she was going to a carol service at St Tydfil's Church that afternoon. No doubt she'd be gone for some time to come.

What could she do now? Feeling the ice-cold chill of the wind, she wrapped her shawl tightly around her shoulders.

Aunt Maggie! She'd go to find her.

As she set off towards Merthyr town, she noticed beneath the glow of the street lamp that it was beginning to snow.

5

The China district of Merthyr Tydfil was an area skirted by the River Taff and looked down upon by a huge, smoking tip. Some people referred to it as 'Pontystorehouse' or 'The Cellars' as some of the rooms were beneath the ground and could be reached by a flight of steps. Many folk thought the name of China strange for part of a Welsh town. The name had stuck even though no one really knew for sure whether it was because the area was once ruled by a man known as 'The Emperor of China', was related to the Opium Wars with Great Britain, or was because of the number of tea shops in the area. Whatever the case, the police even referred to the area by the nickname, calling its inhabitants 'the Chinese'.

The houses in China were arranged in a higgledy-piggledy fashion, many of them in a poor state of repair. There was only one way into the area and one way out through an archway beside a shop where sometimes gatekeepers were employed to keep watch. Betsan recalled Mrs Jenkins mentioning that. Whenever folk spoke about the place it was the usual sort of thing they said, almost as if issuing a warning to people who had never been there.

'Even the Glamorgan Constabulary fear setting foot there!'

'It's a den of iniquity!'

'It's the nearest you'll get to hell on earth!'

Consequently, Betsan had it in her mind that the place was alight with the flames of fire as the Devil himself took residence at the entrance, holding aloft his pitchfork and grinning as he did so. If she managed to get in, would she ever get out again? Yet, surely she must be able to – her mam had once stayed there three years ago when she was looking after Aunt Maggie. If it was all that bad a place, surely her mother would never have set foot inside of it.

Shivering, she drew her shawl tightly around her shoulders, her fingers blue from the biting cold, and realised how unprepared she was for this. She also feared she'd somehow hurt Elinor by shouting at her and causing a ruckus over the sale of Mam's sewing machine. Her father was going to be so angry with her when he returned home. No one would want to see her face ever again. Not Dad, not Elinor, not Florrie and maybe not Mrs Jenkins either. She would be thoroughly ashamed of her torrid behaviour.

Mam had been a gentle sort who'd rarely lost her temper or patience with anyone, even if they were mean to her, and Betsan liked to think she was the same. But in this instance, the missing sewing machine was the straw that had broken the camel's back. She was angry about many things: her father becoming acquainted with Elinor, him marrying the woman he'd known all of five minutes and her taking her mother's place in the house, the portrait being moved to the attic, discovering the twins weren't really her true brother and sister, but most of all –

the thing she was most angry about – was Mam's sad passing away like that.

It had come at a time she'd felt totally unprepared and ill-equipped to cope with it. As she matured into a young lady, it was a time when she needed her mother most. She was the only girl in her class who had lost her mother and she felt even there, as much as she loved school, there was no one who could understand. As a result, she rarely spoke of it. The only person whom she could truly talk to was Bronwen Jenkins. Her father didn't understand as he seemed totally bewitched and beguiled by his new bride.

Betsan drew near to the archway, stopped for a moment and coughed. The smoke emanating from the various street chimneys was strong and a claggy feeling of soot and sulphur permeated the night air, filling her lungs. A couple of young lads in ragged clothing hurled past her, almost knocking her off her feet as they ran, yelling out through the archway. A game, no doubt. Their echoing voices reverberated back at them. Were those the little pickpockets Mrs Jenkins had warned her about?

Taking a deep breath, she followed their path through the arch and down a set of stone steps. Her father had been reading his newspaper aloud to her recently one evening and he'd mentioned a London journalist who'd been a visitor to the town. The man had written an article about the inhabitants of The Cellars, comparing the area with Devil's Acre in London. He'd spoken of those steps and how he feared touching the surrounding walls upon his descent for fear what filth might be on them. For some reason, that part of the story had firmly implanted itself in Betsan's mind. The man had intimated that there'd been all sorts of filth in this 'hellhole' and she figured he was correct as the first thing that hit her on entering the area was the incredible stench that arose from it, reminding her of rotten cabbages.

Surely Aunt Maggie couldn't be living here?

The odour was from all the accumulated filth that flooded the place. Buckets of human waste were often thrown out from doors and windows into the trough-like channels outside the houses. Sometimes the waste ended up washing down as far as the river when it rained, and many a working girl would raise the hem of her frock by bunching it in both hands as she trawled through the area.

Over the years there had been a couple of outbreaks of cholera in the town. Betsan's father had reckoned that those who had survived it had either done so as they were privy to clean sanitation where they lived or else they stuck to drinking the ale instead of the water. Those that could afford to, of course.

Well, if there were another outbreak, Aunt Maggie ought to survive as she clearly stuck to the alcohol.

It was dark as Betsan made her descent. All the while she tried to maintain her balance without touching the stone wall with her hands, as she remembered that newspaper article.

As she reached the final step and gazed around beneath the soft glow of a lamplight, she noticed for the first time some people huddled in a doorway. What were they doing? They appeared to be a husband and wife with four young children between them.

'Arthur, ask him if he'll let us back in and we'll pay him at the weekend!' the woman was saying.

'Aye, I'll try,' the man said in a low voice. 'But the best we can expect from Richards is a hike on the rent when I do!'

'Anything to get out of this bitter cold,' the woman added.

The man strode off in the direction of a house on the corner that seemed larger than the others and also appeared to have more light reflected from inside. As the door swung open, Betsan could smell a familiar odour – beer fumes! It was almost a welcome relief from the other smells around here. Going by the houses and the family she'd seen, the people seemed to be much poorer than those she'd encountered in Plymouth Street.

The woman had a young infant swaddled in a woollen blanket held to her chest to protect him from the cold. Behind her stood three young children of varying ages. Betsan could see that one looked around the age of the twins but the other two were older, their faces steeped in misery. Not one of them was dressed suitably for the weather.

Now was her chance. Swallowing hard, she tugged on the woman's shawl. 'Excuse me, missus...'

The woman's head whipped around in her direction. 'Now what are you wanting from me, good girl?'

The woman frowned. This was obviously the last thing she needed right now, being asked questions by some young girl. There was clearly a large question mark hanging over her regarding whether the family could get a roof over their heads for the night.

Betsan swallowed again. She was nervous but she'd come this far and couldn't leave without enquiring.

'I'm looking for my Aunt Maggie who lives here somewhere,' she said hopefully. 'But I don't know the house.'

'You're not from these parts, are you?' The woman narrowed her gaze.

'Er, no, missus, I'm from Plymouth Street.'

'Oh, very la-de-da!' she said mockingly, but then as if thinking better of her words said, 'You ought to go back there, darling. Why choose to be here all alone on a night such as this? It's not safe here for young girls. They're seen as easy pickings in these parts if there are no adults around.'

'I've run away from home.' Betsan sniffed, the enormity of her actions suddenly penetrating her senses and making her feel sad.

'Oh, dearie me, whatever's happened there has got to be better than what will happen here for you. What's your auntie's name, did you say?'

'Maggie.'

'That might be the woman I know as Mags Hughes. Well, Hughes isn't really her surname, but she lives over the brush with Elgan Hughes, the dealer. Took his name for respectability, I think.'

Betsan brightened up. She had no idea what living 'over the brush' meant – maybe the man owned some sort of store that sold sweeping brushes?

'Yes, that's her,' she said, expecting the woman to expand on her explanation. When nothing was forthcoming, she added, 'Where might I find her?'

The woman coughed as if deliberating on what to say. 'Where she's often to be found – in a pub somewhere, sweetheart. You know she can't keep away from the bottle, don't you?'

Betsan nodded. This wasn't news to her. It was just confirmation of what Mrs Jenkins had already told her.

'Which pub does she drink at mostly?'

'The Vulcan Inn, love, on Merthyr High Street. Though sometimes she drinks there too!' She pointed her bony finger in the direction of where her husband had gone to speak to that rent man. It didn't look much like a pub to Betsan, not like any she'd seen before except it was bigger than the surrounding dwellings.

'Thank you, I'll try there first then.' Betsan smiled.

'Hang on a moment until Arthur returns. He can tell you

whether she's in there or not, save you going inside. It's not a nice place for young girls.'

Betsan nodded gratefully.

It seemed an age until Arthur returned to his wife's side and all the while the snow had begun to fall at an alarming pace. Thick white flakes were now settling on their heads. Arthur, though, was smiling at his wife so that must be a good sign.

'Richards has returned the key!' he said, holding it aloft.

It was then Betsan noticed the mounds of clothing bundled up beside the family; no doubt all their worldly goods were inside those. What had happened to cause them to be locked out of their home?

'How much did he charge for the pleasure?' The woman glared at her husband.

'Two shillings!'

The woman groaned. 'Two shillings we don't have until you get your Christmas pay owed from the ironworks. Two shillings – that might have been better spent on this lot!' She glanced at the kids who were now also smiling though looking slightly concerned. There was a tone of despair to their mother's voice, a tone Betsan guessed they had heard before.

The woman paused for a moment to look at Betsan. 'Better than nothing, I suppose,' she grumbled in a resigned fashion. 'Borrow from Peter to pay back Paul. Anyhow, let's be getting inside. Open up, will you? But first, this young girl is looking for Mags. Was she in the pub just now when you spoke to Richards?'

He shrugged. 'How would I know? I only had Richards and that flamin' key on my mind!'

'Typical man!' The woman gazed heavenward and muttered, 'Lord give me strength!' She returned her gaze to Betsan. 'Come on, I'll go in there with you. Arthur, get the kids inside before they ruddy well collapse from this cold and for goodness' sake bank up that fire before it goes out completely!'

Betsan reckoned the family could not have been homeless for all that long then and maybe it was a regular occurrence for them being late with the rent money and then having the key removed only to get it returned to them with the promise of extra payment. A crafty old trick from that Richards the landlord if ever there was one!

The woman, who introduced herself as Martha, handed the infant to the eldest child, a girl who appeared a little older than Betsan herself, while her husband fumbled with the key in the lock.

* * *

The pub was dimly lit and as they entered all eyes turned towards Martha and Betsan.

'If you're looking for your husband, he's just left here, love!' A large-framed gentleman who stood at the bar with a pewter tankard in his hand chuckled. He looked a little more well-to-do than others at the establishment though his long, dark frock coat might have seen better days and his top hat was lightly battered. This must be the Richards the couple had spoken of.

'I'm well aware!' said Martha crossly. 'And not before you had the bleedin' chance to fleece us once again!'

'Now, now,' said Richards good-naturedly, trying to keep her sweet. 'He had it coming. He's not been coughing up on time – you know that.'

Martha shook her head, as if knowing the truth of it all. It had become apparent to Betsan that maybe Arthur was also at fault here. Was he spending their money unwisely, maybe? And that's why he couldn't seem to pay the rent on time?

'Never mind about that – you'll get your thirty pieces of silver!' Martha snarled. 'This girl, here, is looking for her aunt. Have any of you seen Mags Hughes lately?' She was addressing the whole pub now.

The men shook their heads and returned to supping their pints of ale. It was evident no one had set eyes on Maggie of late, or at least if they had, there was a good reason for not saying so.

Martha glanced at the barman. 'When did you see her last in here, Wilf?'

Wilf had his head lowered as he wiped a glass clean with a dishcloth.

'Well?' Martha was getting impatient now. 'The girl needs to know.'

He looked up at the pair of them and met Martha's persistent gaze, then glanced either side of him as if fearful someone might overhear.

'The constabulary has got her again. Elgan was caught fencing some stolen goods and she got involved, mouthing off at the bobbies, so they locked both of them up. I reckon they'll keep her until Christmas, wanting to make an example of her. Not him though as he's up in front of the judge in a couple of days' time.'

Martha rolled her eyes and tutted.

Draping a reassuring arm around Betsan's shoulders, she walked her to the pub door. The snow was still coming down thick and fast.

'You can forget finding that auntie of yours tonight,' she said with a sigh. 'And it's turning into a blizzard out there. Even if you wanted to return to Plymouth Street, I couldn't allow you to walk home alone in these conditions. You'd better come home with me. We've not got much in and we don't stand on ceremony neither, but you're welcome to whatever we do have.'

By the time they arrived at Martha's rented rooms, which were just across the alley, Arthur was on his knees in front of the hearth, kindling the fire.

He turned when he heard their approach and smiled. 'I've got it underway – don't fret,' he said, pulling himself up onto his feet.

'That's good at least.' Martha nodded, her earlier fury at the situation appearing to have abated. She turned to her eldest child. 'Oh, you've laid the table, Enid, there's a good girl.'

Enid smiled shyly in front of Betsan. The girl had bright titian-coloured hair and the most piercing blue eyes she'd ever seen. On the table was a loaf of bread, a pat of butter and a small hunk of cheese.

Martha removed her shawl and, shaking off the snowflakes, hung it on the nail behind the door. Then she proceeded to saw away at the bread with a long knife.

'It's not all that fresh, granted,' she said, looking at Betsan, 'but I managed to get it cheap from the bakery this afternoon. They sell off stale loaves for a song, once they've lost their springiness, that is...'

After slicing the bread as thinly as she possibly could for it to go around, she asked Enid to butter the slices, then did the same thing with the cheese.

'Take off your shawl, for heaven sake, love,' Martha chided Betsan, who removed it and handed it to the woman where she hung it beside her own. Then the whole family, apart from the baby who, still wrapped in his shawl, had been placed in a wooden drawer near the fireside to keep him warm, took their seats at the table.

Betsan noticed everyone had one slice of bread and cheese except for the father who had two of everything. She felt a pang of guilt for the fact she was depriving the family of a portion. How she now wished she hadn't reacted so badly by turning on Elinor like that, but once the red mist descended, she hadn't been able to help herself. Her selling the sewing machine, it was the final straw, a way to obliterate Mam once and for all from the home and it was underhanded too, for it had not been discussed. Betsan wondered now if her father would be just as upset as she was when he found out what had happened.

'For what we are about to receive...' Martha began, closing her eyes and lowering her head, an action that shook Betsan out of her reverie, 'may the Lord make us truly thankful...'

Which prompted everyone to echo 'amen' in unison.

When the meagre meal was over, Martha looked at Betsan. 'You'll have to bunk in with Enid tonight, darlin'.' She exchanged glances with her eldest daughter who was now clearing away the dishes from the table and then shifted her gaze back to Betsan. 'You haven't even told us your name yet?'

Betsan cleared her throat. 'It's Betsan, Betsan Morgan, missus.'

Martha smiled warmly. 'No need to stand on ceremony here. As you know, I'm Martha, and this is Enid...'

Enid smiled at Betsan and for the first time she noticed the girl had a freckled face and that suited her flaming-red hair. She was really quite pretty. Enid nodded, which reassured her as the girl might well have resented her presence in their home, especially as Betsan had shared the very little food rations they'd had and would now take up space in the girl's bed too.

'And this is Iris and Michael...' Enid gestured with her hand at her two siblings who were still seated at the table. Iris appeared to be around eight years old and Michael a couple of years younger.

'The baby...' Betsan said. 'What's his name?'

'Jonathan,' said Enid, 'though we call him Jonny for short. He's three months old.'

Betsan gasped. Poor Martha had her work cut out for sure with four children to care for and one not far off being a newborn.

'Can I help?' She rose from her chair.

She had been waiting to be excused from the table as Mam used to do at home.

'Betsan,' her mam would say with a smile when she realised her daughter yearned to leave so she could read a book or go out to play in the street with her schoolfriends, 'you are excused from the table.' And Betsan would smile, nod and thank her, then peck a kiss on her cheek. Other times, she'd help clear the table like Enid was doing here but in this house it didn't appear as though there were any formalities, though to be fair, Martha had said grace before they ate. The family seemed content and grateful for the little they had.

'Yes,' replied Martha, 'you can help Enid with the washing-up. Once the kettle has boiled on the fire for a cup of tea, refill it and put it to boil again, please, for hot water to wash up.'

'I'll make the tea if you like,' Betsan offered. 'I used to make it at home for my mam when she had customers calling into the house.'

Martha quirked a curious eyebrow. 'Customers? What does your mother do for a living?'

'Did...' she corrected. 'She was a seamstress.'

Suddenly, Betsan felt heavy-hearted and a lump arose in her throat.

'She died, you see, and that's why I ran away. My dad has now married someone else and today...' She sniffed loudly and swallowed hard. 'I came home from our school party to find Mam's treadle sewing machine was missing. My stepmother had sold it and she never told me she was going to do that so it was quite a shock...'

Betsan's lower lip trembled and Martha stood and wrapped her arms around her, hugging her to her chest. It felt good, someone embracing her like that in a motherly fashion, something Elinor had never done.

Martha broke away and holding Betsan at arm's length to look into her eyes said, 'Now, you listen to me, Betsan Morgan, I can quite understand how upset you've been. Not only have you lost your mam, which is a truly awful thing...' – she glanced at Enid who nodded in agreement – '...but she's been replaced by that other woman and her precious sewing machine sold to boot! You've every right to be upset, darlin'.' She reached into the pocket of her thick woollen dress and handed Betsan a handkerchief. 'Dry your eyes and blow your nose on that. I've got another clean one. Now *I'll* make that tea and we can have a little chat by the fireside before Jonny wakes up, but thanks for your offer.'

Betsan found herself telling Martha all that had occurred of late, from her mother's portrait being relegated to the attic to Elinor completely taking over the house. The suddenness of her mother's illness and consequential death had shocked her to the very core and in the days that followed, she'd found it difficult getting on with her life. But the Christmas school party had been such a lovely time. It had cut through her grief, and winning that special prize of *Mary Jones and Her Bible* had lifted her spirits.

So to then return home in a good mood, with expectations that maybe all was going to bode well for the future, to discover her mother's precious sewing machine had been sold, was all too much, especially as it was for Elinor's flaming dresser, something Mam had wanted herself but could never seem to afford. Yet, now here was Dad splashing his hard-earned money around like water! It just didn't seem fair.

While Martha had been chatting to Betsan over a cup of tea, Arthur had got himself ready for his night shift at the Cyfarthfa Ironworks. He'd not said anything to Betsan about the plight she found herself in but as she spoke she could tell by his sympathetic looks and occasional nods in her direction that he was on her side. Finally, he wrapped his woollen muffler around his neck, donned his flat cap and slipped on his jacket, which was hung near their shawls on the nails behind the door, and before he kissed his wife goodbye, he whispered something in her ear. She smiled at him as he patted her shoulder. Raising his hand in a farewell salute to all, he left the house to make his way to work.

'He's had to go a bit earlier as it'll take him longer to walk there in this weather. That Crawshay family are hard taskmasters. They drive their employees like packhorses.'

Betsan had heard all about that place from her father. Apparently, at one time, there'd been young children working there, some as young as six years old. They were only babies at that age, not that much older than Aled and Alys. She shuddered to even think about such things.

'I'm so sorry,' said Betsan. 'I shouldn't have come here and taken your food from your mouths.'

'Now, I'll hear no more of it!' Martha smiled. 'You're more than welcome here and in any case, a young, slight person such as yourself isn't going to eat all that much!'

'Maybe they'll let my auntie out soon?' Betsan looked at Martha hopefully.

'Aye, maybe, but take care if she welcomes you in, mind. She's been taking in one or two children who are wards of the parish. And something tells me it might not be out of the goodness of her heart.'

'How do you mean?' Betsan blinked.

Martha softened her tone. 'She gets paid to do it and I suspect that money goes straight on her bottles of gin or whatever. She's got one young lad rooming with her that I know of. He's been there for a time. His name is Jimmy Corcoran. His parents came over from southern Ireland to work in the ironworks but they've both since died. His father had a bad accident and burnt himself on the molten iron and his mother died herself afterwards in tragic circumstances. He was at the workhouse for a while but your aunt knew the family and she offered to take him in.'

'I suppose my Aunt Maggie can't be all that bad then?' Betsan frowned.

'I think she gets two shillings a week for his upkeep. Well, you work out the sums. If she can get by with say half of that to keep the lad then the other shilling could well go on booze. I think she had taken in three lads at one time, so she was well in there, but now I only see Jimmy going in and out of the house. He sometimes helps Elgan Hughes to pick up and deliver furniture and other household items on his horse and cart.'

'What happened to Jimmy's mother though?' Betsan asked. 'You said she died?'

'Aye, well, after his father passed away from that dreadful accident, she had no means of support so she became one of the unfortunates – those women who sell their bodies to men for money.'

'I've heard of those. Mrs Jenkins next door told me they sold themselves but I didn't know it was their bodies they were selling.'

Martha angled her head to one side and smiled sympathetically. 'We shouldn't look down on them, oh no, and we don't know all the circumstances of their poor lives. My guess is she needed to feed herself and her Jimmy, so she took to the streets, like. And then it happened one night, and this is a grim tale I'm telling you, she just didn't return home.'

Betsan's eyes widened and a shiver skittered down her spine. 'No?'

Martha shook her head. 'All her friends and neighbours were out in force looking for her. The bobbies arrested a man and took him to the police station for questioning but he was later released. He was some kind of foreman from the ironworks and a married man with children at that. But turned out it weren't him who were responsible.'

'Responsible for what?'

Martha lowered her voice to barely a whisper, the flickering flames of the fire seeming to rise and fall with each word she uttered. 'She was found floating in the river.'

Betsan's mouth opened and closed again. 'You mean?'

'Either someone murdered her or she took her own life. It was never proved or anything but it was my guess that if she cared enough about young Jimmy to try to put food on the table for him and clothes on his young back, then she would not want to take her own life.'

'So who do you think did it?'

'One of the bullies around here and there are a few. They run the girls, you see. The woman would not have been able to make a living without one of the bullies being involved. They generally look out for the girls, sometimes fix them up with men and take a certain amount of their earnings into the bargain. It's a rum life when you get involved in that sort of caper. But then again, I suppose it could well happen to me if our family were to lose the breadwinner, my Arthur.'

Betsan could hardly believe her own ears that women had to resort to that sort of thing. What if it was happening to Aunt

Maggie too? She couldn't bear it if it was. Maybe that's why the police had carted her away like that.

Martha wagged a warning finger at her. 'Now listen, Betsan. Don't go concerning yourself about that kind of thing – not everyone who lives in China is involved in that business. Most are hard-working sorts like my Arthur. I'm just telling you like it is in case you want to go back home – as soon as the weather improves, that is.'

Betsan nodded slowly. For all the woman had told her though, she'd still rather stick it out here and find out how her aunt was. She owed that much to her mother at least. Perhaps once she'd done that, she might consider returning home, but not before.

'Now go and help Enid dry those dishes, then you can both get off to bed. You can top and tail with one another. At least you'll keep yourselves warm tonight, so you'll be doing her a favour. The other kids will come in with me to keep warm; they always do when their father works nights and then he gets the bed to himself all next day, which is a luxury for him. Mind you, it's a devil to keep those kids quiet sometimes when he's trying to sleep, especially the baby.'

Betsan smiled. She was in awe of the woman's kindness and generosity towards her, a stranger. Rising from her chair, she nodded gratefully.

'Thank you,' she said, and then she went off to the scullery in search of Enid.

* * *

The following morning, Betsan awoke to a pair of grubby feet inches from her face. She was puzzled for a moment, but then it dawned on her she had spent the night topping and tailing in a small bed situated against the wall in the one-bedroom dwelling. Across the way, a long sheet that had been draped over what appeared to be some sort of washing line divided the room in two. That's where Martha had slept with the other children last night, all huddled up in the same bed. It wasn't ideal but she figured it could have been worse for the family if Richards had not returned the key to Arthur – granted, for a fee – but fancy if they'd all had to sleep outdoors overnight and in these bitterly cold conditions? Maybe they'd have had to sleep rough with the dossers beneath Jackson's Bridge, warming themselves by the cinder tip that was the mountain of waste from the ironworks. Would Baby Jonny have survived that?

Betsan listened. It was quiet except for the odd gentle snore emanating from behind the curtain. All appeared still outside too and she guessed that was from last night's snowfall – a fall of snow seemed to muffle a lot of sound. Last night she'd chosen to remain fully clothed apart from her boots, as the temperature had dropped dramatically, but her and Enid's combined body warmth had helped them drift off to sleep.

What would Dad be thinking now when he saw her empty bed this morning? Of course, he'd have realised well before now that she was missing because Elinor would have said so. She'd also have told him about her behaviour before she'd run out of the house. But she told herself maybe he'd be glad to get rid of her anyhow as now she was the black sheep of the family. She'd didn't quite fit in and was no longer in the fold.

Hearing a clattering sound down below, she decided to investigate, so she slipped on her black boots over her thick woollen stockings and laced them tightly. The old stone staircase was a winding one, not like the straight staircase with a banister at home. As she reached the bottom step, she saw Martha heading towards her with the baby in her arms.

'Hope this one didn't wake you, love,' she whispered. 'Did you sleep all right?'

Betsan nodded. 'Yes, I did, thank you.'

'I've got some porridge on the boil in the pot on the fire. Can you keep stirring it for me while I feed this one, please?'

Betsan made her way to the hearth, where she knelt to stir the large saucepan of oatmeal on the trivet while Martha seated herself in the armchair, unlaced her dress and exposed her breast for Jonny to suckle on greedily.

'Pass us my shawl,' she said, pointing to the door.

Betsan rose and took it to the woman, who immediately wrapped it around her young son to keep him warm as he made strange suckling sounds.

When Martha had finished feeding Jonny, she said, 'What are your plans today, lovely? It's stopped snowing now so maybe it's best you return to your family. They'll be concerned about you.'

Betsan guessed the woman was right. No matter how angry her father would be about her treatment of Elinor, he wouldn't want her to run away from home and, in any case, Mags was probably still locked up.

'Yes, perhaps I'll return then.' She sighed.

'You don't sound very happy about it?' Martha angled her head to one side.

Betsan carried on stirring the oatmeal with the wooden spoon but now it had turned into a gloopy mess.

'I think this porridge is too thick now, sorry.'

'That's all right, just add some water from the kettle, mix it well and I'll dish up.'

Martha heaved herself and the baby, who was fast asleep now, nicely contented, out of the armchair and placed him in the wooden drawer by the fireside.

'So, what will you do?' she persisted as she laced up the bodice of her dress.

'I guess I'll return home and face the music, but meanwhile if my aunt returns from the police station, would you tell her that I've been looking for her?'

Martha smiled. 'Of course I will. Now, I'd better call the kids. Place that saucepan in the middle of the table, would you?' She winked. 'Arthur'll be home within the hour and after he's been fed, he'll need his bed back.'

The walk home wasn't quite as bad as Betsan had envisaged as the snow had now turned to slush, but the worst part about it was that it seeped into her boots and chilled her feet dreadfully. As she trudged on she desperately hoped she wouldn't now get chilblains. Martha had loaned her a spare shawl to drape over her own and, knowing how poor the family were, she vowed to return it as soon as possible.

As she passed the shops on Merthyr High Street, she had mixed feelings. Usually, she loved gazing into their windows, especially at Christmastime. As a young child, she'd once held Mam's hand and hoped that she'd be given that pretty china doll in Crowther's Toy Shop window. And she had too. She'd awoken on Christmas morning to discover a large box beneath the Christmas tree. She'd never forgotten the delight of undoing the red ribbon to see what was inside. Her mother's eyes had filled with tears as she'd sat in the armchair smiling. This was before the twins had been born and, at the time, she hadn't understood how her mother could look both happy and sad at the same time. But now she understood it, for she now had bittersweet memories of those times. There was an ache in her heart that couldn't seem to go away no matter what she did, an emptiness that was yet to be filled.

The geese hanging from the eaves of the poulterer's shop with their necks dangling downwards appeared to be mocking her. She passed them lots of times but this morning they appeared to be in judgement. Even the pig's head with the apple stuffed in its mouth at Barker's the Butcher Shop seemed to have an evil glare. But deep inside she knew it was all her imagination, all because she felt she had wronged Elinor, even though the woman hadn't been particularly nice to her.

The holly-decorated shop windows with their flickering red candles did nothing to raise her spirits and the bustling crowds now building on the high street seemed to make her misery worse as she studied those happy, hopeful faces appearing to enjoy the festive season. In the distance, she heard a brass band strike up 'Once in Royal David's City' and she realised it was the Salvation Army. They played in the town every year on the approach to Christmas, most days, she recalled.

Swallowing a lump in her throat, she made her way home.

6

Cupping her hands to the glass, Betsan peered through the living room window of her house. There was no sign of any life there so she went next door. Mrs Jenkins failed to answer when Betsan tapped lightly on the back door. She daren't knock too loudly as Bert was on night shift and she didn't want to wake him up. Sighing, she made her way back next door. What if Dad was waiting there to tell her off for the way she'd treated Elinor? But then she noticed a figure through the scullery window; someone was bustling around. Gingerly, she pushed open the back door.

Elinor turned to face her, looking none the worse for wear. Relief flooded through Betsan. She'd been worrying for nothing; Dad wasn't here. At least she'd now have time to talk to Elinor and try to smooth things over between them.

'Well, what do we have here!' her stepmother yelled as she folded her arms across her chest. 'The wanderer returns! You've led us all a fine dance, you little madam!'

Betsan had intended apologising but it was obvious Elinor was in no mood for apologies.

'I... I...' The words just would not come.

'Your father was out of his mind with worry last night and he's really angry about the way you spoke to me. Now get in here and wash up all these breakfast pots!'

Betsan stepped over the threshold with trepidation. Elinor hadn't even asked where she'd spent the night; she was more interested in getting her own mess cleared up.

Betsan glanced nervously at her. 'Where are the twins?'

'That old hag next door has taken them into Merthyr town today. Your father has got her involved as he thought she'd know where you were. Maybe I shouldn't be so ungrateful to her as she's come in handy – now I can put my feet up.'

Betsan removed both shawls and hung them on the peg behind the door. Her feet were like blocks of ice so she went into the living room, removed her stockings, and placed them in the fireplace along with her boots so they could dry off.

'Where's Dad now?'

Elinor had followed her into the living room and was now towering over her. 'Where do you think he might be?' she asked, her voice dripping with sarcasm.

Betsan shrugged. 'I'm sorry, I don't know. At the Star Inn?'

Elinor's eyes gleamed with anger. 'No, he's ruddy not. He's still out looking for you! Now hurry up and wash those pots, then you can make me a cup of tea and toast some bread in front of the fire.'

Hastily, Betsan pulled herself to her feet. 'I'll just go and put on a fresh pair of woollen stockings...'

'No time for that. Now, wash those pots; they won't wash themselves!'

Betsan thought it unfair as she hadn't even been at home when those pots were dirtied but, in a way, it was a relief, as if this was some kind of a penance for yesterday's behaviour. Carefully, she carried the kettle – with the aid of a cloth wrapped around the hot handle from the hearth – out to the scullery. Then she poured the steaming water into the stone sink and topped it up with some cold. After refilling the kettle for tea, she replaced it on the hearth and then set about scrubbing the crockery and pans. It looked as if the family had eaten porridge too, though they didn't have to scrimp and save like poor Martha's family did. This place looked like a bloomin' palace compared to their humble abode.

When Betsan had completed her task, Elinor handed her a dry pair of woollen stockings.

'Here, put these on,' she said. It was the first act of kindness Betsan remembered in a long while from the woman and she nodded at her as she took them. 'Don't go thinking I'm being nice to you for your sake, mind. It's for your father, beside himself he is, and you going missing took the flamin' biscuit last night.'

'Why, what's happened?'

'There was a bit of a fight going on at the pub, which he got himself involved in. He had to step in to break it up for the landlord. He's got a black eye and a few cuts and grazes to his face for his trouble.'

Betsan drew a sharp intake of breath, feeling thoroughly ashamed of herself for causing extra misery for her father.

'I'll toast that bread and make the tea,' she said, glancing at Elinor who had a look in her eye that indicated that she now had a hold over her. Before last night's incident, Betsan had felt justified in her anger but now it seemed the other way around; she was going to have to do everything in her power to keep her new stepmother sweet, else she might upset the whole household and that just wouldn't do.

The sound of the front door opening and approaching footsteps in the passageway caused Betsan to start and then the living room door opened. There stood her father, with a downcast expression upon his bruised and swollen face.

When he saw her, his eyes lit up. She had been wrong, totally wrong! Going by the broad grin on his face and his smiling eyes as he quickly approached, he was extremely pleased to see her.

And then she was swept up in his arms and they were hugging one another tightly as the tears fell from both of them.

'You're home!' he cried. 'But where have you been, Betsan, my darling girl?'

'I'm so sorry, Dad. I stayed with a very kind family overnight. I ran away after I shouted at Elinor as I thought you'd be so cross with me.'

'Oh, dear girl, no, no, no! Nothing could be further from the truth. Elinor explained how upset you've been because she's having a baby and that's why you ran away from here!'

Over her father's shoulder, Betsan glimpsed Elinor's stunned-looking expression. The woman was shaking her head as if to warn Betsan off mentioning the sewing machine incident. So Betsan just nodded blankly at her father.

'All will be well, you'll see. I know this has come as a shock for you but in a few months' time you'll have a new baby brother or sister who will unite this family.'

What on earth was Elinor up to? Betsan narrowed her gaze in the woman's direction. It didn't sit right with her that the woman had lied barefaced like that to her father. Then it dawned on her the reason she'd said such a thing was because she didn't want any light shone upon her getting rid of the sewing machine! But her father would have noticed its disappearance, surely? Especially as a new Welsh dresser now stood in its place.

Deciding to say nothing about it for the time being, Betsan

explained to her father how she'd gone in search of Aunt Maggie but had failed to find her. She told him all about the kind family who had taken her in overnight until the snowfall had ceased.

'So, it looks as though your auntie has been locked up then?' Her father frowned.

'Yes.' Betsan chewed on her bottom lip. 'I was told she's now living with Elgan Hughes and they have a young lad staying with them who she gets money for, for his upkeep, like.'

'Probably getting paid by the parish then.' Her father shook his head. 'No wonder I couldn't find her when I tried – not if she's living with that Hughes fellow. Elgan is a bit of a rogue, what with his wheeling and dealing. You'd do well to keep away from that auntie of yours if she's getting herself into trouble.'

'Oh, no. I think she only tried to help Mr Hughes and they locked her up to make an example of her.'

'Aye. That may be so but your auntie has been known to run her mouth, even when she hasn't had a drink. She's always been outspoken, at least since I've known her. Nothing like the lady your mam was.'

Betsan noticed Elinor roll her eyes when her father spoke of her mother in such an endearing way. Mrs Jenkins had been correct all along: Elinor was jealous of her mother and how much Betsan resembled her, particularly lately. She could see the likeness for herself every time she looked in the mirror.

Her father glanced at his wife. 'Well, have you fed the girl yet?'

His tone wasn't as nice as it usually was towards her and Betsan wondered if maybe they'd had words with one another since she'd left home.

'It's all right, Dad. Martha gave me a bowl of porridge and a cup of tea before I left.'

'And we were about to have some tea and toast, weren't we, Betsan?' Elinor shot her a cautious glance.

'Yes, we were.' Betsan nodded, realising this was an untruth, but not wanting to stir up trouble again, she went along with it to keep the peace.

Her father smiled. 'Then we shall all have some together as we celebrate the lost sheep finding its way back to the fold again!'

For once, Betsan had one over on Elinor and she wondered if her father was now viewing things in an altogether different light. She vowed to ask him about the sewing machine later when Elinor was out of earshot. Maybe she might discover where it was.

* * *

Betsan was sitting at the table in Mrs Jenkins's cosy scullery, sipping a cup of cocoa.

'You mean to tell me that's why you ran off like that, *cariad*?' She looked at her with deep concern in her eyes.

'Yes. I couldn't believe how so much could change in a day. That morning, before I went to the school Christmas party, the sewing machine was there and when I got home it wasn't.' She swallowed hard. 'And to see that new Welsh dresser in its place and all. Mam had always wanted one of those.'

'I can well understand you getting upset by that, Betsan. Your mam worked on that treadle machine day and night; it was just always there, almost like a part of who she was. I think it was most insensitive of your stepmother to sell it like that without your knowledge. Does your father know about it?'

Betsan shrugged. 'I don't think she's told him yet. I plan to ask him when he has a moment alone, maybe tonight before he goes into work at the pub.'

Mrs Jenkins drew a sharp intake of breath and let it out again. 'Well, choose your time wisely if you decide to do that, as you don't want to be the brunt of any discord between your father and Elinor. It might be better to say no more about it, especially as you're unlikely to see it ever again.'

Maybe Mrs Jenkins was right. Betsan tilted her head to one side. 'But the odd thing about it is that Elinor told my father the reason I ran off is because I couldn't cope with the fact she's pregnant, which is untrue. I'm not jealous of the baby coming to live with us.' She shook her head as tears filled her eyes then she sniffed. She hadn't intended to cry but if anyone understood her feelings, it was Bronwen Jenkins.

Mrs Jenkins riffled in her apron pocket and handed Betsan a clean cotton handkerchief. 'Here, dry your eyes with that. I don't know what that young woman is up to, saying that to your father, but she's giving him a false impression of you for some reason.'

It was almost a relief that someone else was saying what Betsan had thought herself. Elinor wasn't going to let her off lightly about that sewing machine and how she'd reacted and maybe this was a means of paying her back. All sweetness and light on the outside but dark with evil intent inside.

'I think you're right.'

'You take care where that woman is concerned, young Betsan. She's not out to do you any favours – that's for sure.'

7

'Get out of here!' Maggie Hughes stumbled and tripped over the threshold of the police station as she found herself propelled forwards, hurtling through the air and landing in a heap on the pavement, pushed with some force by the sergeant.

It was early morning so there weren't that many folk around to witness her sad demise, though better that they witnessed Sergeant Cranbourne ejecting her from the place than the other way around when she'd been arrested. She huffed and puffed as she pulled herself up onto her feet and brushed down the skirts of her dress. Brrr! It was bitterly cold and had been snowing overnight but that had now changed to a dirty grey slush underfoot, particularly where people who had been up early that morning had been walking.

'And I don't want to see you back here ever again. You hear me, Maggie?' the sergeant added, though there was not an unpleasant tone to his voice as one might expect.

Catching the glint in his eyes, she smiled at him and nodded. Although he sounded gruff and even authoritarian to any passers-by, she knew him to be a kind sort really. He and his wife, Mrs Cordelia Cranbourne – Delia for short – lived over the police station where she took care of the policemen, especially the new recruits. The woman had even been so kind as to provide breakfast this morning and goodness knew when she'd have a chance to eat next. She supposed she could have been kicked out of the place on an empty stomach! So, the crust of bread and hunk of cheese washed down with a mug of hot sweetened tea had been a welcome respite.

No, that's how kind the pair were, benevolent sorts to say the least. Mrs Cranbourne had even told her in so many words that she shouldn't have even been locked up as, apart from a few choice swear words when Elgan was arrested for fencing stolen goods and petty affray, she hadn't done a lot wrong. Although inebriated at the time, Maggie was harmless enough. If only that overzealous new constable had not arrived on the scene, the others who knew her would have allowed her to go home.

What was she going to do now though? There hadn't been much food in the house and she knew Jimmy would manage just fine without her. He could survive living off his wits, that one. He was nobody's fool. She hoped he hadn't resorted to thieving while she'd been locked up either. But maybe that young constable, Smith – yes, that was his name, she remembered it when he gave her details to the desk sergeant – maybe he'd done her a favour in the end. In the two and a half days she'd been locked in a cell with three other women, she'd all but sobered up. Two were nymphs of the pave, with such sad circumstances that she didn't feel they should have been locked up at all for plying their wares just to make ends meet. The other was an older lady who had clonked her husband over the head with a saucepan – still with his dinner inside it – when she'd found out he'd taken up with yet another floozie.

Why didn't the police lock up the real criminals? The pimps

who paraded around the China area and often beat and abused
their working girls? Or the rent men who wouldn't even allow
their tenants a day's grace before hurling them out on to the
streets to face the elements? Or even those debt collectors who
came knocking and removing items from folks' houses? Anyone
except those who had just fallen on hard times. Even Elgan
wasn't a bad sort really; he just had one or two nefarious
contacts who supplied him with goods he didn't ask questions
about. That was his failing really – not that he was too trusting,
because he wasn't – he didn't go out of his way to seek trouble,
yet trouble always seemed to find him.

What about Elgan now though? Weren't it today he was up
in front of the judge? There was a chance he might be stuck in
the slammer for his crimes. She considered him very much as
head of the house, the main provider and the man who really
loved her. If only he hadn't been married when she'd conceived
the twins. She often wondered where they were now and what
they were doing but was so thankful her sister and brother-in-
law had taken them on as their own. She didn't want to ruin it
for them. After all, what was she to them anyhow? A loud,
drunken relative. Of no use, no purpose whatsoever.

She took in a deep composing breath, and with her head
down facing the icy wind, trudged through the freezing sludge.

However would she manage without Elgan if he got put
away? She just couldn't imagine life without him.

''Ere, where 'ave you been all this time then, Mags?' Jimmy
looked up from the mountain of leather boots piled up on the
table in front of him. They appeared to be on top of some old
newspapers – with a few small tools and a tin of polish and a

duster beside them. The house was a one-up one-down sort that was common for the area, small and sparsely furnished.

'Never mind where I've been, lovely boy, what have you got there, more like? Those aren't Elgan's for sure. He's only got one pair of boots for work and a pair of shoes for Sunday best! Been on the rob while I've been away, have you?'

Jimmy's face reddened with embarrassment. 'No, I ruddy well haven't!' He picked up a seg from the table and proceeded to hammer it into the sole of a man's leather boot. 'When you were away, Mr Baxter gave me some work to do at home to make ends meet. Said he was sorry for me in my predicament.' Jimmy laid down the boot and shook his head. 'I know about Elgan though,' he said softly. 'But where on earth were you? I was so worried when you didn't come home. You've done it in the past, sure, but that was only one night not two!'

Maggie thought back to those evenings she'd stayed for a lock-in at various pubs on Merthyr High Street and, though not strictly true that she'd disappeared all night long, she had kept some choice hours, not getting to bed before five or six o'clock in the morning.

'Got locked up at the nick, didn't I? It was for mouthing off when they carted Elgan away for handling stolen goods. Even the sergeant and his wife said I shouldn't really have been locked up but a keen new copper who just happens to be the inspector's nephew, disagreed. No doubt Sergeant Cranbourne could hardly send me away else it might have got him in trouble with the inspector. He's all right that Cranbourne.' She sniffed. 'Aye, and his missus an' all – they got what you'd call common sense.' She lifted the boot and peered at the workmanship. 'That's not bad, not bad at all, Jimmy. I would have thought Mr Baxter did that work. Who taught you how to do that? Was it when you were in the workhouse before you came to me?'

Jimmy shook his head. 'No, it was Mr Baxter himself. I've been hanging around his cobbler shop for weeks now. We often have a little chat when it gets quiet. He saw me standing outside peering through the window one day and he called me inside. He's been showing me what to do as it's all getting a bit much for him.'

'Well, that's something, I suppose... You might need to take in work from him as it doesn't look as if Elgan will be able to provide for us any longer and the money I get for you from the parish doesn't stretch all that far.'

Jimmy glanced at her in a curious fashion. 'It would though if you kept off that flamin' gin!'

Maggie's mouth popped open from the shock. She didn't like the way the lad was speaking to her. Maybe her two-day absence had manned him up a little. That and the fact the head of the house hadn't been around either, for he'd have clipped young Jimmy right across the earhole, hearing him speak to her like that. She, who had taken him under their roof not two years since and fed and clothed him.

Jimmy's features softened. 'I'm sorry, Mags. I shouldn't have spoken to you that way. I was a bit scared to be honest when neither of you returned home and I was here all alone. I swear, every creak and groan of this old house set my teeth on edge! Especially at night.'

He stood up and embraced her warmly. A tear trickled down her cheek as she sniffed to keep a full crying bout at bay.

'I am sorry about that. Elgan should have kept away from them ne'er-do-wells if you ask me. At any rate, we'll pay a visit to the courthouse this afternoon to see how his case goes. Can't see him getting anything but a prison sentence, mind. It's not his first offence though Cranbourne did say he'd speak in his favour.'

Jimmy nodded. 'Almost Christmas and Elgan might not be around to share it with us this year...'

'I know, lad. We'll just have to make the best of it.'

A sharp rap on the door startled them both, causing Mags to whip her head around. 'Now, who can that be?'

Taking slow, deliberate steps with hesitation, she went off to answer it. She hadn't even had the time to remove her shawl or have a cup of tea.

She yanked the front door open, which was swollen and stiff from the icy weather, to see a young girl with bright red hair stood on the doorstep. Her nose and cheeks looked scarlet and pinched from the cold.

Maggie blinked a moment as recognition dawned. One of Martha Hardcastle's kids! What was her name now?

'Enid!' said Jimmy behind her.

'Hello, Mrs Hughes, Jimmy,' Enid began. 'My mam sent me over to tell you we had a visitor last night. She just noticed you going in through the front door so sent me to tell you.'

Mags narrowed her gaze. 'Doesn't miss much, does she, your mam?' Then she smiled. Nothing was the girl's fault. 'A visitor, you say? Come on in then out of the cold. It's perishing out there.'

Enid nodded and, gratefully, she stepped into the house.

Jimmy smiled broadly and Mags knew why. He was sweet as anything on the girl and looking quite abashed.

'A girl called Betsan stayed with us last night...'

'Betsan?' Maggie angled her head on one side. 'Betsan Morgan, my niece?' Mags held the palm of her hand to her chest as if she were about to have a heart attack from the surprise. 'But last time I saw her she was only nine years old. She'd be about twelve or thirteen now, I suppose.'

Enid nodded eagerly. 'Yes, she stayed for supper with us and shared my bed, only left to return home this morning.'

'But why? Why was she here in the first place? I don't understand.'

'Seems she came looking for you but the weather was so bad – it was snowing heavily so Mam wouldn't allow her to go back home last night.'

'I can't see either of Betsan's parents allowing her to leave home in search of me, especially not in this area. It's not safe for a young girl to go wandering around here, particularly at night. You know that, don't you, Enid?'

Enid nodded. 'Her father didn't know she was here though.'

'But what about her mother?' Maggie's eyes were wide now.

'Betsan had an argument with her stepmother and that's why she left home, something about her selling her mother's sewing machine.'

Maggie frowned. This wasn't making any sense to her at all. 'Her father has remarried?'

'Yes. She told Mam her mother died a year ago and he met a younger woman who he married quite quickly afterwards. It upset Betsan, dreadfully.'

What Enid was saying took a moment to sink in.

'Gwendolyn died? And I didn't know anything about it? I feel dreadful now. I should have been there for them all...' Tears sprang to her eyes and the room swayed around her.

As if realising what was happening, Jimmy drew a chair out from under the table and brought it over and, taking Maggie's arm, urged her to take a seat. 'Sit a while, Mags, it will do you good. I'll make you a cup of strong sweet tea. It's good for shock.'

'Anything I can do?' Enid asked, looking guilty now, being the bearer of such tragic news.

'It's all right, love. I'll settle her with a cuppa now. You get off back home as I know your mam will want help with the nippers.'

Enid nodded, forcing a smile. 'Right you are then, Jimmy.'

'Don't worry,' he said, catching her eyes, 'you did the right thing informing her. She had to know sometime...'

He glanced at Maggie who now had a catatonic stare. When he turned back to Enid, the front door was just closing behind her.

* * *

Outside the courthouse, which was attached to the police station, it was thronged with people. As Maggie and Jimmy arrived, they could hear some of them chanting, 'Hughes is innocent!' and 'Police corruption!'

Maggie felt as though she were in the middle of a bad dream. This couldn't be happening to her. All of this and finding out her sister had passed away too – it was so much for her to take in. Any moment now she'd wake up in her bed and realise it had never happened at all, any of it.

Jimmy, as though sensing Maggie wasn't really with it, took her hand to lead her through the angry mob, though their anger wasn't directed at either of them.

Sergeant Cranbourne was standing in the doorway, flanked by another policeman of equal stature and presence. He was there, ready to usher the pair inside.

'I'm afraid there's not much room left,' he said, shaking his head, 'but you should be able to squeeze yourselves in some-where at the back of the courtroom.'

Maggie nodded at the man. 'Thank you, sergeant.'

He smiled. 'Now, I shall do my utmost to give your Elgan a good character witness but it's then really out of my hands. It's for the court to decide. The Merthyr Division of the Glamorgan Constabulary has had a job on its hands keeping that lot out there at bay this afternoon and I wouldn't like to be in PC Smith's boots when he leaves here later today. They're gunning for him for sure. I'll probably have to arrange a police escort for him and the inspector too when they leave.'

Maggie drew in a deep, composing breath and let it go again. 'I don't feel any animosity towards him nor the inspector, sergeant. They were just doing their jobs, even if the young recruit was a little "overeager", as it were.'

'That's very good of you to say, Mrs Hughes.'

Maggie drew in nearer to the sergeant so not as to be over-heard, though that might not have been deemed necessary with the sound the baying mob was making outside.

'I warned Elgan to keep away from those sorts, sergeant. Are they being tried along with him this afternoon?'

The sergeant nodded solemnly. 'Yes, and as they have nothing to lose – they'll definitely go down for this – they won't mind who they take down in the process, so don't expect too much grace from His Worship.'

Maggie nodded and gulped. Then, turning towards Jimmy, she said, 'Come on, lad. We better get ourselves a seat in case anyone else shows up.'

He smiled nervously and led her towards the courtroom.

Life had settled back down at home for Betsan. Her father seemed to be doing his best to keep her happy, but keeping two opposing females beneath his roof content was something of a juggling act – if he went out of his way to please Betsan, she could tell by the look on her stepmother's face that he'd offended her. And if he favoured Elinor, then Betsan felt affronted.

But for the time being, there was an uneasy peace in the home. She'd been back for a couple of days and, as there'd been talk of more impending snowfall, she figured she ought to go back to China now to return Martha's shawl and explain that all was well. Meanwhile, maybe her aunt might have returned home. She did not tell her father of her plan but she did inform Mrs Jenkins of what she had in mind.

The woman bit her lip as lines of concern etched her forehead.

'Oh, Betsan, *cariad*. Don't go back there alone,' she said when she found out. 'Not even to return that shawl, at least not without an adult accompanying you.'

'Can you come with me then?'

The woman appeared to be in thought for a moment and then she smiled. 'Yes, I'll come with you but only if you mention this to your father first.'

Betsan's heart sank. Tell her father she was off to that hell-hole again? She could just imagine what he'd say to that: a resounding 'No!'.

'Oh, all right then,' she said, her fingers of both hands crossed behind her back. She told herself that as her father would be at work that afternoon she could pretend that she hadn't been able to find him. She hated lying even if it was by omission but there were a few people she was concerned about she needed to see.

'Good girl,' said Mrs Jenkins, 'you know it makes sense.'

Betsan nodded. 'I'll just pop back next door to tell him and fetch the shawl.'

'Very well. Dress appropriately, mind you. It's freezing out there today.'

'I will, Mrs Jenkins.'

Ten minutes later, they were on their way.

* * *

'And you say,' said the lawyer, 'you were unaware that the items in your possession, which had been purchased on separate occasions from Jeremiah Pinch and one Aldus Hemming, were stolen?'

'Yes, Your Worship,' said Elgan, who appeared to be doing his level best to maintain a steady and composed countenance.

Some of the spectators in the room appeared to be treating this as some kind of peep show as they sat there on the edge of their seats, chewing on something or other or passing around peppermints and apples.

'Looks like half of these are here for the afternoon.' Jimmy chipped into Maggie's thoughts, almost as though he'd read her mind.

'Sssh,' she chided. She wanted to hear what Elgan had to say.

'No, not guilty, Your Worship,' Elgan said, looking at the judge.

'But how can you claim yourself to be innocent when these men, these fine upstanding gentlemen here in the courthouse, have branded you guilty? They claim the goods had nothing whatsoever to do with them and it was you, yourself, who stole them, not they?'

Mags frowned. Anyone with half a brain could see the pair of rotten rogues were guilty just by looking at them.

'Because,' said Elgan, 'I did not know where they had obtained those particular goods from.'

'But,' said the judge, 'did you care to ask them before

purchase how they obtained them if, according to you, they had them in their possession in the first place?'

The lawyer now had a gleam in his eyes.

Elgan shook his head. 'No, Your Worship, I did not care to ask. I just wasn't thinking that way at the time, I suppose.'

* * *

'That's all for the time being, Your Worship,' said the lawyer.

'You may step down for now.' The judge pointed to the dock and two burly police officers who were flanking Elgan led him away.

It was now time for Sergeant Cranbourne to take to the stand. He stood there looking composed and ready with his arms at his sides as he stared straight ahead, making eye contact with the judge.

'What is your name, police rank and where do you currently work?' asked the lawyer.

The sergeant cleared his throat. 'I'm Sergeant Walter William Cranbourne, and I'm the sergeant at this police station, which is the Merthyr Division of the Glamorgan Constabulary, otherwise known as A Division, here in Graham Street.'

The lawyer nodded. 'Now then, could you please tell the court how Mr Elgan Hughes ended up being detained here three days ago?'

'Yes. He was arrested by Police Constable Richard Smith.'

'And why was the suspect arrested?'

The sergeant swallowed and then, directing his gaze at PC Smith who was seated beside his uncle at the opposite end of the court, said, 'Because he was found to be in possession of a large quantity of goods under a tarpaulin on the back of his cart.'

'And where was this, sergeant?'

'According to PC Smith and another junior recruit, it was near High Street Chapel where the site of the outdoor market was pitched that particular day.'

'And what do you suppose it was doing there? I mean, the cart containing the goods, not the market, of course...'

A snigger rippled around the courtroom at that remark and Maggie rolled her eyes. This lawyer fancied himself as a bit of a comedian by the look of it.

The sergeant glanced at Elgan, across the room. 'Well, it's not uncommon for Mr Hughes to offload his goods there for one or two vendors to pitch on their stalls.'

The lawyer pursed his lips then raised a questioning eyebrow. 'Offload, you say? As in he were ditching something "too hot to handle"?'

'No, sir. I didn't say or mean what you are suggesting at all. Mr Hughes is well known at the marketplace and it's common practice for him and others to sell to traders there!'

Across the courtroom, the inspector whispered something in his nephew's ear. PC Smith smiled nervously.

'But this wouldn't be the first time Elgan Hughes has got himself into trouble, would it, Sergeant Cranbourne?'

'No, sir.'

'What about the time he was locked up for causing a disturbance on Glebeland Street? What was that all about?'

'I know the incident you are referring to and Mr Hughes did get into a bit of a fight then, grant you, but—'

'But you see where I am coming from, don't you? The man is a troublemaker, is he not?'

'No, sir, he is not. In that particular incident, there was a man who was abusing his donkey. The donkey was laden down with heavy goods and it could barely stand upright. When Mr Hughes saw the man kick the donkey, it was the final straw – the man removed his belt to thrash the poor beast!'

A loud murmur of disapproval reverberated around the room, resulting in the judge telling the spectators to quieten down.

'Yes, that's all very well,' the lawyer carried on, 'but isn't it true that Mr Hughes and the fellow in question had both been drinking heavily earlier in the Wyndham Arms and had been in one another's company previous to that incident?'

'Yes, but I don't see what that has to do with anything?'

'Don't you? It has everything to do with it. From my inquiries, I discovered that Mr Hughes had lost a serious amount of money in a card game to the man in question earlier that day in the pub and that was why the fight broke out – not because of a donkey being treated like a packhorse!'

The sergeant, who appeared at a loss for words, seemed confused and his face paled. 'I have no knowledge of the card game prior to the incident,' he said, 'which appears to be hearsay if you have it from the pub regulars, but what I do know to be true is that there were several witnesses at the time on Glebe-land Street, who produced written and verbal evidence that the man in question was whipping and kicking the donkey so hard that it made the most awful braying sound. It brought people rushing out of neighbouring pubs, houses and shops!'

'Go on,' urged the judge.

'It was evident that Mr Elgan Hughes probably saved it from a certain death that afternoon. And what you, and most of this court, do not realise...' – the sergeant raised his voice – '...is that afterwards, Mr Hughes threw some money at the owner and said he'd take the poor thing off his hands. He then went on to release the beast from its heavy load, led it home with him where he cared for it, and that donkey is now a picture of health.'

Now it was the lawyer's turn to be at a loss for words, so finally the judge asked, 'So, sergeant, would you like to tell the court your honest opinion of Mr Hughes?'

Sergeant Cranbourne nodded. 'Certainly, Your Worship. Although Mr Hughes hasn't always been on the right side of the law over recent years, I find him to be a man who beneath it all means well. He has a heart of gold and will willingly help others. He has something in common with the police, believe it or not.'

'And what might that be?' The judge quirked a curious eyebrow in his direction.

'He dislikes any sort of injustice towards any man, woman, child or animal, come to that. He's fair-minded, you see.'

The judge nodded. 'I shall return to sum up in one hour. Meanwhile, I'd like to see both lawyers in my chambers.'

'This is it,' said Maggie to Jimmy. 'The sergeant has given a good account of my Elgan. Will it be enough though?'

'We'll just have to see,' Jimmy said, patting her shoulder.

8

As they made their way towards China, passing through the Caedraw area, Betsan looked out at the parish church, which was nestled in amongst the trees with its mother-of-pearl clock face. It was a beacon of hope standing proud in an old grey town, and was a welcome constant in her life. Some things might have changed but that church would be there for many years to come.

If there was one thing in this old world that she could rely on it was God's good grace. Although she had sinned recently – running off like that – last night in her bed, while the twins were fast asleep, she had prayed for forgiveness.

The hands of the clock turned the hour to four o'clock and the bell began to chime.

'It will get dark soon,' warned Mrs Jenkins with a worried look on her face. 'Maybe we'd be better off going in the morning?'

She paused for a moment, laying a hand on the church railings, and huffed out a breath that looked like a puff of steam from a train.

Betsan glanced across at the Star Inn on the opposite side of the road. She'd hoped they'd pass by quickly enough so her father wouldn't glimpse them, but Mrs Jenkins was oblivious to the fact that David Morgan was even at work at all. She'd thought Betsan had gone inside to seek his approval before setting out.

Please hurry up, Mrs Jenkins! Betsan inwardly urged the woman but had the good sense not to verbalise her thoughts as then she would know the truth – her father was unaware his daughter was off to that den of iniquity once again!

Finally, Mrs Jenkins smiled and said, 'It's all right, Betsan. We've come this far so it wouldn't make any sense to return home now, would it?'

As the pair approached the high street, there was the rumble of wooden wheels as a cart laden with goods passed them by and the sound of voices in the distance drifted towards them. This time Betsan could appreciate the holly-decorated shopfronts and the candlelit displays. The marketplace set in front of them was busy too. A man was selling hot chestnuts, warming his hands on the stove used to heat them up in between customers. There were stalls selling all manner of goods from prettily packaged boiled sweets to mouth-watering Christmas cakes covered with a layer of marzipan and icing. There was even a stall selling wooden toys and hand-whittled ornaments.

Centre stage was a handsome doll's house, which drew customers to crowd around to admire the workmanship. Striped awnings covered the stalls to protect them and the traders from inclement weather. The market traders themselves were well swaddled in layers of clothing, from double shawls for the women to thick jackets and mufflers for the men, and most wore fingerless mittens to prevent their hands from turning into blocks of ice.

'Get yer Christmas wreaths here before they've all gone!' shouted a man in a bowler hat.

'Mince pies, custard tarts and loaves of bread here!' shouted another vendor.

But Betsan and Mrs Jenkins did not pause to admire or purchase any of the goods; the marketplace would still be there on their return. Well into the evening, it would remain, at that time lit up with a string of lanterns.

* * *

Across the way at Graham Street, Maggie and Jimmy were leaving the courthouse. The crowd was still outside and chanting.

''Ere, what did your fella get, Mags?' asked an elderly man who sported a flat cap, his rheumy eyes full of concern and his face blue-pinched. He was one of the coal miners at Gethin Pit who had been left with a legacy of blue veins and laboured breathing, both the result of coal dust.

Mags paused for a moment as the crowd hushed, waiting collectively to hear what she had to say. Jimmy linked arms with her as a gesture of support.

She shook her head sadly. 'He's going down for it. My Elgan's going to prison for a year...' Her voice trailed away.

''Tis nothing but a travesty!' shouted a woman from the back of the crowd. 'Elgan is well known to us market traders. He's like one of our own. He's helped me out of many a pickle and the late Mr O'Connell too, ever since we came over from the old country.' The woman had a strong southern Irish accent – there were quite a few living in the town who had come to work at the iron-works, having formerly lived in places like Cork and Donegal.

The woman shook her head in disbelief.

'I know, Mrs O'Connell,' said Mags, 'but the judge did say he could have given my Elgan a longer sentence if he'd a mind to but he didn't as Sergeant Cranbourne gave a good account of him; fair play to the man.'

'Aye, but that bloody young, green-as-grass copper Smith ought to be ashamed of himself, pulling in someone as salt of the earth as your Elgan!' shouted a middle-aged man with a raised fist, prompting the others in the crowd to murmur in agreement.

'Now listen to me,' Mags said, raising her voice and surprising even herself. 'There's no use taking it out on the young recruit. He weren't to know. We have to give him the benefit of the doubt. Just because he was keen as mustard to make his first arrest doesn't mean he ought to be hung, drawn and quartered by the likes of us! In any case, it was those two who offloaded the goods who are to blame. They said nothing in Elgan's defence – just covered their own bleedin' backs!'

The crowd quietened down, most likely understanding and respecting Maggie's viewpoint.

'A few of us were thinking of hanging around here and giving the bobby a hard time!' said the man in the flat cap.

'Save your breath, all of you!' shouted Maggie. 'It's not what Elgan would want and not what I want either!'

The bystanders muttered and then the crowd began to disperse, some walking back towards their market pitches, whilst others headed off home or – if they didn't have a good home to go to – then the pub.

'Let's leave,' said Mags, looking at Jimmy, despair in her heart.

He shot her a rueful smile and, draping a reassuring arm around her, led her away.

* * *

'I can't believe you came to this hovel all alone,' Mrs Jenkins moaned as they passed through the archway and descended the steep steps that led past the cellars.

The truth was neither could Betsan. It wasn't something she'd normally be of a mind to do but now she'd been here the once, she was less fearful.

'They're not all bad sorts here though, Mrs Jenkins.'

On the final step, Bronwen paused for a moment. She seemed breathless again as she had near the parish church but then she inhaled and exhaled and carried on walking.

'Well, of course there are good sorts everywhere, but you were lucky to have encountered that nice family. If you'd have run into one of those pimps we might never have seen you ever again, my girl!'

A shiver coursed down Betsan's spine. She was still unsure exactly what a pimp was. In her young life, she'd heard the term bandied around on more than one occasion. All she knew was that they were some sort of bad man she should keep well away from.

As they approached Martha's house, the stench of the area became obnoxious – intense and overpowering, much like that first night she'd arrived here. Now it smelled like rotten meat and sulphur. Smoke drifted from several chimneys, making the air thick and murky so visibility proved poor.

A young boy in tattered clothing ran past and then Mrs Jenkins squealed loudly. 'What was that?'

Puzzled, Betsan shrugged. 'I didn't see anything?'

'Something scampered over my boot. It must have been a rat! I've heard this place is rampant with rodents, the dwellings being so close to the river and all.'

Truth be told, Betsan hadn't seen any when she'd visited the other evening but it had been snowing heavily at the time.

'Where does this family live?' There was a sharp edge of impatience to her tone.

'I'm not sure now...' Betsan shook her head. 'I thought I'd easily find their place but it's so misty and smoky here – all the houses look the same to me!'

Mrs Jenkins huffed out a breath of exasperation. 'Then we are just going to have to knock on a few doors! I haven't come all this way for nothing!'

The house they approached first had a broken downstairs window, which was stuffed with balls of newspaper. The door was battered and well worn.

Mrs Jenkins lifted her hand to knock and, then glancing at Betsan, asked, 'What's the family's surname?'

'I don't know – all I remember is the woman's name is Martha and her husband, who works at the ironworks, is called Arthur.'

Mrs Jenkins rolled her eyes and then rapped loudly on the door.

After a moment or two an elderly woman appeared. 'Whatcha want?' she growled.

'We're looking for a Martha and an Arthur.'

The woman peered at Bronwen as though she had a screw loose. It was only then that Betsan realised the names rhymed in a funny sort of manner.

Then the woman narrowed her gaze. 'Don't know either of 'em!'

And she shut the door in their faces.

'Well, really! How rude!' Mrs Jenkins pursed her lips.

'I'll try the next house,' Betsan offered. She didn't really want to upset Mrs Jenkins any more than she already was.

* * *

By the time Mags and Jimmy had returned to their humble abode, it was dark and a grey mist had descended.

'This reminds me of the fog in London,' Mags grumbled as she inserted her key into the lock of the front door.

'When did you ever go to London?' Jimmy blinked with surprise.

'Oh, it was about three or four years ago. Elgan took me on the train to stay with his sister in Hackney.' She didn't tell Jimmy the real reason they went was for her to get over the twins' birth and to recuperate. In the event, Elgan had lied to his missus and said he was going away on business for two or three days. What he'd done was stay there for a couple of days to settle her in and then he'd returned home. Maggie had felt so sorrowful at the time. It was almost as though there'd been a death in the family. And maybe there had – she was never to see the twins nor her sister or family ever again. And now she felt that sort of sorrow descend on her like a cloak of darkness. Elgan was being put away for a whole year and she'd never, ever see Gwendolyn again.

'Don't worry, Mags,' Jimmy said cheerfully. 'I'll stick the kettle on to boil!'

Mags smiled ruefully. Someone calls to the house unexpectedly, put the kettle on. Someone passes away, put the kettle on. Someone gets imprisoned, put the bleedin' kettle on!

Oh well, a hot cup of tea would be more than welcome right now.

While Jimmy brewed up, Mags scoured in the back of the scullery cupboard to see what they could have to go with their cuppa. There was a little bit of leftover *bara brith* wrapped in a muslin cloth, a bit stale perhaps but she could divide it in two and slather some of that salted butter on it. She was about to do exactly that when there was a loud rap on the front door.

'I'll get it!' Jimmy yelled cheerfully, and he went off to attend to it.

Mags smiled. The way the boy shot off like that, he obviously thought it was that Enid girl he was sweet over. Thinking on, Mags followed after him in case it was one of the market traders come to pay their respects as Elgan was being put away. But coming from the other side of the door, this wasn't a young girl's voice and it didn't sound like no market traders either. It was a woman, someone she didn't recognise.

'Who wants her?' she heard Jimmy say with a manner of suspicion.

There was further unintelligible conversation that Mags couldn't quite follow, and then Jimmy stepped back inside the house from the doorstep, leaving the door ajar.

'Who is it, lad?' Mags hissed, fearing it might be someone Elgan owed money to.

'Some woman and a young girl!' Jimmy shrugged. 'The girl reckons she's your niece, Mags!'

9

Mags rushed over to the front door. 'Betsan! Oh, Betsan! Is it really you?'

Her eyes took in the young girl, the dark ringleted hair and shiny violet eyes just like her own dear sister's.

The girl looked like what she remembered of Betsan but was now so tall and her hair was much longer. The girl smiled nervously as if unsure what to do, and then, she stepped forward, as did Mags, and they embraced each other.

This girl was blood, a part of her own dear sister.

Mags's eyes brimmed with tears and then she looked at the woman behind Betsan. 'Thank you for bringing her to me, Mrs...?'

'Bron. Bronwen Jenkins. But Betsan came of her own volition to find you. A couple of nights ago, in fact, but you weren't around?'

Mags released Betsan from her embrace and her cheeks reddened. She glanced first at Mrs Jenkins and then her niece.

'I won't lie to either of you. I got locked up by the cops. This time for running off my mouth. Even the sergeant admitted I shouldn't have been taken in, just sent my own way, but a young zealous copper arrested my Elgan and all hell broke loose. We've just returned from the courtroom and, sadly, Elgan has to go to prison for a whole year...' She shook her head and then turned her gaze back to Betsan. 'But I'm so glad to see you, love!' She hugged the girl to her bosom. 'And I'm so sorry to hear what happened to your mam. I've only just heard about it.'

'How?' Betsan asked.

'Those people you stayed with, the Hardcastles, they sent their Enid here to tell me earlier.' Mags stepped back. 'Now, where are my manners? Jimmy here was just on the point of brewing up, weren't you?'

Jimmy nodded, looking quite uncertain. 'Yes. I make the best cup of tea in all of China!' he quipped, which caused Betsan to chuckle along with him.

Betsan gazed around the shabby room with its mismatched furniture and dusty drapes. A single tallow candle stub burned on the windowsill and a small fire was kindling in the grate. Yet, for all its austerity, she could see her aunt had tried to make it a homely place. On the walls were several paintings of familiar scenes: one was of the parish church at the lower end of the town where they'd earlier passed by; another was of Cyfarthfa Castle owned by the ironmaking dynasty, the Crawshay family; and another was of the indoor market.

'You're admiring my paintings there, are you, Betsan?' Auntie Mags smiled at her.

Betsan nodded. 'Yes, they're really good.'

'Elgan got those for me,' she said proudly, clasping her hands together. 'He did a favour for someone, helping them to move house, and they gave them to him. Don't think they're worth anything but I like to look at them, especially if I feel a bit low. I like to imagine what it's like living in that grand castle. I bet they have some lovely balls there!'

Betsan had to admit that if she had that particular painting hung on her wall at home, she'd imagine the exact same thing. It was a little like when she spoke to her mother's portrait in the attic. She imagined she was right there with her and if she had a particular problem, she'd ask her mam and the answer always came in the end, no matter how long it took.

Betsan thought for a moment. She was about to ask her aunt if Elgan had bought a sewing machine from her stepmother and where it might now be, but she thought better of it. Aunt Mags was obviously in shock after learning of Mam's death and her Elgan being put away, so she decided to keep quiet for the time being.

'Well, sit yourselves down!' said Maggie.

Betsan and Mrs Jenkins exchanged uncertain glances. Betsan guessed her friend would not want to stay all that long but it would be rude not to take a seat, so they both sat on the old sofa in front of the window while Aunt Maggie took the armchair opposite.

Betsan's eyes caught a pile of old boots stacked on the table. Were her aunt and Elgan in the shoe business?

There was a slightly uncomfortable silence as if no one knew quite what to say. The ticking of the old clock on the mantelpiece seemed to grow louder with each second, until finally, Maggie spoke. 'I was so sad to hear about your mother's passing, Betsan. I only found out today and along with all the upset about my Elgan, I'm finding it hard to take everything in...' Her voice trailed off and then she cleared her throat. 'But you, darlin', you've had a year to get used to it. It can't have been easy for you during that time?' Mags angled her head to one side in a show of sympathy.

A lump rose in Betsan's throat. She swallowed hard before replying. 'No, it hasn't been easy for any of us.'

'And your father, how is he? I've heard he's since remarried?'

Betsan really didn't want to go into any of that right now, so she was more than happy when Jimmy disturbed them, bringing in the tea on an old tin tray. He handed the mismatched cups around.

Betsan looked up at him shyly and as he winked at her she felt herself blush.

'Thank you.'

Jimmy smiled. 'You can share some of this cake with me, if you like?'

Noticing just how small and thin the slice was, she shook her head and held up a palm. Although quite hungry from her trek from Plymouth Street, she didn't want to deprive the lad.

'No, thank you, I've already eaten.'

Aunt Maggie also offered half of her slice to Mrs Jenkins, who also declined the offer. It was obvious to both of them that Maggie and Jimmy were living on their uppers and to take anything more than a cup of tea right now would deprive the pair further. It reminded Betsan of the night she'd spent with the Hardcastles. She'd felt guilty about that as well.

She took a sip of the weak-looking tea – no doubt they were reusing the tea leaves by drying them out but it was better than nothing; at least the tea was hot – and she watched as Jimmy, now perched on a wooden stool by the fireside, took his time consuming the fruit cake, nibbling slowly and savouring every morsel. Then he licked all the fingers of his right hand one by one and let out a long, appreciative sigh.

Aunt Mags shot him a disapproving glance.

At least now her aunt had forgotten her earlier question about Betsan's father remarrying. Betsan just didn't have the energy for it.

As if sensing this was so, Maggie spoke softly and sympathetically. 'Look, I know things have been difficult for you, Betsan, but at some point, and I don't mean right now as I haven't got the headspace for it with my Elgan being put away, but I'd like to talk to you about your mam. Is that all right?'

Betsan nodded. It was then she noticed Jimmy staring at her. What was the matter? Did she have a smudge of dirt on her nose or something? She shifted about uncomfortably on the settee until he averted his gaze elsewhere.

'So, how long have you lived here?' asked Mrs Jenkins, breaking the silence.

'About two years now since I married Elgan. We did it quietly and anyway, a lot of folk assumed we were living over the brush as I was using his surname anyhow.'

Betsan's mouth opened and closed again. This was news to her. She was sure her mother and father didn't know about that at the time.

As if feeling she needed to provide extra information, Mags added, 'You see, Elgan became widowed and then we married shortly afterwards. But I did know him before that an' all.'

Betsan glanced at Mrs Jenkins, who pursed her lips in disapproval just as she had when her father brought Elinor into their home. That she could well understand but what was the matter with Auntie Mags knowing Elgan *before* his wife died? Then it dawned on her. Elgan was Aled and Alys's father! It all made sense.

After that, Betsan almost expected a question from Mags about the twins but there were none forthcoming.

Finally, Mrs Jenkins laid down her cup of tea on a nearby low wooden table and rose to her feet slowly.

'Well, it's been nice getting to know you and thank you for the tea. We really should be getting back home now. I'm sure Betsan will call again to see you, or maybe it would be better if you call to see her at Plymouth Street instead?'

Mags shook her head. 'I... I don't know if I'd be welcome...'

'Of course you would,' Mrs Jenkins asserted. 'David went in search of you when Gwendolyn passed away but he couldn't find you anywhere.'

'Oh, I never knew...' A tear coursed down Maggie's cheek.

Jimmy rose from his stool, perched on the arm of her chair and draped a comforting arm around her shoulders, which were racked with grief.

Mrs Jenkins exchanged a glance with Betsan. 'Come along, young lady. We'd better be heading home and leaving these people to it!'

Mags glanced up at them and nodded. It was then Betsan remembered Martha's shawl. She was still wearing it over her own. She removed it and handed it to Jimmy.

'This belongs to Mrs Hardcastle,' she said. 'She loaned it to me. Would you see she gets it, please?'

He nodded as confirmation.

As they left the house, Mrs Jenkins closed the door behind them and said, 'I wouldn't like to be in your aunt's shoes right now. A whole year is a long time to be separated from the person you love.'

'Yes, it is. Sorry to have dragged you all this way, Mrs Jenkins. And now we have to walk all the way home again.'

'No doubt my feet will play up tomorrow but at least the exercise might have done me some good. That Jimmy one took a shine to you, Betsan!' Mrs Jenkins swerved sideways to avoid a pile of rubbish in her pathway. 'This place really is the pits. Why don't people keep it cleaned up instead of dumping their rubbish and filth and goodness knows what else on their own doorsteps?'

Betsan had no clue why they did that either but what had come as a surprise for her was Mrs Jenkins saying that about Jimmy. When they'd been in Mags's house, from the way he was staring at her, she'd really got the impression there was something odd about her appearance. She continued to listen to Mrs Jenkins's moans and groans until they emerged from the archway. When they arrived on Bethesda Street, the woman seemed her normal self once again, rubbing the palms of her hands together and brushing down her skirts almost as though taking part in some sort of cleansing ritual after being contaminated by the area.

They passed the outdoor market again, which conjured up an altogether different atmosphere by night, as lanterns and candles lit up the stalls. A juggler was tossing several coloured batons in the air, high above his head and managing to keep them there in some kind of rotation as folk watched in awe. Standing alone, outside the High Street Chapel, was a fiddler who was playing a tune Betsan recognised so well: 'God Rest Ye Merry Gentlemen'.

They passed an elderly vendor, going by the deep wrinkles etched into her weather-beaten face. Mrs Jenkins dropped some copper coins into her open palm in exchange for a sticky toffee apple, which she gave to Betsan, and then moved to another stall, which sold steaming-hot rum punch.

'Just to warm up my cockles!' she said, throwing back her head in merriment.

Why couldn't she have been like that when they were in China? But then again maybe the woman had been anxious there as it was deemed to be dangerous. Though so far, Betsan had seen nothing to alarm her, despite people having warned her about the area.

Mrs Jenkins slowly sipped the punch. 'I'd offer you some to warm you up' – she smiled – 'but I don't think your father would be too pleased about me offering you alcohol.'

Her father! Fear overtook Betsan's being. What time was it? He might be home from work by now and he'd think she'd run off again.

In the distance, she heard the church clock chime the seventh hour and a feeling of dread took over.

'Mrs Jenkins.' She tugged on the woman's sleeve. 'We have got to go *now*!'

'But why? What's wrong, *cariad*?' she asked, her eyes enlarged as she angled her head to one side with curiosity.

'My dad will be home now. I didn't tell him I was going anywhere. I fibbed just so you'd let me come with you.'

'Oh, Betsan,' said Mrs Jenkins, her face crumpled with disappointment. 'You have let your father down, me too and most of all yourself! Now your father will blame me for taking you to China when I had no business to.'

'He won't. I'll be the one who is in trouble, not you.'

'And just when I'd patched things up with him...' She swigged back the last drop of rum punch from her tin mug and placed it down heavily on the wooden stall.

Mrs Jenkins was annoyed with her and so would her father be when they got home.

They began to rush towards the parish church and then Betsan noticed the crowd opposite gathered around the Star Inn.

'What's going on?' She blinked several times as fear hammered at her heart. A policeman was about to enter, followed by another in his wake.

'I've no idea,' said Mrs Jenkins, 'but whatever it is, it appears to be serious.'

* * *

As they approached, Betsan noticed a woman with her head in her hands, sobbing at the pub's entrance, a man next to her, with his arm draped around her shoulders. Betsan thought she recognised her as one of the young barmaids. Several men shook their heads in disbelief, and murmured, whilst another squeezed his flat cap between his hands as if his life depended on it.

'What happened here?' asked the taller of the policemen who identified himself as Sergeant Cranbourne. He cut an imposing figure in his long black cape.

'A fight broke out here the other evening,' explained the man, who continued to squeeze his cap in his hands as if twisting the neck of a chicken. 'Tom McManus was causing trouble again. The barman intervened and got a fist in his face for his trouble, but then he and some of us regulars got the better of the brute and locked him out in the street.'

'So, what happened this evening?' The sergeant began to scribble something down in a small notepad using a pencil.

'Well, Tom returned, didn't he? But this time he brought a couple of heavies with him and they overturned the place, robbed the takings before our very eyes, smashed up our stools and tables and shattered some glasses. They weren't messing around, oh no! They were out to cause as much mayhem as possible!'

The sergeant lowered his voice so Betsan had to strain to hear. 'Look, what's behind this, do you know?'

'Seems McManus had some sort of beef with the landlord, to

do with money owed to him, I reckon. The landlord wasn't in so he took it out on the staff and regulars and the pub itself!'

Suddenly, a shard of fear pierced Betsan's heart. Had Dad gone home before the fight started? And was that the man who had caused his injuries the other night? It must have been as it was too much of a coincidence otherwise.

Mrs Jenkins glanced at Betsan and looked at her full of concern. 'Are you all right, love? Don't fear, your father can handle himself. I'll ask one of the men where he is and they can fetch him out here if needs be to reassure you. I dislike setting foot in a pub – it's unseemly for women to do so.'

Betsan could hardly tell the woman Martha had taken her inside one the other evening when she was searching for Auntie Maggie. She nodded silently.

Mrs Jenkins approached a couple of regulars who were loitering outside, tankards in hand. Betsan couldn't make out what was being said but there was a lot of murmuring, nodding of heads and pointing taking place. Finally, the woman returned to her side.

'Apparently,' she huffed out a breath, 'your father was involved all right. The other barman sent him home as he was knocked flying and might have hit his head in the skirmish. I expect he's all right, *cariad*. Better for him to rest at home.'

Betsan frowned. 'Someone gave him a bruised eye the other night as well!'

'Sounds like it was the same man then.' Mrs Jenkins sniffed. 'Come on, I'll come to your house with you to check on your father and explain where we've been.'

The pair turned away from the scene before them and began to walk home briskly. Arm in arm they walked, as the church clock chimed the half-hour.

10

'He doesn't look well, does he? Oh dearie me,' said Mrs Jenkins as she appraised Betsan's father, who was sprawled out on the old horsehair couch. Beside him, Elinor knelt to mop his brow with a wet cloth, her expression strained.

Betsan swallowed hard. Dad's face looked so pale apart from the bruising around his eye, which now appeared a hue of a purply blue. What on earth was the matter with him?

He suddenly let out a long groan and winced.

'Somebody needs to fetch the doctor!' yelled Mrs Jenkins.

'I'll go!' offered Betsan.

'No, you can't go out on your own at this time, young lady!' She wagged an index finger in her direction. 'I'll pop next door and ask my Bert to go for him.'

She glanced at Elinor for the woman's approval who, eyes brimming with tears, gave it with a smile and a nod. This was obviously a shock for her.

At least the women were no longer at loggerheads with one another.

It was a good half-hour later before Bert returned with

Doctor Llewellyn. Elinor hurriedly explained what had happened to her husband while he laid down his leather bag, hat and coat on the table. He set about examining Betsan's father, asking pertinent questions. Finally, he turned to Elinor and said, 'May I speak to you in private?'

Betsan watched her nod and then she led him into the passageway just outside the living room door, leaving it ajar. Betsan drew near to hear what was being said. She couldn't make out all the conversation but she managed to pick out various words and phrases.

'Concussion...'

What was that?

'Keep him resting. On no account must he return to work right now!'

'Possible memory loss!'

When the doctor had gone, Betsan asked her stepmother what he'd said but all she told her was that her father was to rest and she and the twins must do their best to keep quiet so he might get better. Why wasn't she mentioning anything about concussion or her father's memory? She'd have liked to ask her more but now all Elinor was concerned with was sitting near her husband and wiping his forehead while whispering to him. Betsan felt out of the picture.

When Betsan arose the following day, her father was not on the couch as she'd imagined he'd be.

Elinor was bustling around in the scullery, opening cupboards and taking items out. The bump beneath her pinafore was now really starting to show.

'Where's Dad?' Betsan asked with some alarm.

Elinor turned and smiled at her sweetly. 'He's resting in bed. He will remain there for today. I'm just making breakfast for him.'

Betsan noticed a boiled egg and a slice of bread and butter on a tray, and now Elinor was pouring a cup of tea for him.

'May I take his breakfast up?' Betsan looked at Elinor hopefully.

The woman stopped pouring from the pot and gazed at Betsan. She shook her head. 'No, not today. He's to remain in a darkened room. No visitors allowed.'

That wasn't what Betsan had heard the doctor say, but then again maybe she'd missed that. She frowned and swallowed hard. It wasn't fair at all. She was just as concerned about him as Elinor was, maybe even more so as she'd known him longer and she needed him right now.

Elinor softened her tone. 'It's all right, darlin'. Maybe you can visit him in a day or so.'

A day or so? Was he to remain in his bed until then?

'All right.' She sniffed.

'Look, your father needs his rest right now. He has a headache too and is extremely tired.'

Now Betsan felt guilty. She didn't wish to impede her father's progress.

'Just let me know when I can see him then.'

'I will. I promise. Now there's a cup of tea left in the pot for you and porridge in the pan on the stove. Mrs Jenkins has got Alys and Aled for today.'

This felt so familiar and then Betsan realised why. It was beginning to remind her of when Mam had taken ill. She'd also been bed-bound and in the end she hadn't got out of her bed again.

* * *

Betsan's father didn't get out of bed the following day, nor the day after that. It was becoming apparent after a few days of him being confined to the bedroom that Elinor had it firmly set in her mind that's where he needed to be.

'Aw, don't fret so much, *cariad*,' Mrs Jenkins said later that day when Betsan called around to collect the twins. 'I expect what it is, is Elinor fears losing him. She's trying to keep him out of harm's way. Thinking about it...' She paused for a moment to collect her thoughts. 'Maybe your father would be better off getting another job anyhow. I would have suggested he ask Bert to fix an appointment to see the foreman of the Gethin Coal Pit but that is just as dangerous. There was a bad fall of coal in one of the seams just last week, one of the pit props collapsed. The men and boys were lucky to get out of there alive!'

Betsan gazed around Mrs Jenkins's cosy living room. A fire blazed in the hearth. In front of it the twins were seated on a rag rug playing with two wooden spoons and an upturned saucepan, bashing away at it as if it were a big bass drum. The atmosphere was always warm and welcoming here – not like the frosty reception she sometimes encountered back home. But she had to admit that since she'd run off that time, Elinor had seemed kinder to her. Maybe she regretted selling her mam's sewing machine? Or maybe her father had reprimanded her for doing so?

'Betsan,' Mrs Jenkins said, bringing her back to the present moment, 'don't worry too much. Things have a way of working themselves out – you'll see.'

Betsan smiled. 'I hope so.' Then she glanced at Alys and Aled. 'Come on now, you two, it's time to go back home.'

Aled sighed loudly. 'Me no want to go back home!' His lips formed a pout.

'Well, you have to come now!' Betsan said firmly.

Mrs Jenkins ruffled Aled's hair in a good-natured way. 'They've both had their tea.' Then she clapped her hands together to get their attention. 'Come on, you two! Do as your sister says!'

It seemed strange now to think of herself as their sister, now she knew their mother was in fact her aunt, Maggie. Betsan wondered too if the reason they didn't want to leave Mrs Jenkins's home was because they too were finding it a little frosty next door at times. She hoped not.

* * *

Sergeant Cranbourne called to the house the following day to inform them that Tom McManus had been captured at long last and was now safely in police custody. He enquired after David Morgan but Elinor said her husband was resting in bed. The sergeant made no bones about it and just said for her to pass the news on to him.

It had now been five whole days since Betsan had laid eyes on her father; all she'd heard were muffled voices in his bedroom and the odd groan from him. It was beginning to feel as though Elinor were keeping him as a prisoner. Locked up and far away from everyone else. But if that were the case then why was she doing so?

Even Mrs Jenkins was beginning to wonder why David Morgan had not been seen of late and why he wasn't up and around by now. She voiced her concerns quite animatedly, which caused Elinor to return to her argumentative behaviour, which created an even worse atmosphere.

Finally, one Sunday afternoon, Betsan heard thumps and voices overhead and then footsteps descending down the stairs.

There stood her father framed in the doorway with a blanket draped around his shoulders.

Betsan gulped. Dad appeared so much thinner now. His bruises had turned a yellowy-green and his shirt hung on him like an old sack. The hollows beneath his eyes were prominent as his cheekbones stood out, his face appearing drawn. He seemed old, weary and worn, not the same man who had recently teased and tickled her and laughed as he did so. Not the same man who had wept for joy to have her back home, clinging on to her as if his very life depended on it. This man before her was like some sort of ghost, a shadow of the father she had known. The light had dimmed from his eyes.

'Dad!' she said, stepping forward to greet him, but there was little response. He just stared at her as though she were a stranger to him. The twins, who were sitting on the couch, appeared confused and Alys burst into tears, her shoulders shuddering as she bawled. Betsan lifted her from the couch into her arms, holding her close to soothe her whilst Aled remained where he was as though in a daydream.

Betsan looked at Elinor for some sort of explanation and since none was forthcoming, she turned towards her father, who was swaying from side to side, and softly said, 'Dad, you should sit down. You look a little unsteady on your feet there.'

He nodded blankly as he headed, trembling, towards his favourite armchair. Aled sat staring at him all the while, his mouth open wide.

'Come into the scullery. I need to explain something to you,' said Elinor, clearly sensing Betsan's distress. Betsan nodded and followed her out. 'You may be wondering what's going on, and you have a right to, of course. Your father seems to have some sort of memory loss.' Elinor shook her head. 'He thinks I'm just a barmaid from the pub – not his wife.'

Betsan could hardly believe her ears, though she didn't doubt the woman's words. 'But how is that?' She blinked.

'Doctor Llewellyn did say memory loss is not that uncommon after a blow to the head and that it should return given time. Now,' she warned, 'he doesn't remember me as his wife but that doesn't mean he won't remember you or the twins. Go and have a little chat with him while I brew up; see what he says. But don't get upset if he fails to respond.'

Betsan nodded and returned to the living room.

* * *

Maggie awoke all of a fluster. Something was different. Now what was it? She stretched her arm across the bed to touch the cold spot beside her. He wasn't here any more. Elgan was gone. It felt as though she were a widow when, in reality, he was only locked up in a prison cell.

How was she going to go on? It was a relief for her to have Jimmy around and the lad must feel upset too. He had to, as he'd been that close to Elgan – almost like a son to him. So close Elgan even took him out on the cart with him to help him trade goods. What would happen to his business now? And the horse and cart too? There wasn't just the horse to care for but that old donkey Elgan had once rescued and he'd almost got himself into trouble over that too.

Sergeant Cranbourne had seen to it that the horse and cart were returned to Mags the day following the court case, but it did nothing to assuage her fears.

She sat herself up and inched out from under the bedclothes. Brrr! It was bloomin' freezing. Tentatively, she made her way to the old chair where she'd tossed her clothing last night, the cracked linoleum beneath her feet feeling as cold as ice. After dressing in her thickest blouse and woollen skirt, she sat on the chair to pull up her stockings, securing them with pieces of elastic. Then she yanked on her leather boots and tied the laces tightly – no good slipping in this weather going to the outside lavvy.

Next she poured some water from the jug into the basin on top of the oak washstand and she washed her face. A cat's lick was all it was – no use stripping off as it was perishing cold. The bowl and jug matched, adorned with pretty pink roses either side. They had been a surprise from Elgan after he'd bought some goods from an elderly lady living in one of those big houses at the top of the town. They were well used, but she was so grateful for the gift. There was a small hairline crack on the side of the basin but that didn't seem to matter. The set was the nicest thing she owned and they meant the world to her as they were a gift from Elgan, a treasure amongst her trash.

As she descended the creaking stairs, Jimmy entered through the front door bringing a blast of cold air in with him. He closed the door firmly behind him and stamped his snow-covered boots on the doormat.

'Where have you been?' she asked as she reached the bottom step.

Jimmy's eyes were shiny and bright and his cheeks pinched red from the cold. 'Out to see to Casper and Jasper.' He smiled.

'There's a good lad, you are. Did they take their feed?'

He nodded vigorously. 'Oh yes, and I broke through the ice in their drinking trough for them to get at their water.' He paused for a moment before asking, 'Why do you think Elgan called the donkey a name that rhymed with Casper?'

Maggie chuckled. 'Because he's a daft so-and-so – that's why!' It had often amused her that he did that, but from the moment he'd arrived home with that old donkey, they'd both fallen in love with him.

They seemed to take in all the waifs and strays, like with Jimmy. The other lads who had boarded with them had now gone on their way as they were old enough to care for themselves, but Mags had to admit that money from the parish for their keep had been helpful – though there was more than a time or two she'd spent some of it on gin.

Jimmy nodded. 'Well, the two of them seem to get on with one another. What are we going to do about Elgan's round though?'

Maggie shrugged. 'I'm not sure. I never got the chance to discuss it with him before he was taken down. Sell it maybe?'

'Oh no!' said Jimmy, his face crestfallen. 'He's taken a long time to build up that business and who knows what would become of Casper and Jasper? They might not get such a kind owner as Elgan.'

'You're fond of those beasts, aren't you, lad?' Maggie tilted her head to one side.

'Yes, I suppose I am. But I don't think I could run that business on my own.'

'You could do it if I helped you,' said Maggie thoughtfully. 'Stick that kettle on the fire to boil and we'll have a little chat about it over a cuppa.'

Jimmy grinned wholeheartedly.

A decision was finally made that the pair would try to keep Elgan's business going as long as he remained in prison, though Maggie realised she would now have to keep away from gin shops and taverns. Her drinking had been her way of soothing herself, applying a balm on an open sore that somehow had failed to heal. As a young girl, becoming pregnant to a then married man hadn't been what she'd had in mind. Back then, she'd dreamt of her prince whisking her away to his ivory tower and had believed in her happy ever after.

But the reality had been a relationship with an older, married man. And although she'd never doubted Elgan's love for her – not once in all that time – society had dictated that she was then a loose woman with dubious morals. Elgan had been unable to leave his sick wife even though the light of his love for the woman had long since dimmed. So the twins had been born under a cloak of secrecy. And fair play to Gwendolyn and David, they'd taken the pair on as their own.

She'd often wondered this past couple of years how they were doing after she'd been banished from the Morgan family home. When did the twins begin to walk? Who was first? Aled or Alys? How old were they when they each cut their first tooth? All these things were painful for her so she tried not to think too much. But what she had realised was that by giving them away to her sister and brother-in-law she had been providing them with a better life.

But now things had changed – she was off the booze and she'd more than proved herself by caring for Jimmy. She wondered about having them back, to heal that gulf in her life. And anyhow now Gwennie was no longer here, was it fair for David's new wife to take them on as her own?

'I think I'll go to pay my respects to my brother-in-law later today,' she declared, glancing at Jimmy.

His eyebrows shot up in surprise.

'Are you sure that's a good idea, after all you told me about what went on?'

'Sure it is. It's been a long time coming and I want to find out how Gwennie died.' Her shoulders slumped as she uttered the name she used for her sister – she was the only one who had called her 'Gwennie'.

This felt all too much to take. The loss of her Elgan and the loss of her dear sister too, all within a couple of days. Although she'd not seen her for over three years, there'd always been the hope that someday they might be reunited once again. Now that hope had been extinguished forever like a burnt-out candle. She didn't want to allow that to ever happen again with any other loved one. A valuable lesson had been learnt that day: the lights could go out completely at any time and she bitterly regretted not getting herself off the booze sooner, as then she might have been accepted back into the bosom of the family.

She made a vow there and then to hang on to Betsan and the twins at any cost, even if it meant she'd never touch another drop of 'mother's ruin' ever again.

* * *

'Dad...' Betsan said tentatively as she approached her father, who was still sitting in the armchair. Now he was staring into the flames of the fire in the hearth.

Slowly, he turned to face her and lifted his head. To her utter relief, there was recognition in his eyes.

'Betsan.' He reached out his arms towards her and she stepped forward, stooping to embrace him as he drew her in close.

When she finally pulled away, she asked, 'How are you feeling now?'

'I'm feeling so much better, poppet. But where is your mother? She should be here by now. Is she nattering with Bronwen next door as usual?' He chuckled.

A surge of shock socked her in the gut. Oh, no! Betsan's hands flew to her face. Her father was making no sense whatsoever. Mam had been gone for over a year. But how could she possibly tell him that without upsetting him all over again?

Her father's eyes diverted towards the corner of the room where the Singer sewing machine once stood. He frowned. 'Where's your mother's sewing machine, then? Now tell me where is it? And where is she?'

He seemed to be getting agitated now, just as Elinor came hurrying in from the scullery. Aled and Alys sat there in stony, stunned silence.

'David,' Elinor said softly, 'I sold the old sewing machine. I put it in part exchange for our lovely new dresser! Don't you remember?'

He turned his head and, trembling, stood. His eyes were fixed and beady. This was a side of her father Betsan had not seen before and it scared her half to death.

Elinor sent Betsan a frightened glance. Neither of them knew what to say to calm him, and then Alys began to break down in tears once again. Fortunately, this managed to distract her father. He seemed to forget what was said and he reseated himself, asking, 'Did someone say they were making a cup of tea?'

Elinor nodded, her eyes brimming with tears. She whispered to Betsan, 'This is the reason I've been keeping him away from you children.'

Betsan nodded. Now she understood and, for the first time ever, she actually felt sympathy for the woman.

Not long later, when the scene had settled down, while everyone was sipping their tea and the twins were playing on the fireside rug, there was a knock on the front door.

'That's all I need.' Elinor sighed and she went off to answer it.

11

Maggie waited patiently on the doorstep of the house in Plymouth Street as a curtain twitched in the house next door. Finally, the door swung open. What she saw before her was a young woman, around ten years or so younger than her sister would have been. From the swell beneath her rose-print gown, it was obvious she was with child.

So this was the woman who had slipped so easily into her sister's shoes before even a full year of respectful mourning had taken place?

The woman appeared flustered as she scraped back a strand of hair behind her ear that had worked loose from her coiled, pinned-back style. She narrowed her eyes with suspicion. 'Yes?'

'I'm here to see the family. I'm Betsan's Aunt Maggie. Gwendolyn was my sister...'

Recognition dawned and the woman's eyes widened. 'Hey, I've seen you plastered many a time around the town and when I worked at the Vulcan Inn before I took to working at the Star. You'd best be off. The family won't want to see the likes of you!'

She shooed Maggie with her hand as though she were an annoying wasp.

But Maggie remained where she was, firm-footed on the doorstep. 'That's as may be. I don't deny I had a drink problem in the past, but that's all over and done with now and I've come to pay the family a visit!'

Maggie began to stare the young woman out who, after all, was in reality just a chit of a girl. The woman turned her back and, for a moment, Maggie feared she might slam the door in her face, but instead she disappeared down the passageway and didn't return, leaving the door partially open. What now? Should she remain where she was or follow after her? As she hesitated, Betsan appeared at the door.

'Come inside, Aunt Maggie.'

Maggie nodded gratefully, tears in her eyes. At least someone was pleased to see her. 'Thank you, darlin'.'

'Dad hasn't been himself lately,' Betsan whispered behind the palm of her hand. 'He had a blow to the head.'

'Oh?' Maggie's eyes widened. 'What happened to him?' She lowered her voice to match her niece's for fear of being over-heard inside the house.

'A man at the Star Inn caused trouble and punched him. He was knocked out for a while. But he seems to have forgotten stuff. He can't even remember marrying Elinor; she's almost like a stranger to him now.'

'I'm assuming that was her at the door?' Maggie sniffed loudly.

'Yes. I don't think she's very pleased that you've called at the moment.'

'Don't you worry, Betsan. I haven't come here to make trouble. Quite the opposite. I won't outstay my welcome but I admit

I've stayed away far too long when I should have been here for you all.'

'Come with me,' said Betsan, taking Maggie's hand.

Betsan led her to the half-open door of the living room and as she pushed it open, Maggie saw a picture of perfection. Her two babies, who were not babies any longer, were sitting on the rug in front of the fireplace. Alys, who had beautiful large blue eyes framed with thick dark lashes, was playing with her rag doll, and Aled was engrossed in his play as he wheeled a wooden train across the floor. They both looked up as she entered, their eyes full of wonderment.

She was about to rush over to them and draw them to her, feeling such a huge rush of love towards them – it was almost as though it were a torrent that had swelled up inside of her for three long years that needed release – but then she thought better of it. For all intents and purposes, she'd left her kids with David and Gwennie and what would Betsan's father say to that now? But when she glanced from the twins to his direction, he was smiling broadly as though pleased to see her.

'Oh, Mags!' he said, rising from his armchair. 'I don't know what on earth has happened to Gwendolyn. I expect she's still out at the marketplace or something. She'll be so disappointed to have missed you...'

Maggie glanced at Betsan who shrugged her shoulders. Just as well her niece had informed her of this situation otherwise she'd have wondered what was going on.

Maggie returned the smile feeling genuinely pleased to see her brother-in-law, but didn't he look thin and gaunt now? Not the strapping chap she remembered so well.

'Sit yourself down, Mags!' he said warmly.

She was about to seat herself on the couch when the young

woman, Elinor, entered. She also nodded as if to say she could sit down.

'Betsan, make your aunt a cuppa,' said David in a cheerful manner.

'It's all right, I'll do it,' said Elinor, a stony expression on her face.

David Morgan glared at the woman, his sunny demeanour now suddenly gone. 'I've no idea what you're doing here in my house!' he yelled harshly, causing Maggie to flinch.

Why was he being so nasty towards Elinor? It really wasn't like him at all. She'd never seen him like this in all the years he was married to her sister.

Elinor frowned. 'I live here with you, David. Don't you remember marrying me?'

'What kind of a fool do you take me for?' he shouted as he rose from the armchair and raised his hand above her head as if about to strike her, but she fled the room in tears before he could do anything. Then glancing at Maggie, he said in a normal tone of voice, 'I don't know who that flibbertigibbet thinks she is coming into my house and taking over while Gwendolyn is out!'

'Who is she then?' Maggie asked, curious to see who he believed she was.

'Elinor Evans, a young barmaid who works with me at the Star Inn. Bit of a floozie, if you ask me!'

So it was evident he did know who she was – there was some recognition at least – but he didn't realise he'd since married her and thought Gwennie was still alive.

Maggie smiled in nervous reassurance at Betsan as she hovered between the living room and the scullery, not quite knowing what to do or how to react.

'I'll tell you what,' said Maggie, as her lower lip quivered with apprehension, 'how about I make the tea instead? Always could brew a good cuppa me!'

David smiled broadly. 'Splendid idea!' he said, rubbing the palms of his hands together.

* * *

Betsan frowned as she sipped her cup of tea. Why was Dad acting so strangely these days? She'd never seen him in such a rage as he'd been when he'd raised his hand to Elinor. No wonder her stepmother had kept him upstairs in the bedroom. Since he'd turned on her, Elinor hadn't returned to the room. Betsan guessed she'd taken herself to bed. Even at her tender age, she realised it couldn't be good for a pregnant woman to get upset like that.

Deciding to have a word with her aunt to see what her thoughts were, she followed her to the door when she made to leave. At least Dad seemed warm and approving towards her, not knowing that she'd once been banished from the house.

'Now, don't you go worrying yourself, Betsan,' her aunt said softly on the doorstep. 'You know if there's any trouble you can always come to me. I expect this blow to the head is making your father act so strangely...' She paused for a moment.

'What is it, Auntie?' Betsan blinked several times while her aunt chewed on her bottom lip.

'I'm thinking about the twins, how maybe I should offer to take them to my house to ease the load for Elinor – she's pregnant, after all, and has to look after your father.'

Betsan deliberated a moment before blurting out, 'I know about the twins.'

Maggie's eyes widened. 'Know what about them, darlin'?'

Now Betsan wished she hadn't said anything in case she upset her aunt, but she'd started so she decided to carry on. Whispering, she said, 'That they're yours really...'

Maggie's mouth popped open. 'How do you know that?'

'Mrs Jenkins next door told me.'

Maggie shook her head. 'So, it was her who was curtain twitching when I arrived. She's not some sort of gossip, is she? She seemed all right when she called with you the other day.'

'No, she's not a gossip. She's most kind. Mam told her about the twins. Mrs Jenkins found it hard to tell me but I got it out of her. She won't go spreading it around; she's not like that.'

Maggie nodded and then laid a hand on Betsan's shoulder. 'Yes, they're my children but I couldn't cope with them at the time. I was unwell but your mother and father did a fine job bringing them up. But I want you to let me know if you and Elinor can't cope. You hear?'

Betsan nodded. 'I will. I promise.'

'There's a good girl. Now give your auntie a big kiss!' She leaned forward to embrace her and Betsan inhaled the comforting scent of lavender one more time. It was so good to have Aunt Maggie back in her life.

* * *

Although Aunt Maggie's visit had bucked Betsan up no end, as she watched her walk away from the house, her stomach lurched.

When she returned indoors, there was still no sign of Elinor. She'd assumed that as soon as Auntie left the house, Elinor would show her face again, but maybe she was now afraid to; after all, her father had shown a side of himself that even Betsan had not witnessed before in all her young life. Had he been nasty like that to her mother? Hopefully not. She decided to probe Mrs Jenkins about the matter later.

Her father smiled as she entered the living room. 'Your mother will be sorry she missed Maggie,' he said, shaking his head. 'Now, where can she have got to? Be a good girl and pop around next door to ask Mrs Jenkins if she's seen her?'

Oh dear, what should she do now? She didn't want to leave the twins in her father's care in case he should lose his temper again. So instead, she nodded, but went in search of her step-mother upstairs.

She knocked on her bedroom door softly and it was a time before Elinor opened it. Her eyes looked puffy and sore from crying.

'Dad wants me to go next door to ask what's keeping my mother...' she whispered. 'He seems to think she's still alive...' She gulped for air for a moment at the mention of her. 'And I don't want to leave my brother and sister alone with him just in case...'

Elinor nodded. 'Don't worry, I'll come downstairs and sit with them. This can't go on though, Betsan. I don't think I can live here for much longer. You saw how he made to strike me. He no longer recognises me as his wife and it's not good for the baby either if he continues shouting at me like that.'

She sniffed loudly and reached for her handkerchief from her skirt pocket to dab at the tears that had formed.

Betsan nodded. A few weeks ago, she'd have given anything for the woman to have walked out on her father. But now, in the cold light of day, she recognised Elinor as a young woman who had done her best to take on an older man and three young children.

'Don't worry,' she said as she touched the woman's forearm lightly in reassurance. 'I won't let anything happen to you or my new brother or sister.'

Elinor's smile illuminated her eyes. 'I used to think you were a right little madam, especially that time you kicked off about your mam's sewing machine.' She took in a deep breath and released it. 'But I can see now how much it meant to you and I was wrong to sell it like that.'

Betsan nodded and, with a lump in her throat, said, 'I'm going to have a word with Mrs Jenkins to see what she thinks of all this, if you don't mind?'

Elinor shook her head. 'No, I don't mind. She has a right to know as he could get a bit sharp with her too.'

'I won't be too long,' Betsan said reassuringly.

* * *

As Maggie walked back home, she felt deeply troubled. What on earth had come over David for him to raise his hand like that to a woman? In all the years she'd known him as her brother-in-law, he'd been quite a gentle sort of soul who, although he could handle himself when it came to any trouble brewing at the pub, was in general a peaceable sort of a fella. Were the kids safe staying with him now? His character seemed volatile and unpredictable. And what about his new wife? She'd seemed sparky on the doorstep. Though in her defence, she had allowed her admittance into the house; she might well have slammed the door in her face.

But there was one prevailing thought running through Maggie's mind: would the twins be better off living with her now? That young woman, Elinor, was pregnant with her own child. However would she cope with four of them when it arrived?

By the time she returned home, Jimmy was concerned and looking out on the doorstep for her.

'I was just about to send out a search party!' he teased.

Maggie shook her head as she puffed out a cloud of steam. It was bitterly cold. She couldn't wait to get inside and as soon as she followed him indoors, she removed her shawl and hung it on the peg behind the door.

'I stayed a little longer than intended,' she explained, 'due to my concerns...'

She gravitated towards the fireplace to thaw out her blue and stiffened fingers.

'Oh?'

'Betsan's father has suffered a blow to the head and he's not himself. He thinks my sister is still alive!'

'Huh?' Jimmy's eyes widened.

'Not only that, he shouted at his new wife – in front of me! – and raised his hand as if to strike her. He didn't in the end, but it concerns me – and she's pregnant an' all.'

'That's not good,' said Jimmy. 'My dad was like that with my mam before he died. But what about your twins?'

'They're proper little darlings.' Maggie's eyes shone as she spoke about them. 'They looked clean and well fed but in view of what I witnessed, I'm going to get them out of there.'

Jimmy's mouth fell open. 'B... but how will we manage? This house is pretty small and there's the business to run.'

'Don't you worry about that now. We managed all right while the other parish lads were dossing here. The twins can bunch up with me in my double bed. Now Elgan's inside there's plenty of room.'

'Aye, maybe.'

But Maggie could tell by the look on the lad's face that he had concerns. And to be truthful, so did she. What could she do though? As far as she was concerned, she had little choice.

PART II

12

_____

Elinor was in the middle of packing a carpetbag of her belongings.

'Fetch my hairbrush and mirror from upstairs, darlin'.' She glanced at Betsan, whose bottom lip was trembling. 'And make sure you're quiet about doing so, not to wake your father. I can't have him shouting at me again.' She hesitated a moment, before placing the palms of her hands on Betsan's shoulders. 'I'm sorry, I have the baby to think about.'

A tear coursed down Betsan's cheek. Now she was beginning to warm to Elinor and appreciating the things she had done for the family, it was time for her to leave them all.

'B... but where will you go?' She sniffed loudly.

'Florrie will take me in at her place. She's got rooms at a pub in Church Street.'

Betsan nodded and then she quietly left to fetch the hairbrush and matching hand mirror for her stepmother. Softly, she pushed open the bedroom door to see her father lying there on his back gently snoring. To look at him now, he was a different person to how he'd been last night when he'd yelled loudly at Elinor and threatened to push her down the stairs. She'd 'wormed her way into his house' according to him, which had made his wife leave!

Whatever was he thinking? From his viewpoint, Mam was still alive, no matter what anyone told him. His mind was fixed on that, and it was causing him a great deal of distress.

She padded tentatively to the dressing table, located the hairbrush set and lifted it. As she did so, her father let out a loud snorting noise, which startled her, causing her to drop the set on the wooden floorboards.

This awoke him.

Trembling, she looked at her father and gulped.

'Where are you going with those?' He blinked and, rubbing his eyes, sat up in bed.

'Just taking them to Mam. She's asked for them,' she lied.

Feeling satisfied with her answer, he nodded. 'When did she say supper would be ready?'

'N... not for ages yet...' Her voice trailed off into barely a whisper and she swallowed hard, her mouth as dry as parchment paper.

Her father reclined his head on the pillow and, closing his eyes, appeared to drift off back to sleep.

That had been a close one.

Quickly, she picked up the hairbrush set from the floor and took it downstairs where she handed it to Elinor.

Elinor's eyes seemed large and shiny. It really felt like it was hurting the woman to have to leave, but she had her unborn child and her own health to think of.

'Thank you,' she said, taking the set from Betsan's outstretched hand, and then she hugged her warmly, planted a kiss on her cheek and placed the set in her bag and closed it. She took her cape from the arm of the chair and draped it around her shoulders, tied the ribbons of her bonnet and took the bag in her hand. 'Now, I've told Bronwen what's going to happen and she's agreed with me. Said she'll keep Aled and Alys there for today, not to upset them with my leaving, but darlin' you must ask your auntie to take them with her. Bronwen told me they are her children and that you know about it, so they are her responsibility. And providing she keeps off the drink, then they will be safer with her than here.'

Betsan nodded soberly. She had to agree with that statement. 'I'll miss you,' she said, and gulped, fighting to hold back the tears.

'After all the spats we had? No, you won't!' Elinor chuckled.

'I will. I am so sorry for upsetting you.'

'Me too.' Elinor smiled. 'Now, I best be going before it gets dark. Mrs Jenkins knows the address I'm off to but, for now, please don't tell your father, will you?'

Betsan shook her head, realising that all of this was for the best even if it hurt so very much.

'Don't look so worried. I'll still be around and if your father gets his memory back and calms down then I shall return, but for the time being this is the best way.' She nodded and Betsan mirrored the gesture.

And then she watched her stepmother leave the living room with her large, bulky carpetbag in hand. Would Dad even notice she'd left the house?

The only thing she could think to do was to climb up to the attic and have a word with her mother's portrait.

* * *

When Betsan's father rose from bed later that evening, he was more concerned about filling his stomach than asking where Elinor was. She appeared to have gone right out of his mind. Thankfully, Elinor had made a large pot of cawl before her departure, which would see them through a couple of days, especially if Betsan then made dumplings to go along with it. But what then? Would her father throw a fit of temper if she asked him for some housekeeping money?

After warming and ladling up the cawl for her father and placing the bowl in front of him at the scullery table, she informed him she was popping next door to see Mrs Jenkins. She didn't mention the twins and neither did he ask about them.

All he said to her was: 'Tell your mam to hurry up in there. I know she likes a natter with Bronwen but she wasn't even here to serve up my supper – you had to do it!' Though this he said with a good deal of humour and she noticed a playful glint in his eyes as she left for next door.

'I really don't know what to do, Mrs Jenkins,' Betsan explained next door as Aled and Alys chewed on buttered crusts of bread.

Bert was stood at the sink with his braces dangling down from his waist as he washed his top half thoroughly over the stone sink. He was getting ready for a night shift at the coal pit. Betsan realised the couple could well do without any problems from the family next door.

'Betsan,' said Bert tentatively, 'you need to ask your father for that housekeeping money now your stepmother has left home.'

'But I don't know what to say in case he gets nasty again!' She shook her head as memories of him raising his hand to Elinor came flooding back to her.

Bronwen and Bert exchanged worried glances.

'That doesn't sound much like your father to me,' said Bert, frowning. 'I've always known him to be an affable sort of a fella.'

Betsan didn't know what affable meant but she guessed it was probably something good as she'd never in all her young life heard anyone say a bad word against her father, not ever. Even Elinor, who had been through so much of late and borne the brunt of his bad temper, did not run him down. She understood it was the blow to the head that had caused this to happen and she was just protecting herself and their unborn child by leaving.

'I had a thought...' Betsan began. 'Well, it was something Elinor said – that maybe the twins ought to return to their mother.'

'Oh for goodness' sake!' said Mrs Jenkins. 'I don't know if that's a good idea!' She glanced at Bert for reassurance.

Her husband slowly shook his head. 'From what I know of Maggie, she'll be back on the booze anytime soon, if she's not already.'

Betsan exhaled a shuddering breath. Maybe they were right and she ought to do all she could to keep the family together. Would the twins be safer staying put?

'I don't know what I'm going to tell Dad about Mam when I go back home.'

'Pardon?' Mrs Jenkins frowned.

'He thinks she's over here with you chatting away. He told me to remind her to stop nattering and return home. He doesn't even remember Elinor is his wife any more.'

Mrs Jenkins tutted. 'I know I've said a lot in the past about that one but she's to be commended for how she's handled the situation up until now.'

Betsan had to agree with that.

* * *

Elinor's presence was missed the following day. Betsan found it difficult with her not being around. Up until recently, she hadn't appreciated quite what her stepmother was doing for the family. Before her father's amnesia, Elinor had made him happy. He'd had a purpose in life, something to live for, something to get up for in the morning and start the day with a view to working for his family. Now, it appeared as if it was all too much effort for him to drag himself out of bed.

This couldn't go on. She had the twins to see to. She'd already lost one parent and didn't intend on losing the other.

Although Mrs Jenkins was kind and helpful, she could hardly expect the woman to tend to their needs all day long, especially as she seemed to be lacking energy these days. The truth of the matter was the woman wasn't getting any younger and maybe now caring for the twins was getting too much for her, but even if this was indeed the case, she didn't like to complain.

By the end of the day, Betsan had realised she couldn't cope with stepping into Elinor's shoes – they just weren't a good fit at all. And despite what Mrs Jenkins had said, the twins were now Aunt Maggie's responsibility; they were her own flesh and blood. So she dressed them warmly: Alys in her thick woollen dress with two shawls draped around her shoulders and her bonnet, and Aled in his long trousers, jacket and muffler with two shirts on his back and his tweed flat cap.

It wasn't that long a walk over to the China district but it would be a bitterly cold one. With any luck, they'd arrive before dark. But what if Aunt Maggie refused to take the pair? What then?

But something inside her told her that she would take them in, would be delighted to even. She'd seen the way her aunt had gazed at them when she'd paid her recent visit. And the twins had taken to her immediately, something they weren't prone to doing with strangers. But maybe Maggie did not look like a stranger to them as she resembled Mam so very much – except her figure was curvaceous and her manner quite coarse at times.

'Are we going shopping?' asked Alys as she watched Betsan fetch the wicker basket from the scullery.

'No, we're not going shopping but I will be after I've dropped you off with your m— Er, I mean, Aunt Maggie.' She smiled, having almost slipped up.

Aled frowned. 'Where's Aunt Magsie?' he asked, not quite getting the name right.

'Her house isn't far away,' Betsan reassured, lowering her voice. 'Now then, you pair, Dad needs his rest, so we must keep quiet as little mice leaving here. No chatter, all right?' The pair nodded in unison. 'Fingers on lips like this then!' She placed an index finger to her own lips and the pair did the same with theirs.

She led them out to the passageway, and softly closed the living room door behind them. She had a few pennies in her purse that Elinor had left behind, which should be enough to purchase a loaf of bread and a hunk of cheese from the market-place. She reckoned she could buy a few tangerines and a bag of mixed nuts too. It was Christmas week, after all. But what then? As far as she knew, there was no other money left lying around the house. Did Dad have any? And if he did, would he remember where he kept it?

As she closed the front door behind them, she noticed the dove-grey sky overhead, which promised the threat of snow.

Sniffing loudly, she walked her brother and sister along the street whilst holding their hands firmly, with the basket over the crook of her arm. With any luck, she might be able to return home before her father awoke.

Rooftops glistened shiny and white, and shapes became silhouettes against the landscape in the frosty late afternoon air. It was that time of day when the light faded away to be met with its nemesis: darkness.

Darkness was no one's friend. When darkness appeared, the criminal element hid in doorways or shadows to capture their unsuspecting prey. And it was then under its cloak that nefarious deeds were doled out. It was the time when Betsan preferred to be in the safe sanctuary of home and how she wished she had set out a little sooner. She should have left before darkness finally fell like a curtain at the theatre.

Aled and Alys were working hard to keep up with her quick pace, their little legs doing twice the work. Every so often, either or both of them would give an upward glance at her as they wondered what on earth was going on.

Finally, when they reached Bethesda Street, now in close proximity to China, Betsan rested a moment to catch her breath. The freezing cold air was making her lungs ache; it hit her full force so that she gasped for breath. By now, the twins were almost in tears. She knelt so she was at the same level and hugged them closely.

'Sorry, kids. I wanted to rush to get here before it got too dark.' Then she kissed Alys, who had tears streaming down both cheeks. 'Sorry, darling.'

She handed her sister her favourite rag doll, which she'd had stuffed in her basket.

Alys immediately smiled and ceased crying. Aled was doing

his best to stem his flow of tears. He sniffed loudly and swallowed.

'Sorry, Aled.' She kissed him too and then stood.

'Where's Elinor?' he asked, looking up at her with such doleful eyes her heart went out to him. Of course both children missed her, as they had taken to her; she'd been a mother to them.

'She's gone to live at Florrie's place for the time being,' she explained, but she could tell by the blank look on his face he just didn't understand why his new stepmother would leave them like that.

It was going to be hard for her to part with the pair of them, but like Elinor, she realised it was all for the best.

Mags wrapped the gin bottle up in an old tray cloth and placed it in her shopping basket. She planned to see the twins tomorrow, but tonight she needed the comfort. Parting with Elgan had been bad enough to contend with but realising her own dear sister had left this earthly realm was really getting under her skin and the guilt of not seeing her or even being there for the family as she lay dying was a bitter pill to swallow.

Soon she'd be home and she could sit in front of the fire with her feet up.

Oh, Elgan, why did you have to leave me right now when I need you so much?

There were so many things she relied on him for. Not just him bringing an income into the house but little things like how he rubbed her back when she felt unwell, how sometimes he knelt at her feet to unlace her boots when she'd had a hard day and wanted to kick them off. The bed was far too empty without him in it. She'd known him most of her adult life. He was all she'd known really. Oh, there'd been flirtations with other men over the years, but that's all they'd been. She wasn't as promiscuous as folk liked to imagine. Elgan was the only man who'd had proper carnal knowledge of her body and soul, and that was the way she wanted it to remain.

She had felt guilty though when she'd first met him; she'd not known he was a married man but by then he'd pled undying love towards her and it was only after that night he'd taken her virginity that he thought to tell her he had a wife.

Although it had upset her so and she'd broken off relations with him for a time, she'd found it hard to stay away from him, and him from her. She'd known of his wife, Thelma – had even spoken to her on occasion over the years. She'd seemed a kind, homely sort, but apparently, things had soured with time and in the end there was little love between them. Out of duty, Elgan had stayed with his wife, even when Mags had borne their twins. It wasn't until after the woman had passed away that Elgan felt able to move Mags into his house and beggar what any of the neighbours made of that. It had been their business and their business alone. But she had to admit, she didn't feel real happiness and peace about the situation until the day he'd married her.

To have and to hold, from this day forward...

Well, you can't bleedin' hold me now, can you, Elgan?

A warm tear trickled down her cheek.

* * *

Jimmy was visiting the marketplace to see if he could persuade any of Elgan's trading customers to purchase some of the items Elgan had stowed away in the old stable where he kept the horse and donkey. There were some nice pieces of furniture there, which ought to bring a bob or two. A table and matching chairs, a wardrobe and dresser, some pieces of pottery and the best of all was a Singer sewing machine. He was thinking that maybe Mrs O'Connell who ran the clothing stall might purchase that.

Mags wouldn't inspect any of the items herself; she'd just instructed him to get on with it as she nipped out for a while. She'd told him he'd been helping Elgan long enough to have some kind of an idea of their worth. Though to be honest, it was the sewing machine he had no clue about. What did one of those fetch? There was a shop that sold new ones on the high street – he'd have a wander over there before he called to see Mrs O'Connell, but thinking about it, maybe that shop purchased second-hand ones as well.

It had been a total surprise to discover it at the back of the stable under an old dusty tarpaulin. Elgan hadn't even mentioned it to him when they'd worked together last. Had he been saving it for a special customer? But Mags had told him to sell as much of the stuff as he could. So that's precisely what he'd do.

Mags was about to pour herself a swig of gin when there was a rap on the front door. Surely Jimmy wasn't back so soon? He hadn't all that long left home. She replaced the cork in the bottle, wrapped it up once again in the tray cloth and hid it in the cupboard behind an old tin where she kept the cake. Then brushing down her worsted skirt and patting her hair, she headed towards the door.

After unbolting it and turning the key in the lock, she gasped with surprise. There, stood on the doorstep, was Betsan with

Aled and Alys either side, their faces pinched red from the cold. A trickle of snot had found its way out of Aled's nostrils and was hovering between there and his upper lip. She reached into her pocket for her handkerchief and wiped it for him, before replacing the hankie in her pocket as she smiled at them all.

'Oh, come in, you lot!' she said, all thoughts of the gin bottle going out of her head. 'You look half perished to death!'

Betsan nodded gratefully. 'I... I've come to ask you a favour, Auntie Mags,' she said tentatively.

'Don't stand there on ceremony on the doorstep – come inside!' She beckoned them to step over the threshold and then all three entered her humble abode. 'Now, remove your outer garments and take a seat by the fireside and I'll fetch something warm to drink. Will the little ones drink tea?'

Betsan nodded eagerly. 'They will if you put a little bit of sugar in it if you have some?'

Auntie smiled and nodded. 'Not a problem, darlin', and I'll ensure I don't give it too hot to them either.' She watched Betsan remove her shawl and bonnet and then help her siblings off with their outer garments.

'It's lovely and warm in here, Aunt Mags.' She beamed as she placed their belongings on the table and took a seat in the armchair.

'Just as well as it's perishing outside.'

'You've been out yourself then?'

'Oh, yes. I only popped out to pick up some bits and pieces.' Mags failed to tell her that her shopping had been just a bottle of alcohol, or 'mother's ruin' as folk deemed it. Maybe it was just as well they'd arrived when they had, as now she'd not put a single drop to her lips.

And maybe it ought to stay that way.

Soon they were all warmed up and seated with a cup of tea,

and Mags set out a plate of jam tarts. She'd baked them fresh that morning and watched in awe as the little ones eagerly consumed them.

'So, what's the favour you wanted to ask then?' She tilted her head to one side curiously.

'Er...' Betsan hesitated before taking a deep breath and blurting out, 'Elinor has left home to move in with her friend Florrie from the pub. I thought that maybe, er, maybe Aled and Alys might stay here for a while under the circumstances, at least until she returns.'

Mags smiled. 'I'd be delighted to have them stop here with me and Jimmy. I was going to suggest it anyhow.' She lowered her voice to barely a whisper so that Betsan had to lean in to listen. 'They don't know I'm their... m.o.t.h.e.r?'

'Oh, no, not as yet,' Betsan reassured her.

'They're more than welcome.' She raised her voice to its normal pitch to address them. 'Would you like to stay with your Auntie Mags for a while, kids?' Both children looked a little uncertain, their wide eyes searching Betsan's for her approval. But then Mags added, 'You can help me feed Casper and Jasper in the morning if you stay here.'

'Who... who's Casper and Jasper?' Aled said with a slight lisp.

'One is a horse and the other a donkey,' she explained.

Aled's face immediately lit up and Alys smiled.

'So, what do you say?' Mags held her breath, hoping they'd say yes. It would be the first night her own flesh and blood had stayed under the same roof as her since she'd fled, leaving them with her sister. What on earth had she been thinking of back then? The truth was her mind had been in utter turmoil and, if she was being less harsh with herself, she would have recognised it as the melancholia some women experienced following childbirth. But in her case, it had been severe: a kind of madness had set in. It was a place in her mind she never wished to revisit.

Her heart leapt as both children nodded eagerly.

'Good, that's settled then!' She beckoned Betsan to follow her to the scullery where they could talk freely and, when they were out of earshot of the children, she asked her niece, 'So, just why did Elinor leave?'

Betsan's face reddened. 'It's Dad. He's become quite nasty towards her. She felt it unsafe to stay for her and the baby's sake. He almost pushed her down the stairs last night.'

Mags gasped. 'I witnessed enough when I paid you a visit. He's not been aggressive towards you and the twins though, has he?'

'Oh no.' Betsan shook her head vehemently. 'He's been nice as pie to us. It's just Elinor he's taken a strong dislike to. He seems to think Mam is still alive and Elinor has taken her place and pushed her out of the house. Well, that's what he thinks sometimes; other times when Elinor's out of the room, he believes Mam is still living at home and either out shopping or talking to Mrs Jenkins in her house next door.'

'Elinor did take your mam's place in a sense but your father was responsible for that. Still,' Mags sighed deeply, 'it sounds as if his mind will no longer accept that fact. When did he last see a doctor?'

'Not since a day or two after the blow to his head. Doctor Llewellyn visited that same night and he checked him over a couple of days later, but he wasn't as bad then as he is now.'

'Hmmm. I don't know what to suggest – doctors do cost money. Money most folk don't have. Which brings me to you. Have you money to live on?'

Betsan shook her head. 'Only a few pennies Elinor left for us from the housekeeping jar, which I'll spend at the marketplace later on my way home from here. After that I don't know how we'll survive as Dad can hardly return to work right now, and if he has some money somewhere, I don't know if he'll remember where he's put it.'

Mags swallowed a lump of sadness that had formed in her throat. Her niece seemed so desperate to take care of them all. Her heart went out to her.

'Look, when you leave here, buy what you intended from the market and then tomorrow, catch your father when he's in a good mood. Not when he's just risen from bed, mind you – give him time to come around and make sure he's eaten. Most folk get angry or upset if they're tired or hungry. If he has no money to give you then come back to me and I'll help you out.'

Betsan nodded. Mags hated to see her niece in this sort of position – not when the person who ought to have been caring for her, particularly since her mother's death, needed taking care of himself.

Finally, it was time for Betsan to go shopping. The market-place was open until late in the run-up to Christmas, but Mags didn't want her to hang around and, in any case, Betsan didn't want to leave her father unattended for too long either.

'Don't worry none, darlin',' Mags said optimistically. 'Aled and Alys can bunk in my bedroom tonight now your Uncle Elgan is no longer here. We'll keep one another warm and then tomorrow morning I'll take them to the stable to feed Casper and Jasper. They'll enjoy that.'

Betsan nodded. Then, as if she suddenly remembered something, she stood and lifted her basket from the table. 'I've packed a change of clothing for the twins. But if you need any more, you'll have to call to the house for them.' She handed the neatly folded garments to her.

'They'll be fine, don't fret none,' Mags said, wagging an index finger in the air. 'If your father gives you any grief, come to me. I'll sort him out for you. I always did have a way with him.'

'I will, Auntie, that's a good idea. I noticed when you visited the house, Dad seemed pleased to see you.' She stooped to kiss the twins. 'You be good, both of you and I'll call to see how you're doing tomorrow.'

'Don't go worrying about that. I'll bring them to you. Now take care leaving here as it's dark outside. Wish our Jimmy were here to walk you home.' Mags frowned.

'I'll be all right. I'll go quickly now.'

'Don't stop to talk to any men, you hear?' This time she wagged an index finger in Betsan's direction.

'I won't, Auntie. Right, I'm going!'

She blew a kiss to the twins and she was gone, out into the night air. A nefarious, uncertain place to enter, particularly during the hours of darkness.

* * *

'A penny for a fumble!' Betsan heard a woman's provocative cry as a man, who appeared to be swaying back and forth, left the inn she'd been in with Martha recently.

Betsan watched the woman, under the glow of the lamplight, who appeared to be a suggestive sort in a low-cut dress – and in this freezing weather too. If Mrs Jenkins thought that Elinor was some sort of hussy, she was nothing in comparison to this sort stood bold as brass here, exposing parts of herself to men leaving the pub and asking them for pennies!

The man grinned at the woman and then she heard him tossing coins in her direction, which landed at her feet.

The man, as if realising he had thrown more money than he cared to, dropped to his knees and then down onto all fours to scour the ground but the woman placed one ankle-booted foot on his back, pinioning him there. Daringly, she lifted her skirts and as she did so revealed a shapely calf.

'Got you!' she chuckled, throwing her head back.

'Eirwen! Flipping heck! Lemme get up!' the man grunted, which made the woman laugh even more. It was obvious to Betsan the pair were familiar with one another and she watched the woman remove her foot from the man's back as requested.

'Get on your way, Bill!' she yelled. 'But do leave the rest of the money for the pleasure of having my heel stuck in your back! I know how much you like it!'

What on earth did she mean by that and why would Bill like it? Betsan wrinkled her nose in disgust.

Bill scrambled to his feet and, shaking his head, began to stagger away, moving from side to side like a crab as he did so. It was obvious he was in no state to find the money in the dark but the woman was a dab hand at it. She collected it and placed the coins in a small purse that dangled on a string around her neck. When she'd finished, she tucked it firmly away beneath the folds of her breasts.

Betsan, taken aback, stood motionless as the yellow gaslight made an eerie shadow of the woman's form, and she was about to step away when the woman spotted her.

'What you looking at, lovely girl?'

Betsan swallowed. 'Sorry, miss. I was just passing through, that's all.' She lowered her head.

'You want to take care around these parts, see. It's not safe for a young girl to be around here alone, particularly after dark.' The woman's tone had softened now. 'If you come across a man called Dan Griffin, stay well away, dear!'

Betsan lifted her head to look at the woman. 'Who is he?'

'Someone you need to keep away from. He'd put someone

like you, who has a lot of years in you, to work for him. Make you one of his girls.'

Betsan thought for a moment. If she had a job she could help her father out.

'What sort of work do his girls do? Do you mean working at the inn there?' She pointed.

'Well, in a manner of speaking, but it's not nice work. That's how I started off and not much older than you are now, either.' She sighed loudly. 'Where have you been anyhow? How come you're traipsing through these parts?'

'I went to see my Auntie Mags.'

'Mags Hughes?' The woman seemed interested now.

'Yes, that's the one.'

'I know her. She's a good sort with a heart of gold. Now then, let me accompany you out of here.'

Betsan smiled, feeling safer with this woman around – it looked as if she could handle herself.

They chatted amicably as the woman, who told Betsan her full name was Eirwen Powell, linked arms with her. As they approached the steps leading out of the cellars and back up to Bethesda Street, she whispered, 'Go on, gal... You'll be safer up there on the street than down here.'

Betsan thanked the woman and she began to ascend the stone steps, clutching her basket, all the while being mindful not to come into contact with the wall that the journalist had written about in the newspaper. For some reason, that had stuck in her mind, yet she'd touched all sorts in the China area itself, so it didn't make sense why that wall might be more disease-ridden than anywhere else.

As she almost reached the top step, she heard a man's gruff voice cry out.

'Eirwen, get over here! Not thinking of leaving us, are you?'

Thinking initially that the drunken man may have returned, she glanced behind to see a tall man in a top hat grab hold of the woman by the arm and shake her forcibly.

What should she do? Try to help her? But that man appeared mean and scary, so she figured the best thing she could do right now was to get as far away from China as possible.

13

It was obvious the snotty-nosed gentleman at the sewing machine shop didn't believe a word Jimmy was saying to him.

'I'm telling you, mister. I've got a nice Singer treadle sewing machine back at home...'

The man, who was wearing a crisp, clean suit and a white waistcoat, exchanged a glance with his female assistant behind the counter before rolling his eyes. Then he whispered something unintelligible behind his lily-white hand as he appeared to look Jimmy up and down. It was evident the man didn't know what a hard day's graft was with hands like that.

Jimmy became aware of his own dishevelled appearance and hid his filthy, dirt-caked hands. He realised he really should have had a good wash and brush-up before calling at the shop but as initially he'd been bound to visit the market traders, it hadn't occurred to him to clean himself up until now.

He heard the words 'vagabond' and 'one of the Rodnies' mentioned, which caused him great offence. He was definitely not one of those bad lads, no matter what that gentleman thought!

Finally, the man glared hard at him.

'If you don't leave the premises this very second then I'll dispatch one of my assistants over to the police station who shall fetch a police constable to forcibly remove you forthwith!'

Graham Street, where the police station was located, was only a few hundred yards away, a cock's stride, some might say. It just wasn't worth the flaming hassle.

'Look, mister. I'm leaving,' said Jimmy, holding up both his palms as if in defence. 'Did you think I was going to snatch a sewing machine and shove it under my jacket or something?'

The man stood open-mouthed until the female assistant beside him said, 'No, but you might have got those rancid, dirty paws of yours on our till!'

What could he do? They wouldn't believe he had a business proposition for them. That was the advantage Elgan had over him when it came to business transactions. They'd have listened to him as he was a grown-up and, besides, he had the 'gift of the gab'. Well, someday he, Jimmy Corcoran, would do the same thing and he'd wear a fancy suit with a white waistcoat and then he'd return to this very shop. But by then, he'd be in a very different position indeed!

Betsan had managed to purchase a loaf of bread, a hunk of Caerphilly cheese, a few tangerines, nuts and dates and, best of all, she'd had enough left over to buy a couple of slices of cured ham. Even if Dad had no money in the house, it was enough to last a day or two. There were plenty of sacks of oatmeal and potatoes in the scullery, and Mrs Jenkins wouldn't see them go short either.

She turned around after paying the stallholder when she

noticed a familiar-looking face emerging through the crowd, heading in her direction.

Jimmy!

Even though she'd only met the lad the once, he had made an impression upon her. He'd seemed friendly and kind but now he looked irate as he walked with some purpose, taking large strides and brushing rudely past her so that he jostled her arm, not having noticed who she was as the brim of her bonnet shaded her face.

'Jimmy!' she cried after him.

He stopped in his tracks and then turned to face her. As she drew near to him, recognition dawned beneath the lamplight.

'You're Mags's niece, aren't you?' He pushed back the peak of his flat cap as if to get a better view of her.

'Yes, of course it's me.'

'But what are you doing out alone at this time of an evening?' He frowned.

'I've been to drop the twins off, my younger brother and sister, with my aunt.'

He nodded as if he was expecting something of the kind.

'You know about Mags and the twins?' Betsan blinked. 'That they're really her kids?'

He folded his arms and softened his stance. 'Yes. I do indeed. I've known about them since she took me in. There's not a day gone by when she hasn't thought of them.'

'I didn't realise...' said Betsan barely in a whisper. 'I only discovered she was their mother fairly recently.'

'What did you believe about them then, love?'

'That my mam and dad were their real parents. My neighbour, Mrs Jenkins, the lady who called to see Aunt Mags with me the other day, she told me. I was shocked.'

'I bet you were.' He hesitated a moment. 'Here, let me take

your basket, and I'll walk home with you. It's not safe for a young lady to be out unescorted at this time of the night.'

She smiled and thanked him. 'What are you doing at the market yourself, Jimmy? Running an errand for my auntie?'

'In a manner of speaking. Now that Elgan's in prison, we've got to make a go of the business on our own. Mags wants to see if any of the market traders he sold to will purchase any leftover stock from the stable.'

'Oh, what sort of things did he buy and sell?'

'Bits and pieces from folks' houses, mostly, that they no longer needed or they wished to part-exchange for something else. Sometimes he bought goods too if the owners were selling their house or someone had passed away. I don't think I arrived at the best time to speak to the market traders though as they've had a long day and want to pack up to go home. So, I'll try again tomorrow. Truth is, I spent too much time trying to flog something to that toffee-nosed git in that shop there!'

He pointed towards the sewing shop.

Betsan followed his finger. That was the shop her mam used to buy material and cotton threads from. Though it was expensive, so she mostly purchased what she needed from a market stall instead.

'What were you trying to sell him? Material? That sort of thing?'

'Oh no, love. It's a sewing machine. You ought to see it. Nice piece of machinery and all. A Singer treadle machine, no less. It's like a work of art.'

Suddenly, and out of nowhere, Betsan found her shoulders shaking with grief as tears streamed down her cheeks. The mention of a sewing machine had evoked such a powerful memory for her. It was almost as though a picture of her mother working at the treadle was dancing before her eyes, so much so, she could hardly bear it. It was emotionally painful.

'Aw, why are you upset, sweetheart?' Jimmy draped a comforting arm around her shoulders.

'It's my mam. You know she died last year?'

'Yes, Mags's sister, weren't she?'

'Yes.' Betsan took a shuddering breath. 'She was a seamstress. That was her profession. Loved it, she did, and I liked to watch her at work and I know this sounds silly...'

'No, it don't, love. Go on...'

'But I liked helping her, fetching things from her work basket or making cups of tea for her customers while they waited. She was ever so clever and kind too.'

'I bet you miss her a lot. I miss my mam too.'

'Oh, I forgot about your parents. I'm so sorry, Jimmy. So you know what it's like then?'

'Yes, I do, love.' He took her hand and gave it a reassuring squeeze, which comforted her.

'So, you still have her sewing machine then, do you?'

'No, I don't. My father remarried and my stepmother got rid of it one day when I was at school. It broke my heart.'

Jimmy frowned and he tilted his head in a sympathetic manner. 'What a terrible thing to do without telling you. Why would she go and do a thing like that?'

'She had fanciful ideas and wanted a Welsh dresser for the living room. She traded the sewing machine for one and some fancy pieces to display on it – blue and white crockery that we have to keep for best!'

Suddenly, Jimmy released her hand. 'Blow me down with a feather! I might be wrong and shall have to check, but I remember helping Elgan load a Welsh dresser onto the cart along with some crockery like that. I think he was taking it to a house in Plymouth Street. Is that where you live?'

'Yes! Yes!' Betsan gasped, hardly believing her ears.

'So, Elgan must have left the sewing machine in the stable all this time. But I don't think Mags knows about it as it was covered up. Tomorrow, you must pay a visit and we'll see if you think it might be the same one.'

In spite of all the recent upset with her father and Elinor leaving them, Betsan found herself crying once again. Only this time they were tears of joy.

14

Betsan decided to stack the grocery items away in the scullery cupboard to keep herself occupied. The house was in darkness as she approached and she found that her father was not at home. Might Dad have gone next door? She'd ask. Then she remembered Mr Jenkins was on night shifts again and when he was, Mrs Jenkins tended to go to bed earlier than usual as she disliked being alone at night-time in the house.

Betsan lit the oil lamp on the windowsill in the living room. If it was daylight, she could have gone outside and searched for Dad but she was just too fearful right now. She was so grateful that Jimmy had walked her home earlier.

Her previous moment of joy about the sewing machine had now turned to despair.

As the hours ticked away on the mantel clock, sitting in her father's armchair, she found herself nodding off, until suddenly there was a tapping sound at the front door, which made her sit bolt upright, wondering if she'd dreamt it or not.

And then, she was out of the chair and rushing to the door to answer.

'Who's there?' She was aware of her voice trembling now.

'It's me – Florrie!' yelled a familiar high-pitched voice.

Relief flooded through her and she scrambled to unbolt the heavy front door. Then she yanked it towards her to open it. There, stood on the doorstep, was her father with Florrie, as she supported him beneath his arm. He appeared to be somewhat unsteady on his feet.

'What happened to you, Dad?'

Her father just stood there staring blankly at her, as if he too was wondering what had happened.

'Let's get you inside then, David,' said Florrie gently. She glanced at Betsan who, after all, deserved some sort of explanation. 'I'll explain what's gone on after he's inside by the fire. Make him a cup of something hot, darlin'. No alcohol, mind. He's had quite enough already!'

Betsan nodded apprehensively. This was so unlike her father. He hardly ever touched alcohol and even when he did it was only a drop and only for a special occasion like on Christmas Day or at a wedding. That's why he'd been able to work at the Star as he didn't succumb, as many did, to the perils of drink. That's why he was so good at his job.

David Morgan took small steps to get to the armchair and slowly eased himself into it and then he closed his eyes, as if wanting to shut out the world.

'Now, try to stay awake, David,' Florrie scolded and then glanced apprehensively at Betsan. 'Be quick about that hot drink!'

Thankfully, the kettle hadn't long boiled and was still simmering away on the fire. So to avoid burning herself, Betsan took a tray cloth to lift it carefully and carry it to the scullery to make the tea.

'Would you like a cup?' she asked, looking at the woman who she realised had put herself out to bring her father home.

Florrie smiled. 'Yes, please. It's brass-monkey weather out there tonight!'

She nodded, the sharp edge disappearing from her voice. No doubt she was concerned as she would never have seen Betsan's father in this condition before. Maybe it had shocked her to do so.

Betsan returned the smile. The woman wasn't wrong about the weather: it had been the coldest night she remembered for a long time. She wet the tea leaves in the awaiting earthenware teapot and, while it brewed, asked, 'Where did you find him?'

'At the Star Inn, lovely. He turned up there thinking he was supposed to work his usual shift. He's dreadfully confused. He didn't mention Elinor nor the baby she's expecting at all but he did mention your mother a few times. Elinor has told me all about how he's been acting this past week or so.'

Betsan nodded, tears in her eyes, her vision now blurred. There was a lump in her throat that was refusing to go away, so she sniffed and turned away for a moment.

'It's all my fault! I shouldn't have left him alone but I thought, and so did Elinor, that my brother and sister would be better off with their real mother, my Aunt Mags.' She turned back to face Florrie.

'I understand,' said Florrie, a sympathetic tone to her voice. 'I don't know what the answer is, to be honest with you. Elinor is fine staying at my digs for the time being but she's very concerned about you, lovely.'

She laid a reassuring hand on Betsan's shoulder and looked deep into her eyes.

'She is?'

'Oh, yes. She cares more about you than you'll ever know. I

realise you got off to a shaky start with her because you miss your mother but she's not a bad sort and she does make your father happy. Well, not at the moment as his mind is disturbed.' She paused. 'Hey, you'd better pour that brew before it gets stewed, ducks!'

Betsan giggled through her tears and then she finally managed to swallow the lump in her throat. She poured the steaming tea into the awaiting cups and Florrie carried the tray into the living room where her father was sitting, staring into the flames of the fire as if all the answers lay there.

Oh, Dad, where have you disappeared to?

* * *

Mags glanced up as Jimmy entered the house, a wide smile on his face. How was she going to tell him the twins were already here? She took a deep breath before speaking.

'We'll have to be quiet as Betsan dropped Aled and Alys off here earlier. I was intending to fetch them in a day or two but she brought them this evening as she's concerned about her father.'

'Don't worry, I already know,' he said, keeping his voice low.

Mags sat up in the armchair. 'You do? How's that?'

'I bumped into Betsan at the marketplace and walked her back home. I even carried her basket for her!'

Mags smiled. 'Good lad...'

She was about to say something else when Jimmy interrupted her train of thought. 'There's something in the stable I discovered last night that I think you ought to know about.'

'Oh?' She furrowed her brow.

'I know you told me to try selling as much of what's there as possible to get us through but did you realise there's a treadle sewing machine under the old tarpaulin?'

Mags shook her head slowly. 'No, I did not.'

'But that's not all...' Jimmy, in his excitement, forgot to keep his voice low. 'It belonged to your sister!'

'Never, lad! How did you come to that conclusion?'

'I worked it out for myself. You see, Betsan mentioned her stepmother had sold the treadle machine in exchange for a Welsh dresser and some blue and white crockery. It was then I remembered that Elgan took something in part exchange from a lady in Plymouth Street!'

Mags couldn't fathom it out. 'But my Elgan would have known that was my brother-in-law's house. Why didn't he tell me? I just don't understand.'

'The only way you'll find the truth is if you ask,' Jimmy said thoughtfully. 'Either write to him or go to the prison itself.'

'Yes, but I find it hurtful if it's true that he knew whose house that was and that the sewing machine was my sister's...' She sniffed loudly.

'Talk about condemning someone before they're even found guilty, Mags! Give him at least a chance to explain it to you. And don't forget, he wouldn't have known who Elinor was when he took it from there, would he? He might have assumed someone else had moved into the house and said nothing about it to not upset you.'

'That's true, I suppose.'

'Betsan's over the moon about it, though, to be reunited with her mam's sewing machine.'

Mags didn't know how she was going to explain the situation to Jimmy, but felt she had to.

Shaking her head, she said, 'It might not be that simple though, lad. That sewing machine now legally belongs to Elgan and is worth a bit of money. Money that he probably needs. Money we'll need while he's doing time in prison. And there's not much income coming into this house...' Her voice trailed off into barely a whisper.

'But it should have been passed on to Betsan anyhow,' Jimmy protested.

'I know that,' said Mags softly. 'If it were mine to give, I'd let her have it.'

'It's a sign though,' said Jimmy. 'I tried to flog it at that upmarket sewing shop on the high street and that snotty-nosed gentleman wouldn't take me seriously. That was before I knew it was your sister's, of course.'

Mags nodded. Maybe it was a sign Betsan was meant to have it. Who knew?

One person knew, that's for sure. The only person who knew anything about the intentions of purchasing that machine and that was Elgan himself. But he had told her she could sell the things from the stable to keep finances ticking over. So why was there no mention of the most expensive item of all?

* * *

The gaoler frowned as he scratched his bald pate. It wasn't that he'd never been offered a bribe before to allow someone in; it was more that the woman standing before him seemed desperate somehow. Far more desperate than most he saw entering the premises with a view to seeing a loved one.

'Look, 'ave a heart,' she was pleading. 'My husband will be incarcerated here for one whole year. I only want to see him for a few minutes to sort out something about the family business. I want to keep it running for him while he's inside. He was carted off straight after the court case so there was no real chance then.

I just need to ask him a few questions about something – issues that need resolving.'

The gaoler peered at her through narrowed eyes. Was this woman telling the truth or was it simply a ploy so she could smuggle something in to him to provide him with some sort of contraband, or even help him escape? It had happened before now, a wife had smuggled a file in her shopping basket and, as a result, her husband had attempted to file away at the bars of his cell window. Thankfully, he'd been caught in the act and got a further six months in custody for his misdemeanour, while his wife was ordered to spend one month in prison. She had known it was wrong, so needed to be made an example of. It was a cautionary tale indeed.

Another had managed to bribe a guard to allow her time with her husband. The prisoner had then changed into women's clothing along with a bonnet his wife had brought with her to help conceal his identity, escaping that way. So 'two women' had walked out of the prison that day. The pair was never seen again.

So to accept a bribe might mean losing his job, if something were to go wrong, but on the other hand, he could do with the extra money with Christmas on the approach.

He decided he had to be sensible about it. For the woman to visit her husband, someone would need to keep an eye on them. Putting his thumb and forefinger in his mouth, he whistled loudly, which brought a young guard running towards him from the exercise yard.

The lad came bounding over, appearing out of breath. 'Yes, guv?'

'Take Mrs er... What's your name, love?'

The woman immediately brightened up. 'Mrs Hughes. I'm Elgan Hughes's wife.'

He smiled at her. Maybe he could make her Christmas for her and his own into the bargain.

'Take Mrs Hughes over to the restroom and fetch the prisoner, Elgan Hughes, to see her. He's from Merthyr Tydfil and should be in the new admissions wing.'

'I know who he is, guv!' The lad smiled as though he liked and respected Elgan.

'Go along now, Mrs Hughes. I'll allow you just ten minutes as the restroom will be empty right now; any time after that and I might get in trouble for it. Understood?'

'Thank you, sir!' She placed a silver shilling in the palm of his hand and he nodded at her.

'Better grease the young guard's palm as well,' he whispered in her ear. 'That way you'll keep him sweet.'

At least he'd made someone else's day too.

He watched her go on her way. She was a fine-looking woman at that. Elgan Hughes was a lucky man indeed.

* * *

Maggie waited patiently in the small room, which appeared to belong to the prison guards. An old horsehair sofa was placed at one end, its straw stuffing spewing out of it, and an old battered armchair stood near the open fireplace. She guessed that, on a bitterly cold day like today, it would be the most coveted seat in the room. Against the wall beneath the barred window was a small table with two chairs. On top of the table was an earthenware teapot and several unwashed tin mugs. Holding the palm of her hand to the pot, she noticed it was lukewarm – so someone had been here fairly recently, but it appeared that most prisoners were out having yard exercise; that's why this room was currently free.

It seemed an age since the young guard had gone to fetch Elgan. What if it was a ruse cooked up between himself and the gaoler at the gate? What if they did this to gullible folk just to get money from them? Maybe if they complained, the pair would say they were bribed.

Now her imagination was running riot. Her stomach churned over.

Taking the train all the way from Merthyr Tydfil to Cardiff and bribing the guards was costing her dearly and she hoped it was worth it.

A click of the door lock and then Elgan came shuffling into the room with the guard in his wake. Why was he walking like that? Had he injured himself or been beaten? Then she noticed the iron clamps and chains around his feet. Her heart pained to see the dark rings beneath her husband's eyes. His white matching prison jacket and trousers with arrows marked on them were hanging off his form. On his head was a white pill-box-style cap.

'Oh, Elgan,' she said, rushing towards him as tears spilled down her cheeks.

The guard, as if realising she needed to hug her husband, allowed her to do so.

Elgan felt like a bag of bones in her embrace.

'Are we allowed to sit at that table here?' She glanced at the man for confirmation.

He nodded and cleared the teapot and mugs away, before taking them over to a wooden counter set at the far end of the room.

It was then she noticed the tears in the corners of Elgan's brown eyes. Her husband was not one for tears usually but it was evident that being confined here was breaking him down.

The guard coughed into his fist to get her attention. 'I'll just be outside the door. Best to keep to the allotted ten-minute visit,' he advised, no doubt having done this many times before. 'I'll let you know when visiting time is over!' he said cheerfully, and he closed the door behind him as he left the room.

Mags nodded gratefully as she took a seat and watched Elgan draw out the chair opposite.

'Are you all right, my love?' She reached out and squeezed his hand across the table.

'Yes, don't you worry about me. The food in here is almost as good as I get back home!' He chuckled as it was a running gag how bad Maggie's cookery skills were. She'd never been handy like Gwennie had been.

Mags wiped away a tear with the back of her hand. 'I couldn't believe you were carted away from the courthouse like that!'

'Nor could I.' He shook his head. 'Sergeant Cranbourne was the one most shocked of all, I think. He thought his character witness would have been successful but it was the wrong judge that bloody day!'

'I know.' She shrugged. 'He told me he thought that maybe the judge wanted to make an example of you. He said he'd seen men kept out of prison for doing far more than you did.'

'I know.' His features softened. 'But the truth of it was that I knew those were wrong sorts I was doing business with, so I didn't ask any questions.'

She nodded. 'Well, I wanted to let you know that me and Jimmy will carry on running the business for you.' Elgan's eyes lit up – he now had something to hope for. 'The year will soon pass and you can return home to us where you belong.'

'That's good to know.' He returned the squeeze of the hand. 'But one thing, do not do business with any dodgy dealers like I did, do you hear?'

'I hear you loud and clear, Elgan.' She beamed at him.

'Jimmy is trying to sell the items from the stable but there's one object we're both puzzled about.'

'Oh, what's that, my sweet?'

'It's the Singer treadle sewing machine. How did you come by it?'

'Oh.' Elgan now too wiped away a tear with the back of his hand. 'It was intended as a Christmas gift for you, my love.'

There was so much tenderness in his voice, Mags didn't doubt that for a second, but wonderful though it was, did he realise the circumstances of his purchase? Even the misery behind it?

'Thank you. So it's really mine? My property to do what I wish with?' Mags brightened and sat forward in her seat with a measure of expectation.

He looked at her with questioning eyes. 'Of course.'

'It's just that... Oh, I don't quite know how to say this, but did you realise the house you bought it from was Gwennie's?'

He nodded. 'Yes, and I realised it's your sister's sewing machine. A young woman sold it to me.'

It was then she realised that of course he wouldn't have even known her sister had passed away as she, herself, didn't until after he was carted away to prison.

'Elgan,' she said softly. 'Gwennie, bless her soul, passed away about a year ago. The young woman who sold you the machine is David's new wife.'

If she had knocked the wind out of his sails with a sledge-hammer, she could not have matched his reaction in that particular moment.

Elgan shook his head and stared at the table in disbelief.

'I've only just discovered this myself and it's been a terrible shock...' she said, a catch to her voice as the grief of losing her only sister prevailed. She sat forward in her chair. 'Who did you think the woman was then?'

He lifted his head and made eye contact. 'To be truthful, I thought maybe she was her sister-in-law or someone employed at the house. And as you'd been estranged from her, I thought it was a gift you might appreciate, but now I appear to have upset you?'

'Oh, I do appreciate it, Elgan. I really do. It's just that young Betsan was very upset to discover her stepmother had sold her mother's sewing machine. No one had discussed it with her and even her father didn't know until afterwards.'

Elgan held up his palms as if in defence. 'I am sorry. The woman gave me the impression that the machine was no longer required at the house and that I'd be doing them all a favour by taking it in part exchange. She chose a Welsh dresser from the cart and some crockery in payment.'

'I know about all of that. I'm not angry with you, Elgan.' Maggie smiled at him. 'I'm just trying to establish the facts. So as the sewing machine is now mine to do with as I like, is it all right if Betsan makes use of it? I can show her how to thread the bobbin and how to get started, though she's watched her mam do it so many times, she probably knows how to do so already.'

'Yes, yes, you must do as you see fit, my dear.'

At that moment, the young guard came rushing into the room to inform them the visit was now over – no doubt so was prisoner exercise in the yard. Mags and Elgan stood and embraced once again, Elgan hanging on to his wife as if his life depended on it, until the guard coughed to remind them they needed to be on their way. Who knew when they'd next embrace or even set eyes on one another?

That sewing machine might come in useful though. And Maggie had an idea.

15

'Betsan, this can't go on, *cariad*,' Mrs Jenkins said when she called around to see her the following morning. They were both stood in the scullery while her father napped in the armchair in the living room. He seemed none the worse for his little escapade the previous night but, nevertheless, although not violent or demanding, he now seemed subdued, which greatly concerned her.

Betsan drew in a composing breath and let it out again. 'Dad went missing last night. I'd left him asleep in his bedroom and took the twins to my aunt's house.'

'I see,' said Mrs Jenkins thoughtfully. 'So you decided to leave them with Maggie after all?'

Betsan nodded. 'I had to think of them...'

'But what happened then?'

'He wasn't here when I returned with the shopping. Oh, Mrs Jenkins, my heart sank to find he'd gone.'

'I bet it did.' The woman nodded sympathetically.

'It was much later when Florrie knocked on the door. He'd turned up at the Star Inn thinking he had a shift to work and then as the landlord said no to him, he must have got himself drunk. It's so unlike Dad to do a thing like that.'

Mrs Jenkins tutted. 'This is a real dilemma. You're too young to be shouldering all of this and taking care of him on your own. I really don't know what to suggest other than to get Doctor Llewellyn back here to assess him. But I really don't think there's any magic medicine for his condition.'

Betsan nodded, realising that she was speaking sense. 'I still don't know if there's any money lying around the house. How will I buy anything else we need?'

'I could loan you some to get the doctor out for a visit but that's about it, or I won't have enough to pay the rent. There's not enough spare for me to give you any more and believe me, I would if I could. I'd give you all I have.'

Betsan felt deeply touched to hear her say that and she didn't doubt it for a second. Mrs Jenkins had such a big heart. As if to show this even further, the woman stepped forward to caress Betsan's cheeks, gazing into her eyes as she wiped them with her handkerchief. Then she planted a kiss on her forehead in a motherly fashion.

'I'll be back in a moment with the money for the doctor,' she said softly. 'Call to his house to see if you can get him out to pay a visit here as soon as possible.'

Betsan nodded, feeling as though there was little choice in the matter.

The doctor couldn't call immediately as he had several house calls to make but he arrived promptly at four o'clock with his Gladstone bag at the ready. He examined her father and spoke to him at length before making a detour to the scullery to have a word with Betsan and Mrs Jenkins who were patiently awaiting his verdict.

Doctor Llewellyn slowly shook his head.

'It's not good, I'm afraid. I had hopes that he'd have recovered his memory fully by now but it's almost as though his recollections are absent from the time of your mother's illness onwards. That can happen sometimes when the mind doesn't wish to deal with something, as a form of protection, if you like. I got the impression that he's speaking of your mother as though she's still around here somewhere.'

'That's right,' said Mrs Jenkins. 'He's been thinking Gwendolyn's next door talking to me or otherwise out shopping. What do you advise?'

The doctor rubbed his bearded chin in contemplation. 'That he gets plenty of rest and if he mentions your mother, Betsan, you go along with it and you too, Mrs Jenkins.' Both nodded. 'You see, the shock of hearing she's passed away and no longer here with him might make his mind already more troubled than it already is.'

'Doctor,' said Mrs Jenkins, 'I'm concerned for Betsan staying here with him as he seems prone to violent outbursts. It's too much for a young girl to contend with alone.'

Doctor Llewellyn furrowed his brow. 'But where is the new Mrs Morgan? Is she no longer here?'

'No, she's gone to stay with a friend. The stress of caring for him was too much for her as she's with child.' Mrs Jenkins shook her head.

'Then...' The doctor hesitated. 'I do have a suggestion but I don't know how you'd feel about it.' He turned towards Betsan.

'Go on, doctor,' Mrs Jenkins urged.

'I'm on the board of guardians at the St Tydfil's Workhouse.

We could admit your father for a spell? It might be an idea to provide you with some respite.'

Betsan opened her mouth and closed it again. She exchanged a worried glance with Mrs Jenkins.

'But it would only be for an interim period,' the doctor reassured her. 'Then when I'm satisfied his memory has returned and he's no longer a danger to anyone, he can return home again.'

Mrs Jenkins huffed out a breath as though what the doctor had just said was a relief. 'Don't worry, *cariad*. You can stay here with me and Bert while your dad goes inside the spike for a while.'

'No,' said Betsan firmly. 'If Dad is to go there, then I want to go too, to keep an eye on him. At least he knows who I am!'

The doctor shook his head. 'Please, young lady, it's not a place for you...'

'But there's no money coming into the house any more. We won't be able to pay the rent soon. I am now like an orphan: my mam has gone for good and my father is no longer a father to me!' She shut her eyes tightly to prevent the tears that were threatening to spill before opening them again and blinking several times.

'You really are a determined young lady, aren't you?' Doctor Llewellyn chuckled as he looked at Mrs Jenkins, who smiled in agreement.

* * *

And so it was arranged that David Morgan, along with his daughter, both be admitted into the St Tydfil's Union Workhouse on the east side of Thomas Street. There had been paperwork that needed filling in regarding their admission and both would now need to stand in front of the board of guardians while Doctor Llewellyn presented their case, explaining how they'd fallen on hard times with no income to speak of coming in. David Morgan's recent amnesia was highlighted as the doctor spoke of how a hard-working man who had once seen to the running of a popular Merthyr inn now found it impossible to carry on in the same manner. Indeed, he'd been a fine, respectable, mainly teetotal gentleman, a good husband and father to his children who'd had the misfortune of losing his wife and, potentially, now his job within the space of one year.

'And,' continued Doctor Llewellyn sombrely, 'had he not sustained a severe blow to the head from a local thug, causing him to lose his recent memory, then he might not be stood in front of us all right now. David Morgan had pulled himself up by his bootstraps following his wife's tragic death. He had taken care of his children, provided for them and paid the rent so they might have a roof over their heads. In fact, he did everything he could possibly do. He'd also recently remarried but his young wife, who I hasten to add is pregnant with their child, has found it fit to flee their abode as he is no longer the man he once was. He can't even remember marrying her in the first place!'

The doctor glanced at the members of the board for their reactions. One or two were nodding or murmuring amongst themselves. A gentleman named Mr Hargreaves, who was a well-known grocer in the town with a chain of shops, asked, 'So then, doctor, how do you think Mr Morgan will fare in the workhouse?'

'It's my belief,' said the doctor, 'that he needs some sort of supervised routine and hard work, of course, and he's no stranger to either of those. It's just to get himself and his daughter over a difficult time. Then, hopefully, in a matter of months, he may leave here, maybe with his memory intact. It is too much to expect a young girl of thirteen years old to provide and care for a grown man.'

There were further murmurs as the board members glanced at one another.

'The daughter,' said Anthony Windsor, who owned a couple of jewellery shops, one in Aberdare and the other in Merthyr, 'is she in fine fettle, as it were? Could she be put to work? Maybe even boarded out somewhere?'

'Yes, that's entirely possible,' he replied. 'She used to help her mother who was a successful seamstress, so she might be useful in the sewing room here or else in service somewhere.'

'I see,' said Mr Windsor in a thoughtful manner. 'Well, it's evident that both can work for their keep and may even be useful to the workhouse. Bring them both in and we'll address them personally.'

The doctor nodded and went off to fetch the pair who were seated on a wooden bench outside the door.

David Morgan was staring blankly at the opposite wall. He did not even seem to be reading the large sign in front of him, which read:

The Lord will fight for you;
You need only be still.
Exodus 14:14

Strange, in all his years of duty here, both on the board of guardians and as a doctor, he'd never paid much attention to that sign before, but he was noticing it now. The words seemed appropriate somehow and he thought about how the workhouse was a window of humanity; all sorts of people walked through its doors – young, old, destitute, poor, even those who had once had it all but had now fallen on hard times, the sick and those in good health. If anyone wanted a glimpse of society, it was here for all to see and they were all here under its roof. Some for a short period of time, some for many years and some, maybe, forever.

The girl looked up as he approached and he smiled at her pretty face.

'They're ready for you both now.'

* * *

As soon as they entered the workhouse, to Betsan's dismay, she was separated from her father. He was sent to the men's wing while she had to go to the girls' dormitory and she found herself in a room with a long row of beds with other girls of varying ages. Some were quite young, while several were older and taller than her. It became obvious who controlled the girls here and it wasn't the supervisor, Mrs Parry-Jones. It was Dora. Dora Phillips who stood a full head and shoulders taller than the rest.

The younger girls appeared petrified of her. Everyone was, except for Betsan. Betsan had learned to stand up for herself. She had stood up to her stepmother and hadn't feared her at all, so no jumped-up bullying inmate was going to drag her down. After all she'd been through with Mam's sudden illness and ensuing death, followed by a brand-new stepmother whom she'd disliked with a vengeance (though she no longer felt that way about Elinor), no one and nobody was ever going to push her around again.

Going through the humiliation of entering this place had been bad enough. She'd had to remove all her clothing and stand naked in front of the supervisor. Then she was ordered to submerge herself in a hot bath where she was scrubbed all over with carbolic soap, using a stiff bristled brush. Her hair was washed thoroughly and rinsed in vinegar after being shorn short, close-cropped. She hadn't realised she'd have to lose her lovely chestnut hair, even if it got a little wiry in wild weather. Her head was even checked for nits! Thankfully, no head lice were found.

And then to add insult to injury, she was made to wear a baggy calico dress with a pinafore, a linsey-woolsey petticoat, thick worsted stockings and leather lace-up boots that hurt like the devil when she walked as they'd not been broken in and were causing blisters on her feet. The day cap she wore made her feel as foolish as those white frilly pantaloons Elinor had insisted she wear for her wedding to her father.

So far, despite this, she knew she could adapt to the work-house regime as long as Dad was all right. He'd had such sad-looking eyes when they'd left home together for the last time. Her one solace was that she'd been allowed to take her *Mary Jones and Her Bible* book into the workhouse. If Mary could cope with hardship, so could she.

She'd handed the key to the house over to Mrs Jenkins who promised to keep an eye on the place. A letter had been written to the rent man, endorsed by Doctor Llewellyn, informing him of the current situation. With Mrs Jenkins's help, they managed to leave what was owed to him but she'd said she'd ask her Bert to remove the painting of Betsan's mother from the attic for the time being and they'd put it in storage at their house in case another family were moved in. Mrs Jenkins also took their clothing and one or two other items.

Betsan hadn't realised that the furniture they used, apart from Elinor's precious Welsh dresser, belonged to the landlord. Mrs Jenkins, who had the same landlord herself said if needs be she'd offer the ruddy dresser as payment for the next few months. Betsan had smiled at that. It was the exchange of the sewing machine for the ruddy dresser that had caused so much trouble in the first place!

* * *

By the time Mags returned to Merthyr, darkness had all but descended. The train from Cardiff had been full to bursting and it hadn't been a comfortable journey by any means and now she had to walk back home from Plymouth Gate railway station to China. Maybe she could call to see how Betsan was doing? She'd be able to give her the good news that as the sewing machine was a gift from Elgan she was quite happy to allow her niece to take it over. In fact, she had an idea that maybe they could both set up a business together making garments and doing repairs like Gwennie had. She wondered what Betsan would make of that.

As she approached the house, she noticed there were no lights in the window. That was odd. Shouldn't there be someone there at this time of an evening?

Rapping on the door knocker several times, she received no reply, so she cupped her hands to peer in through the window. Nothing to see, all was in darkness. It was too early for bedtime. Even though her brother-in-law might have taken to his bed, Betsan wouldn't have.

She was about to make her way home, as she didn't want to leave the twins with Jimmy much longer – even though he seemed to adore them both, it just wasn't fair on him – when Bronwen Jenkins emerged from her house. The woman appeared a little out of puff.

'I'm glad I caught you, Mags,' she said as she approached.

'Why? Whatever's the matter?' Mags blinked.

'It's Betsan and her father...' She took a gulp of air. The woman wasn't looking too good.

'Take your time now.'

'They've been... taken to the w... workhouse.'

'The workhouse!' Mags swallowed hard. This couldn't possibly be true. 'But how? Why?'

'Betsan got the doctor out to assess her father and he suggested David go in there for a short spell and Betsan insisted on going with him! I offered her a place here, honestly I did.'

Mags touched the woman's shoulder gently. 'I'm sure you did all you could.'

Bronwen nodded. 'I did, I really did. I loaned them money to get the doctor here but he refused payment, so I have it here to pay the rent for them instead. But who knows if they will ever return home again? You know what it's like. Betsan can't support herself, can she?'

Mags shook her head, her dream about setting up a business with her niece disappearing into the ether. She said nothing about it to Bronwen though.

'Rest assured,' she said, 'I shall pay them both a visit there tomorrow if they'll allow me inside.'

Bronwen nodded. 'Thank goodness you have the twins in your care. Who has them now?'

'Jimmy, the lad you met when you called. I had to leave them with him all day as I've been to visit Elgan in Cardiff Gaol.'

'How come they let you in?'

'I had to give them a little sweetener, shall we say. I might have to do that tomorrow too at the spike, if no one will allow me to see my niece.'

Bronwen smiled. 'I can see where Betsan gets her feistiness from. Her mother was a quiet sort, but I think you'll fight tooth and nail for what you want.'

'Oh, I will. I do. I just wish I'd fought tooth and nail for my own offspring at the time.'

'Ah, but...' said Bronwen with a note of sympathy, 'from what I was told, you weren't in your right mind after the birth of the twins. It could happen to anyone.'

'Thank you.' She sniffed. 'My Gwennie was a great sister and I'll never be able to repay her for her kindness now she's gone.' She turned away as tears formed.

'But you're already repaying her by taking your children back where they belong and looking out for Betsan and her father.'

It was true and those were just the words Mags needed to hear.

She turned back to face the woman. 'Go inside now, Bronwen. It's cold out here and you don't seem well to me.'

'I'll be all right, Mags. I'm glad you called. Let me know if there's any way I can help.'

Mags nodded gratefully as she watched the woman return to the house next door.

No, the poor dab didn't look well at all.

16

———

Betsan hadn't set eyes on her father since entering the workhouse and she wondered how he was faring.

'Miss Morgan!' A shrill female voice called out her name while she was hovering in one of the corridors she was supposed to be cleaning. Every inmate, unless sick, was expected to carry out daily chores. For the males it was usually oakum picking, bone crushing or working in the vegetable garden, for the females it was mainly the cleaning of the workhouse, toiling in the laundry or helping in the busy kitchen.

In the corner of the corridor stood a metal pail of soapy water with a scrubbing brush and cloth. The water had long since gone cold as Betsan had been that intent on locating her father's whereabouts. She'd scurried from corridor to corridor, peeking through various unfamiliar windows and behind several doors, many of which, upon trying, turned out to be locked. But so far, nothing. There was no sign of Dad whatsoever. Hearing the voice, her neck shrank down into the shoulders of her shift dress and, slowly, she turned to face its owner.

Mrs Parry-Jones, who had seemed quite affable towards her, now had a sharp edge to the tone of her voice.

'Just what exactly are you doing here?' she chastised, narrowing her gaze.

Betsan's bottom lip trembled, though she wasn't frightened of the woman herself. She had been spun such lurid tales of inmate punishment by some of the other girls that she didn't intend blotting her copybook so soon, so she decided to come clean about her quest.

'I'm sorry, miss. It's just that I've been in here for a couple of days now and I was hoping to catch sight of my father. I'm worried about him, you see...'

The woman, in a long dark-grey dress with a high lace collar, glared at her over her gold-rimmed spectacles and her thin lips curved into a smile.

'That's all right. Perfectly understandable as I've heard about his problems. I'll check later for you to see how he's getting on. But for the time being, you need to work if you are to avoid punishment. So get cracking. Clean the corridor floor, please!'

Betsan returned the smile. 'Thank you, miss.' She then proceeded to roll up her sleeves and knelt to submerge the cloth in the soapy suds of the pail.

'You'll get used to it,' Mrs Parry-Jones said. 'One little tip so the floor dries quickly: ensure you don't make the cloth too wet, rinse it well between each use.'

Betsan looked up at her. 'Thank you, miss.'

'One more thing: when you're finished here and you've put your equipment away, go over to the sewing room. Miss Marston would like to have a word with you.'

Betsan nodded. Then she watched the supervisor walk away, the sound of her heeled boots click-clacking, echoing down the corridor.

Doctor Llewellyn had said he'd try to secure her a position in the sewing room. Her spirit had lifted to hear that and she still hoped that that might be the case. Now, as long as the supervisor brought back positive news about her father, she'd survive.

'Madam, I can't possibly allow you in here without official notification,' said the man on the workhouse door. The building was quite imposing with its grey-brick exterior and arched entrance windows, to the side of which stood the porters' room.

'It's just that my niece, Betsan, was admitted here along with her father, David Morgan,' Mags said in a persuasive, flirtatious manner. 'And no one had thought to inform me...'

She twirled her long blonde hair around her index finger and licked her full lips. Then she looked down at the ground as if in a bashful manner. The truth was she knew every trick in the trade to get her way – when she'd hit her difficult time three years ago she had resorted to such tactics to obtain alcoholic drinks from local men. And hadn't they fallen for it an' all? Of course, they'd expected something for it at the end of the night, something in return for their bountiful generosity, but by then they were too pie-eyed to chase her when she'd run off with a pair of their trousers or a bulging wallet. She had stopped all that kind of caper though when Elgan had come back into her life. But on this occasion, she needed to employ her womanly wiles once again.

The porter, who had a thick grey bushy moustache and matching sideburns, smiled as his eyes illuminated with a sense of mischief. This was going to be easy. Even though he was turning her down, she knew he had warmed to her. Nothing would deter Mags, not for a moment if it meant checking on her niece's welfare. She was doing it for Gwennie. She hadn't been there when her sister was ill but she could be there for her daughter.

'Has anyone ever told you how handsome you are?' She smiled coquettishly.

'Go on, yer pulling me leg!' The porter knew it too, and still he chuckled. The truth was he seemed to relish the attention.

'Now, if you were to pay me a visit sometime, I'd see what I could do for you, if you do this one teeny, tiny little thing for me...' she teased.

He didn't know who she was or where she lived so what was the harm in a little come-on?

Finally, he let out a long breath and shook his head. 'All right. I can't allow you over the threshold without prior agreement but I'll see if I can get either your niece or her father to come to you.'

She smiled broadly. 'That's the ticket, er? Mr...?'

'Edwyn. Edwyn Tripper, ma'am.' He doffed his peaked cap in her direction and then replaced it on his head. Then he dispatched a young lad to see if he could locate either David or Betsan Morgan.

It was a good ten minutes of making idle chit-chat with the man before the lad returned with Betsan in tow. Wide-eyed, she spoke excitedly when she set eyes on her aunt.

'Auntie, what are you doing here?'

Mags looked her niece up and down. Although the girl appeared well enough, that horrible uniform was shapeless, like a coal sack covering her slight figure.

'I heard from Mrs Jenkins you and your father had been admitted here. Can you remove that cap for me, please?'

Betsan did as she was told. Mags bit her lip to hold back the tears that were beginning to fill the corners of her eyes.

'Why on earth did they cut your beautiful hair?'

'Because it had to be done for me to enter here. They check your hair for head lice, see. I didn't have any, but I suppose they need to be sure as it could cause an outbreak. Doctor Llewellyn had to examine me too. He told me it was to ensure I didn't have a 'fectious disease.'

Mags smiled. 'You mean an infectious disease, darlin'.'

'Yes, that's right. Like small pox or scarlet fever, something like those. He said I passed my examination with flying colours though!' she said proudly, her eyes lighting up.

'Of course you did, Betsan. You were perfectly clean and tidy, healthy too, before entering. I just hope now you don't pick something up whilst you stay here. Why didn't you come to me for help though? I'd have let you bunk in with us. Jimmy would have given up his bed for you and slept on the living room couch.'

Betsan shook her head. 'Oh, no. I wouldn't have wanted him to do that for me. Besides, would you have taken Dad in as well?'

Mags hesitated. The truth was, no, she couldn't. It wouldn't be fair on the twins while his behaviour was so unpredictable. She shook her head.

'Sorry, you're right. I wouldn't have right now as he's being aggressive towards people. You're a loyal daughter; he should be proud the way you're standing by him. Your mam would be too.' She tickled Betsan affectionately beneath her chin like she had when she was a toddler. Then she noticed the girl's glazed eyes. 'Hey,' she said suddenly to change the subject. She didn't want to upset her niece for all the world. 'I've been to see Elgan at Cardiff nick to check out that sewing machine and stuff about the business he might want sorted. The machine was intended as a Christmas present for me so that means when you're out of here, you can use it any time you like! It's yours by right!'

'Thank you, Auntie!' Betsan stepped forward to embrace her

and Mags clung on as if her life depended on it. Tears fell from the both of them but they were tears of joy.

When the pair had composed themselves and broken away from one another, Betsan looked up at her aunt.

'You'll never guess what?'

'I don't know?' Mags shrugged.

'I was summoned to the sewing room earlier and spoke to Miss Marston, the sewing teacher. Doctor Llewellyn put in a good word for me, so I'll be helping there now most days! Not only learning more about being a seamstress but repairing workhouse clothing as well. So hopefully, I won't have to clean too many corridors during my stay!'

'That's fine and dandy!' Mags exclaimed. 'I have big plans that you and I shall go into business together making and selling garments on the market someday!'

Betsan's lips curved into a smile. 'Oh, I'd love that!'

'It's settled then. Now, is there anything I can do to help you or your father?'

Betsan hesitated a moment. 'Maybe you could pay Elinor a visit to tell her we're here now? As she's married to my father, they might allow her to visit. I don't know if he'll want to see her but I'd welcome a visit. I want to see how she's getting on. The baby will be due in a couple of months – her tummy was ever so big last time I saw her.'

'Very well, darlin'. Where is she staying now?'

'With Florrie, the other barmaid she used to work with. She's at the Brunswick Inn. It's on the corner of this street and Church Street.'

'I know it, of course. That's convenient with her being just a stone's throw away!' Mags smiled. 'Not far for me to go. But...' She chewed on her bottom lip. 'Are they allowing you to see your father?'

Betsan shook her head. 'Not so far, no. Mrs Parry-Jones, the supervisor, said she'll try to find out how he's getting on for me.'

'That's good.' Mags let out a loud sigh. 'I'll return soon now I've softened up the porter.' She chuckled. Then glancing at him in the distance, she noticed he was watching her with interest. 'I was promised a few minutes with you, so I'd better not outstay my welcome. You run along too as I don't want you getting in any bother because of me.'

Betsan smiled at that, and in that moment, Mags realised her niece was going to be all right. She couldn't say the same for her brother-in-law. Who knew what might become of him in a place like this – hard labour, meagre rations and a strict regime to follow. She'd heard of troubled folk who'd entered here being described as 'idiots' and 'imbeciles' when the poor inmates had probably just suffered a great deal of mental distress.

Suffer no more, dear David, she thought as she hugged her niece one final time and then went on her way.

* * *

Dora was throwing her weight around. Already she'd made two of the younger girls cry that particular day. One had even wet herself as she was that scared of the girl. By the time Betsan returned to the dormitory, Dora was on fire, carried away with the feeling of power and authority and how she had total reign over all the girls in the dorm.

'Well, look who we have here!' she scoffed as she tossed her raven-haired locks, her eyes glittering with resentment. She was out to stir up a storm and the other girls sensed it. They all stopped what they were doing, all eyes on Betsan.

It was supposed to be a quiet rest period where the girls could either lie down on their beds for half an hour or take on tasks they'd not previously had much time for, like writing a letter to a loved one or reading a book from the workhouse library.

Now though, all girls were on their feet and drawing near. There was the feeling that if Betsan didn't do something right now, then she'd be forever overshadowed by Dora, Queen of the Dorm!

'Where 'ave ya been?' The girl loomed over her, but Betsan did not flinch.

'Out to the entrance to meet my auntie,' Betsan said in a matter-of-fact tone.

'Hear that, girls?' said Dora, her hands on her hips. Her eyes surveyed the room as if to ensure all were watching the spectacle about to take place. 'She's been out to meet her auntie!'

Some of the girls laughed, but the rest chose to remain silent.

'And what's the matter with that?' Betsan asked, sticking out her chin in defiance.

'Because you're new here and not allowed any special privileges unless I say so!' She pushed Betsan in the chest roughly with the palms of her hands, causing her to stumble backwards so she had to fight to retain her balance. But this only served to incur Betsan's wrath.

The girls gasped collectively as Betsan, maintaining eye contact, moved slowly towards Dora until she was just inches away. Then, widening her eyes, she snarled, 'Think I'm scared of some sad ragamuffin like you? I've seen off bigger and better than your sort!' Which wasn't strictly true, though she had stood up to her stepmother on many an occasion. A flood of anger coursed through her body and she fisted her hands at her sides as she thought how unjust it was to lose her mother and now her father too though in an altogether different manner.

Dora raised the flat palm of her hand as if to swipe her across the head but, instead, Betsan caught the girl's arm and then twisted it behind her back. It was evident the girl was doing her best to regain her composure and break out of the stronghold.

'Go on, Dora!' a girl called Beryl urged. 'Give that little scrote a backhander!'

But as hard as she tried, Dora couldn't release herself from Betsan's grasp. Some of the girls who weren't in Dora's close circle were now egging Betsan on but she wasn't someone who wanted to inflict pain on a bully; she was just someone who wanted to show Dora and her kind that she wasn't to be messed with.

Finally, she relaxed her grip and pushed the girl roughly in the back, in the same manner Dora had pushed her a couple of minutes ago.

Dora turned towards her, face red and with evil intent in her eyes. 'You'll pay for this, you little witch! You see if you don't, Little Miss High And Mighty! Thinks she's better than everyone else.'

Dora wiped her snot-filled nostrils with the sleeve of her dress and began to leave the room, her close friends running after her.

'Oooh! I'm shaking in my boots!' Betsan shouted after her. It was then she noticed the admiring glances from some of the other girls.

But Dora's words were not a threat to be taken lightly, for she realised the girl meant every word. She'd been humiliated, badly. Now she would want to exact her revenge.

* * *

Jimmy stood outside J. D. Baxter Boot and Shoe Repairs, the small cobbler shop on the high street near the Vulcan Inn. He hesitated a moment before pushing the door to enter. When he did, a little bell above him tinkled. Repairing footwear at home had been going so well that now he had something he wanted to put forward to the man.

Mr Baxter, who was sitting on a stool, head down, absorbed in his work, looked up at the sound of the bell. He wore a long leather apron and his shirtsleeves were rolled up to his elbows. Between his legs was an iron shoe last with a man's shoe fitted on it. He spat out some tacks that were in his mouth, ready for use, into the palm of his gnarled hand. Jimmy noticed when he was deep in concentration how his eyes became screwed up.

'Hello, Jimmy!' he said, looking up and smiling. 'What brings you here today, lad? Have you come to watch me at work so I can pass my skills on to you like I promised?'

Jimmy cleared his throat. 'Er, not exactly. I mean I love to watch you at work and learn from the master, of course, but I have a proposition to put to you...' he said nervously as he didn't know how his idea would be received.

'Oh, yes?'

Mr Baxter was elderly and so was his wife, who often helped at the shop, and it was evident he needed additional help. Now his grey eyes were questioning as he angled his head to one side, waiting for Jimmy's answer.

* * *

There was an uneasy peace in the dorm that evening and during the following few days. Dora and her gang kept well away from Betsan and they didn't pick on any of the younger girls either.

Meanwhile, Betsan worked hard in the sewing room, acquiring new skills from Miss Marston who was an excellent seamstress and teacher. Mrs Parry-Jones had got word to her that her father was managing well, taking on various workhouse tasks, eating his meals and resting at night-time, which he'd had trouble with before entering the workhouse. Though there was still no sign of his memory returning.

It was a few days later when things took a turn for the worse. Betsan had been dispatched to work in the laundry room as they were short-handed there following an outbreak of something that was causing diarrhoea and vomiting amongst the inmates. A finger had been pointed towards the kitchen as the supplier of meat had been changed as the workhouse master, Mr Aldridge, had started a cost-cutting measure that involved paring everything to the bone. As a consequence, cheaper offcuts of meat were used even though Cook objected to this, though it was yet to be proven that any meat cooked was rancid or undercooked or even whether some sort of hygiene measures at the workhouse were under par. It might even have been some other sort of illness. Who knew for certain?

Doctor Llewellyn was baffled. Whatever was causing it, inmates were dropping like flies and Betsan hoped her father would not succumb to it, nor she herself for that matter.

That Thursday morning, Betsan found herself in the laundry room with Dora, who initially kept to herself. But as the morning wore on, she noticed the girl and two of her cronies glancing sideways in her direction as they muttered behind the palms of their hands. There was a lot of nodding of heads and pointing of fingers. Then Mrs Laine, the laundry mistress, left the room unexpectedly.

Betsan glanced around her warily. It was quiet, far too quiet.

A strange sort of silence descended over the room as all chatter ceased; all that could be heard was the bubbling of the boiling water in the large copper vat that was used to wash the clothes and the hard steam press of several irons hissing as they pressed over thick cotton bedsheets.

'Quick, grab her, girls!' Dora yelled and her friends, Connie and Beryl, took strides towards her with a look of menace in their eyes.

Betsan, who stood rooted to the spot with a towel she was in the midst of folding in her hand, took in a deep breath and exhaled. Then her eyes widened as she saw Dora lift one of the irons from the ironing bench and slowly but deliberately head towards her.

'I said grab her!' she shouted.

Betsan shivered.

Connie and Beryl roughly grabbed an arm each as the towel fell to the floor, while Dora held the iron inches from Betsan's face.

'You little witch!' she yelled with such force that spittle sprayed from her mouth. Her dark eyes were like two lumps of coal, hard and beady. 'I'm going to show you who's boss around here and I'll ruin your features forever!'

For the first time since entering the workhouse, Betsan felt real fear. The iron made a sizzling sound but then Betsan watched in disbelief as Dora, as if realising she was going too far, walked away and replaced the iron on the bench.

Betsan emitted a sigh of relief, expecting Connie and Beryl to loosen their grip, but when they failed to do so she realised they didn't intend to punish her with the iron, but something else.

'Now!' yelled Dora as the two marched Betsan to the far end of the room where the sluice cupboard lay. It was there soiled bedding was stored ready for sorting, soaking and then boiling in the copper.

Betsan gulped as Beryl yanked open the door and the pair shoved her inside.

'*Ych a fi!*' she shouted as they slammed the door shut behind her. *Yuck!*

'How very disgusting of you, Beryl!' Connie laughed as Dora joined in with the merriment.

The room had no windows so inside was pitch-black and if there was some sort of light source, Betsan had no idea where it was. The sluice stank to high heaven of the inmates' waste products. She gagged from the overpowering stench of it all, not knowing which was worse, the vomit or the diarrhoea.

But realising that Dora would relish the thought of her crying out for help, she remained silent. Instead, she removed her cap and held it firmly over her mouth and nose to stifle the odour but even the smell of starch did little to abate the disgusting stench. She screwed her eyes shut as she did her utmost to think of something else but the stifling cupboard she found herself in. Even though she tried desperately to imagine the sweet perfume of roses, her stomach continued to heave until eventually she expelled the contents of it over her boots and down her pinafore and dress.

Then the door was opened suddenly and all was bright again. But it wasn't Dora standing in front of her laughing her socks off, it was Mrs Laine with a shocked expression on her face. Behind her stood Dora, Beryl and Connie, who were pinching their noses tightly with sour expressions on their faces.

'Who locked you in here, girl?' Mrs Laine gasped and, as she did so, the three girls dropped their hands to their sides as if now fearful how Betsan might respond to that question.

Betsan shook her head before replying. 'I don't know, miss. I didn't see who did it.'

Mrs Laine narrowed her eyes with suspicion. 'And you've vomited, I see, not surprising after being locked in there with all that filthy laundry! I'm not taking any chances now – not if you've got the workhouse sickness. Now get off to the washroom and have a good soak in the bath, wash your hair too and tell whoever's there that I've said you are to have clean clothing from the storeroom as we're behind with all this laundry now. I don't know if they'll provide new boots for you though. I shouldn't think so but they can be cleaned up – they don't look too bad. Your pinafore has taken the brunt of it.'

Betsan glanced at her boots. There was more vomit on the pinafore and she guessed it was because she'd turned to one side as soon as it happened and the rest must have hit the floor. At least she wasn't going to have to clean it up!

She stared over Mrs Laine's shoulder to see Dora standing there open-mouthed, as if shocked that Betsan hadn't told the woman the truth, informing her who really was to blame.

'Now off you go!' said Mrs Laine brusquely. 'Then when you're all spruced up and have been given fresh clothing, return to your dorm and lie down for the rest of the day in case you come down with the sickness too, and we'll send the doctor to examine you.'

'Yes, miss!' she said and made her way out of the room, the group of girls parting like the Red Sea to allow her to pass, as if she were now contaminated. As she did so, she paused to address Dora and her friends. 'You can all close your mouths now, girls!' she said, her lips curving into a big smile. 'You look as if you're catching flies there!'

Their plan to hurt and humiliate her had failed dismally, as now she could enjoy a nice hot bath, would be given fresh clothing to wear and get to lie on her bed in peace as the rest of the girls carried on with their daily chores. It wasn't such a bad life as now she could read her prized *Mary Jones and Her Bible* book from cover to cover without being disturbed by anyone.

17

Mags was becoming quite concerned about Jimmy. As yet, the lad hadn't returned home. Where was he? He had said earlier he was off to visit the market traders to see if any of them would purchase the goods from the stable. What if he'd got himself into trouble though? One or two of them were associated with the men who had caused Elgan's imprisonment in the first place, though the vast majority of traders were law-abiding and most definitely on Elgan's side.

It was a good hour later before she heard Jimmy's key in the lock and he burst into the room out of breath, his eyes shining brightly.

'Where on earth have you been, lad?' Mags stood with her hands on her hips. The twins had been put to bed hours ago.

'Sorry, didn't have time to let you know.' He drew out a chair from the table and sat. 'I'm a bit out of puff as I've been rushing to stable the horse for the night and feed him and the donkey.'

'But why were you gone for so long?' Mags frowned. He really could be an unpredictable sort sometimes, could Jimmy.

He took a deep, composing breath and then exhaled slowly.

'Well, I went to the market like I said I was going to do, as I chose a bad time the other evening when all they wanted to do was to close down their stalls and—'

'Yes, go on,' she urged impatiently.

'I covered most of the stalls asking if they were interested in purchasing goods of Elgan's. Most stallholders recognised me, of course, but—'

'Spit it out, lad!' Mags said, voice raised, for a moment forgetting Alys and Aled were sound asleep upstairs.

Jimmy smiled at her impatience. 'I was just coming to it. Anyhow, none were interested in purchasing anything at all though most asked about how he was getting on in the nick so I told them how you'd been to visit and bribed your way in there!'

'I'll thump you in a minute!' said Mags, raising her fist. Why was he taking so long to get to the point?

'But then,' said Jimmy with a gleam in his eyes, 'I came upon a marvellous idea!'

'Idea?'

Had the lad found her gin bottle or something and taken a few tots from it?

'Yes, an idea, Mags. One that might help us over a lean period!' He leapt out of the chair, causing her to startle at the suddenness of it all.

'What sort of an idea?'

'I thought maybe I could use the horse and cart for another purpose instead. I could go around the doors offering to pick up any boots and shoes that need repairs and take them to Mr Baxter's shop to provide the option of a delivery service, footwear all mended and polished shiny bright!'

Mags frowned and rubbed her chin in contemplation. 'Sounds good but people might not want to pay for that sort of service when they don't have two ha'pennies to rub together.'

'Maybe not in some cases but I thought of knocking on some of the larger houses in the town. You know those that have servants and such.'

Mags mulled it over. 'Might not be such a bad idea at that but will Mr Baxter go for it? And pay you into the bargain?'

'Yes, he's already agreed. And as he'll have to take on more work if my plan is successful, I'll also end up doing more repairs like you saw me doing the other day. Those were easy but he's offered to pass his skills on to me so I can learn the craft, an apprentice, like.'

'Oh, Jimmy!' She hugged him to her. 'I'm so proud of you, lad.' When she finally broke away, she looked at him and said, 'I won't be sitting on my backside neither when Elgan's inside. I had an idea too. Now that he's told me Gwennie's sewing machine is mine to do what I like with, I'm going to do what she did!'

Jimmy angled his head to one side. 'Do what?'

'Why, be a seamstress of course!'

Jimmy opened and closed his mouth. 'But do you know how? You're not exactly domesticated, are you, Mags?'

She chuckled. 'Maybe not. Perhaps I'm not the best cook or homemaker in the world but I can use a sewing machine, so I will be sitting on my backside in a manner but working at the same time!' She chuckled. 'At one time I used to help my sister. If she had a large order to get out and her eyes were tired, I was able to take over from her.'

'I see,' he said. 'But what about Betsan? She had her heart set on that sewing machine, didn't she?'

'Yes. When she leaves that blessed workhouse, I want her to come into business with me, making garments and taking in repairs. I've got it all worked out. We might even set up our own market stall together someday but for the time being I'm going to have a word with Mrs O'Connell on the market about selling some of the items we make and taking in repairs for her.'

'Then I think we should raise a toast to our new ventures!' Jimmy beamed.

For a brief moment, Mags pictured the gin bottle wrapped in the tray cloth at the back of the cupboard, so far untouched.

'I'll say amen to that, but it'll have to be that ginger beer I made, none of the hard stuff!' She laughed.

A couple of miracles occurred for Betsan: the first was that Dora and her friends were now no longer her enemies. After the incident with the sluice cupboard, they showed her some kind of respect as, after all, she would have been well within her rights to complain to Mrs Laine about the three of them. Mrs Laine, in turn, could have taken it upon herself to inform the supervisor who would have certainly spoken to the workhouse master about it. Suitable punishment would undoubtedly have been meted out to all three girls, which may have resulted in removal of particular privileges, extra chores and possible actual physical punishment from the swish of the birch. So now realising Betsan was no snitch and she'd had the good sense to remain quiet on the matter, they were deeply indebted to her. But in reality, all Betsan sought was peace.

The second miracle to occur was that Mrs Parry-Jones came to tell her there was a great improvement in her father's condition and it was arranged that Sunday afternoon Betsan should be allowed to visit him. All week the excitement mounted for her. How would Dad look? Would he speak to her? Would he even recognise her? After all, back home, his mood and memory differed day by day. It had been hard to predict his reactions to those around him.

The day finally arrived as promised and she was able to meet with her father in the exercise yard. To her surprise, he appeared to have gained a little weight since the last time she'd set eyes on him and now had a spring in his step as he strode briskly towards her. The light had finally returned to his eyes.

'Hello, sweetheart!' he greeted as he hugged her to his chest.

'Dad!' she cried as she fought to hold back the tears. 'I've missed you so much.'

'I know you have, my darling. I'm sorry I've been difficult to live with lately. I feel bad that I've landed us both up in here.' He drew away for a moment to gaze into her eyes. 'How are the twins?'

'They're fine, Dad. They're living with Aunt Mags now.' She looked at him to gauge his reaction.

'That's good. They're where they should be. I'm sorry you had to find out like that – that they're really your cousins and not your brother and sister. How did you know?'

'I got it out of Mrs Jenkins and then spoke to Aunt Mags about it.'

'And you're all right with that?'

She shrugged. 'It doesn't matter. To me, they will always be my brother and sister.'

'It's good you feel that way. Elinor has said she'll return home when we leave here. But Mrs Jenkins told her she had to sell that Welsh dresser to ensure the rent was paid. All I can hope now is that the landlord at the Star Inn will employ me again as we need the money. Florrie's going to put a good word in for me.'

Betsan nodded. 'Did Elinor say how Mrs Jenkins was doing?'

He shook his head, frowning. 'No, and why do you ask?'

'She's been out of breath lately.' Betsan bit her lower lip.

'Yes, come to mention it, she hasn't seemed her sprightly self for some time now. And to think of all the help she's given us since your mam passed on. She's been a treasure. Don't you fret none – we'll come through all of this and soon we'll be back in our old home and you'll have a new baby brother or sister in a couple of months.'

Betsan smiled, thinking how it wasn't so very long ago she had dreaded the thought, but now she was quite looking forward to it.

* * *

Mrs Parry-Jones told Betsan that it was Elinor paying her father a couple of visits that had triggered his memory but even though things were much better for him, after being examined and assessed by Doctor Llewellyn, the decision was made that he should remain in the workhouse for a while longer. So it would mean Christmas in the workhouse for both Betsan and her father, but she didn't mind too much. It was now Christmas Eve and visits were allowed from loved ones.

With Miss Marston's assistance, Betsan had managed to embroider a tablecloth for Auntie Mags. The woman had taught her several embroidery stitches including back stitch, feather stitch, stem stitch, running stitch and several others but her favourite was the French knot, which involved wrapping thread around the sewing needle to form a knot on the surface of the fabric. Oh, the linen tablecloth did look pretty and all as Betsan had embroidered it with a buttercups-and-daisies design, which would cover Mags's old scuffed table a treat.

For Alys, Betsan had made a brand-new rag doll from the leftover scraps from the cutting-room floor, using two bright blue buttons for the eyes. Thick yellow wool was sewn onto the head and then braided into two long plaits.

For Aled, she'd sewn a rag book where she'd cut out shapes of trains and ships from coloured felt and stitched them onto each page, which had an embroidered word on it to help him learn to read.

Finally, for Mrs Jenkins, she'd sewn a green felt case for her to slip her spectacles into. She had intended making something for her father – since being in the workhouse she had also learned how to knit, so she'd thought of a scarf, though she had yet to finish it. But her father had insisted she concentrate her efforts elsewhere as they both had all they needed right now, which was one another, and they were allowed to meet up for one hour on Christmas Day itself.

Mags and Betsan were seated in a large dining room opposite one another as various conversations from other inmates and their visitors echoed around the room. The dining room was in the workhouse chapel, doubling both as a chapel and a refectory.

Christmastime was good for the inmates because as well as being allowed a visit from loved ones on Christmas Eve, tomorrow would be a day to look forward to as Cook would be preparing a fine festive meal for them all, or so Mrs Parry-Jones informed them. Local businesses in the town donated various food items for the inmates and even gifts, alcohol too, which was permitted on that one day of the year. The reality was most would dine far better inside here than if they were at home. For those who had previously lived alone or on the streets, it provided jovial company too.

'Are you taking care of yourself, darlin'?' Aunt Mags asked.

'Yes, I am, Auntie.' She smiled.

'Remove your cap – there's a good girl.'

Thankfully, Betsan's hair was now beginning to grow again and was no longer tuft-like, as it had been when it was first shorn, and she was relieved about that. She'd felt ugly with hardly any hair on her head.

'Ah, that's much better,' Mags enthused. 'It won't be too long before your lovely locks grow back again!'

Betsan nodded in agreement and then she replaced her cap. 'How's Mrs Jenkins?'

'I haven't had time to call to see her but I will. Why do you ask? Have you been concerned about her, darlin'?'

Betsan frowned. 'Yes, sometimes she seems out of breath and her lips turn blue. I thought she might have tried to visit here by now...' Her voice trailed away into nothingness.

Mags let out a long breath. 'I suppose she's been busy or maybe she tried to visit but wasn't allowed in. Do you know when they're next having a visiting day like this?'

'New Year's Day, I think. Oh, would you ask her to come to see me, Auntie?'

Mags nodded. 'I'll do my best, love. I'll call to her house to check on her when I leave here. How about your stepmother? Has she called to see you yet?'

Betsan shook her head. 'She's been to see Dad though and he's perked up since, seems more his old self.'

'And his memory?'

'Most of it seems to have returned, though he can't remember that man attacking him that night.'

'Well, that sounds promising. Now I've brought some good news...'

Betsan's eyes glistened and she shaded them as the light

reflecting from the arched leaded window behind Aunt Maggie momentarily dazzled her vision. 'Oh, yes?'

'I've had a word with Mrs O'Connell, the Irish lady, who has a clothing stall on the outdoor market and she says she would definitely be interested if we can sew some new garments for her stall and also take in repairs. The pay won't be a lot but it will be enough to get us started and keep the wolf from the door. So when you've left here, we can get cracking on our new business! Of course, you'll have to carry on with your schooling. I know you read and write well enough, but I don't want you missing out on any of that.'

Betsan beamed. 'I want to be a seamstress just like Mam was,' she said proudly.

Mags leaned across the table to pat her niece's hand.

'How are Aled and Alys?'

'Oh, they've been doing just dandy, darlin'. Jimmy's been taking them out on the horse and cart as he's been making deliveries for Mr Baxter, the cobbler.'

'Yes. I remember seeing a pile of footwear on the table when I first met him.'

'He's got big ideas. Wouldn't mind betting one day he'll end up with a shop of his own.' Mags chuckled.

On Christmas morning, there was an early service held at the workhouse chapel before breakfast and then afterwards gifts were handed out to the inmates. Betsan received a brush and hand mirror set, which was emblazoned with pretty colourful flowers. Then she was allowed to open the gifts Auntie had brought for her, which included several satin ribbons of various colours, which she probably wouldn't be allowed to wear right now, but as soon as she was allowed home she vowed she'd wear one of them in her hair on her day of departure. It would have grown to a more reasonable length by then.

There was also a small box of pink and white sugared almonds and a tin of toffees, but best of all, Auntie had given her the little cameo brooch with the edged-out shape of a white rose on it that her mother had gifted her sister one year for her birthday. She intended to somehow wear it every day, even if it meant pinning it to her undergarments or beneath her pinafore. She'd need to ensure no one stole her items from her before she left here, so she intended to hide them beneath her mattress. And Aunt Mags had insisted Betsan take it as she also had another reminder of her sister now, being reunited with her niece.

The Christmas dinner itself, the following day, was roast beef with all the trimmings: crispy-edged roast potatoes, sweet carrots, parsnips and sprouts with lashings of tasty gravy made from the juices from the roasting pan. The odour wafting towards her made her mouth water at the thought of it all. This was followed by a plum pudding drenched in brandy and set alight as Cook proudly brought it in to be served on a silver platter with a dash of cream. She'd never tasted such a delicious feast and the inmates had cheered when Cook set the pudding alight. The noise didn't die down until long after the blue and red flames disappeared and it was ready to be devoured by all.

Mrs Parry-Jones had informed her that it was the one day of the year when workhouse inmates up and down the land dined almost as well as kings and queens. The fine feast was followed with bowls full of tangerines and nuts being passed around and hot punch ladled into the inmates' tin mugs. Betsan, who had never tasted alcohol in her life, loved the taste of the rum in the punch, though one of the older inmates told her there wouldn't be all that much in it because one Christmas the inmates were given too much alcohol and it had almost caused a riot.

They were all encouraged to take a walk in the exercise yard, which Betsan was glad of as she felt she could consume no more and needed a breather. Looking up at the grey leaden sky, she closed her eyes and gave thanks to God that things were improving for them all. It wasn't quite the Christmas she'd hoped for but life now seemed on the up once again.

* * *

'What's the matter, Mags?'

She was in the middle of preparing a Christmas dinner for them all, but her forehead had creased into a frown. She'd managed to acquire a goose cheaply from one of the market traders who had taken pity on her particular plight with Elgan being put away. Another stallholder gave her some potatoes, carrots and a nice leafy green cabbage and a neighbour had made a plum pudding for her. All of this was without her even asking; people were being kind as they loved her and Elgan so much, realising how tight things now were for the woman and Jimmy. So now they had plenty to eat, he couldn't fathom why she was being so glum. Why today of all days? Particularly as her own offspring were now under the same roof.

'Are you worried about Elgan, Mags? Thinking of him today in particular?'

She shook her head as she carried on peeling a carrot and then she set it down on the wooden chopping board. 'No, it's not that so much; it's something Betsan said to me yesterday.'

He wrinkled his nose. 'About what?'

'Bronwen Jenkins. She asked if I'd seen her lately. She's concerned as the woman has been breathless lately.'

Jimmy sighed. 'To tell you the truth, when the pair of them first called here, I noticed Mrs Jenkins was a bit out of puff. Thought walking here all that way from Plymouth Street was too much for her at her age.'

'Possibly. I didn't notice that day as I was so overwhelmed by the court case and seeing Betsan again. I did notice it when I spoke to Bronwen last but I didn't mention it to Betsan. Don't know how old the woman is but she was a good friend and neighbour to Gwennie and when she passed, she took care of Aled and Alys like they were her own.' She began to chop the carrots vigorously, then she scooped the slices into a saucepan of water. 'The vegetables are all prepared and the goose is cooking nicely.'

She untied the strings of her pinafore and tossed it on the table and went to grab her thickest shawl from the peg at the back of the front door.

'I won't be gone too long,' she said, draping the shawl around her shoulders, 'just put the saucepans on to boil in about an hour if I haven't returned by then.'

Jimmy nodded. He was familiar with Mags and her methods of doing things and in the past couple of years he'd often helped her out. In fact, he now knew how to cook a roast dinner or a stew after spending many a time watching her at work. She claimed to be a terrible cook and he teased her on occasion when she burnt something, but the truth was that, mainly, her meals were very tasty indeed.

* * *

The twins were playing in front of the hearth with the toys Betsan had given them for Christmas: the rag doll for Alys and the rag book for Aled. There were other toys too that Mags had managed to buy cheaply from the market. A toy drum with sticks that made a terrible racket but the twins enjoyed creating it. There was also an old doll's house that Elgan had stored in the stable. It wasn't in the best state of repair but Jimmy had painted it up and hammered a couple of nails into the sides to prevent it from collapsing completely. And finally, a wooden boat that Jimmy had whittled for them from a piece of wood. He promised to take them to a local pond to sail it when the weather improved.

About to leave, Mags looked down at the pair of them, and they looked back up at her with wide eyes. 'I won't be long,' she reassured them, blowing them a kiss. 'Jimmy will be looking after you while I've gone.'

They both beamed as they adored Jimmy; he was like a big brother to them and so full of fun.

As Mags left the house, a few snowflakes settled on her face and the shoulders of her shawl. Looking heavenward, she tutted. It would have to snow right now! She couldn't be with her niece on Christmas Day, so this was something she could do for her: to check on the welfare of her dear neighbour. If she'd been in her right senses, she ought to have remained indoors but this was just too important.

An icy blast of wind blew hard in her direction, causing her to wrap her shawl tightly around herself and put her head down against the bracing elements. The bitterly cold weather almost took her breath away, but still she persisted in placing one foot in front of the other. There weren't many folk out on the streets today as most were at home. The ones she saw she guessed were returning from a church or chapel service somewhere. She wondered what Elgan was doing right now. Would he dine as well as those at the workhouse? She very much doubted it. Maybe he'd be lucky to get bread and water dished up.

As she approached Plymouth Street, a swirl of snowflakes obscured her vision, causing her to blink her eyes to clear her line of sight. Not much further now. Nearly there.

She let out a sigh of relief when she reached Bronwen's door and she rapped so hard on the knocker that her knuckles hurt. There was no sign of life inside. No sign of any smoke billowing from the chimney and no excited children glimpsed through the window. All was in darkness.

Finally, the door drew open and there stood Bronwen, her eyes widening to see it was Mags on the step.

'Hello, Mags,' she greeted. 'What brings you here?'

'I've come to see how you are on behalf of Betsan,' she explained.

'Oh, come on in. It's perishing cold to be stood on the doorstep.'

Mags stamped her snow-covered feet on the doormat and entered the house.

'We'll have to keep our voices down as Bert's asleep. He worked a night shift at Gethin Pit last night, you see. Come through to the scullery.'

Gratefully, Mags followed the woman along a narrow passageway and into a small back room where there was a cosy fire lit in the hearth. Several saucepans bubbled merrily away on the hob.

'Take a seat.' Bronwen gestured towards the pine table in the centre of the room. Both women seated themselves. 'How is Betsan doing these days?'

'She's fine,' said Mags. 'I visited her just yesterday and she's doing very well. Hopefully someday soon she and her father can return home. The landlord hasn't moved any new tenants in, has he?'

'No, he can't,' said Bronwen firmly. 'The sale of that dresser has given them three months' grace at least.'

Mags exhaled. 'Thank goodness for that. Though Betsan was wondering why you haven't been to pay her a visit as yet?'

'Aw, has she? I have tried to get past that porter on the door a couple of times but as I'm not family, he was having none of it, said I needed an authorised visit, whatever that is!'

'Yes, that is a problem. I had one official visit on Christmas Eve but the one before that I had to sweet-talk the man into and even then I could only see her briefly at the entrance. Someone had to fetch her for me.'

'Aye, well, you've still got the looks for it!' Bronwen chuckled.

Mags smiled. 'Yes, but I doubt Elgan would approve!' She rolled her eyes and then sat further forward in her chair, leaning across the table with her chin resting on her fist, as though there was an important question that needed addressing. 'Betsan has been concerned about your health. That's really why I'm here today.'

'Oh?' Bronwen's eyes widened.

'She said you've been breathless of late and, on occasion, your lips have turned blue? You were a little breathless last time we met...'

Bronwen nodded. 'Aye, she's right enough. But I have seen Doctor Llewellyn and he's advised me to rest up more. Said I can't go carrying on like a spring chicken any longer. I need to change my lifestyle and improve my diet.'

Mags smiled sympathetically. 'I just want to thank you for all you've done lately for the twins.' She reached out appreciatively to pat the woman's hand.

Bronwen beamed. 'They were a pleasure to care for and I'm so pleased they're back with their mother as it should be.'

Tears pricked the backs of Mags's eyes, as she became overwhelmed with gratitude towards the woman for all she'd done for both children. Without her help, they might have had to go into an orphanage or the workhouse. Bronwen had given them both her time and her heart.

'Now, where are my manners? You've walked all this way to see how I am and I haven't even offered you a cup of something hot to drink nor wished you a merry Christmas!'

Mags smiled as she gazed at the woman through glazed eyes. This Christmas was going to be different in so many ways.

'Thank you, I'd love a cup of tea.' She sniffed. 'And a merry Christmas to you, Bronwen.' She handed the woman the gift her niece had made for her. 'This is from Betsan for you!'

A couple of days after Christmas, Betsan was working in the sewing room when Miss Marston sent her on an errand – a handwritten note for her to take to the supervisor's room.

As she walked down the corridor, she became aware of a group of people who were being ushered in through the main door.

'You need to go to the receiving ward,' said the porter as he directed the group. It appeared as though a family was being admitted to the workhouse. She guessed they'd fallen on hard times. Betsan knew what that felt like. How awful though for it to happen over the Christmas period.

As she drew near, the mother of the family, who cradled a young baby in her arms, turned her head in Betsan's direction. It took a while for recognition to dawn.

It was Martha! Martha Hardcastle and her family. The younger children were whimpering and their father had a defeated look on his face. Enid, though, held herself straight with her chin jutting out as if to say, *I still have my pride!*

'Mrs Hardcastle!' she cried out.

'Oh, Betsan dear!' Martha kissed her on the cheek, the porter standing impatiently behind her. No doubt he wanted to return to his position at the main door as soon as possible.

'What's happened?' Betsan frowned.

'The landlord has finally thrown us all out for good. We just can't make the last rent payment as he's hiked up the price again! So we have no other choice than to see if they'll accept us here. I'm just hoping now they'll see fit to admitting us.'

Mr Hardcastle nodded. 'I feel I'm to blame. If I'd kept up payments to begin with. Demanded my pay on time from the foreman at the ironworks...' He gritted his teeth in anger.

'Now, none of this is your doing,' soothed his wife as she jiggled Baby Jonathan in her arms.

Enid smiled at Betsan. 'Hello again. How did you end up here too?'

Betsan sighed. 'My father. He suffered a blow to the head at work and lost his memory for a time. He was in no fit state to work so there was no money coming in and the doctor decided it was best to admit him here. I could have stayed with my neighbour or Auntie Mags, but I didn't want to leave him – my stepmother has moved out and the twins are now with my aunt.'

'You did right,' said Mrs Hardcastle, laying a sympathetic hand on her shoulder. 'You're a good daughter to him. I'm just hoping we can all stick together in here!'

Betsan hesitated before speaking. 'But didn't you know? You won't be able to stay together as a family. Mr Hardcastle will be sent to the men's wing where my father is. Mrs Hardcastle, you'll be allowed to keep the baby with you in the women's wing as he's under two years old, but Enid will be in the girl's dorm with me and any children under seven will be in the children's wing.'

Martha frowned. 'Well, I'm glad you've explained it to us, Betsan, and it's reassuring that we will know a friendly face in here already. I was told they'll be putting our case before the Board of Guardians. We better get a shift on as I don't want us to spend the night on the streets.'

Betsan nodded. It was so unfair that a lovely, hard-working couple like the Hardcastles had to come to this, seeking refuge for themselves and their family in the workhouse. Truth be told, there were worse places, and out on the street in this awful weather was one of them.

18

The Hardcastle family were formally admitted to the workhouse and Enid ended up in the dorm with Betsan, just as she had predicted. Betsan was glad of the fact she was still in there to keep an eye on the girl in case Dora tried to pick on her. But so far, Enid had settled in well, though she had been most unhappy about having her beautiful flame-coloured hair cut so short. As they both sat on her bed, she wrapped a reassuring arm around the girl, comforting her.

'It's all right, Enid,' Betsan soothed as the girl blinked away the tears. 'Your lovely hair won't take long to grow again.'

She whipped off her own cap to demonstrate how much her hair was growing now, and ran her hand through it – so much neater than when Aunt Maggie had first set eyes on it.

Enid continued to bawl, so Betsan handed her a clean handkerchief from her pocket, which she gratefully took to dab at her watery eyes.

'Thank you. I wouldn't mind so much but I'd hate it if Jimmy saw me looking like this...' She sniffed.

Betsan nodded. 'You're sweet on him, aren't you?'

Enid beamed. 'Yes.'

'And does he like you in the same way?'

'I don't know, to be honest. I mean, he's cheeky with me sometimes. Teases me and all.'

To be truthful, Betsan wasn't entirely sure of Jimmy's feelings towards Enid. When he'd helped her home that night with her shopping from the marketplace she'd got the impression that it was herself he had eyes for. But maybe she was mistaken and she wouldn't wish to upset Enid for all the world. There was no way she'd ever want a lad to get in the path of their friendship. In any case, she didn't have the time to go courting as she had her father and her new business venture with Aunt Maggie to think of. But of course, there'd be no way of avoiding Jimmy as he lived with Auntie.

'Lads can be a bit strange,' said Betsan. 'It's hard to fathom whether they like us or not so, for some, teasing might be a way of getting our attention, but to be honest...' She paused for a moment.

'But what?' Enid's forehead creased into a frown.

'But sometimes teasing might just be that. Jimmy is a character, a cheeky sort of lad. Maybe don't read too much into it – that way you'll never be disappointed.'

Enid shrugged and let out a long breath. 'I guess you're right, Betsan. I shouldn't get my hopes up. In my mind, I've pictured myself marrying him and that we'll have a houseful of children!'

'Blimey, Enid! You'd better slow down.' Betsan chuckled. Then more seriously she added, 'Don't you have any ambitions though? I mean, don't you want more out of life?'

'No,' said Enid firmly, 'I'd be content to be Jimmy's wife and to keep house for him and any children we might have.'

Betsan felt a pang of sadness that the girl wanted no more than that. Things were harder for girls than they were for boys.

It was a month later when Enid received the news she was to be boarded out as a maid to one of the big houses in the town. The Clarkson family were well off and their vast house overshadowed the others in the area. It had large columns outside the front door and a long drive that led to a flight of stone steps, with a concrete lion's head mounted either side.

Most of the girls in the dorm were envious of Enid being selected to go and, for one or two, green-eyed envy took over.

'It's just not fair!' Dora complained as she stomped around the dorm. 'I've been here much longer than Enid and I haven't been sent into service anywhere yet!'

'Neither have I!' yelled Beryl, who folded her arms in defiance.

'When Enid returns,' said Betsan to the girls, after Enid had left the dorm to discuss the position with the workhouse master and his wife, 'please don't let on how you're feeling about any of this.'

'I don't see why not!' Dora's lips formed into a pout.

'The family has been through so much lately. Just be happy for her. Your turn may come soon enough and if Enid does well there, then maybe they'll take more of you at the house.'

Several girls nodded but Beryl narrowed her gaze.

'Don't you want to go there too though, Betsan?'

'No, certainly not!' Betsan held her head high. In reality she could think of nothing worse. 'I'm going home in a couple of weeks once the doctor gives my father a clean bill of health.'

Beryl nodded. 'Well, I won't say anything when Enid returns.' She turned towards Dora as if seeking approval. 'Will you?'

Reluctantly, Dora shook her head. 'No, at least not for the time being. She can let us know what it's like to work at the big house first. I've heard the Clarksons are one of the wealthiest families in the whole of Merthyr!'

'Maybe,' said Betsan, 'but I would think it's the Crawshay family who have the most wealth and influence in this town, as they own coal pits and ironworks.'

The remainder of the girls murmured and nodded their heads in agreement.

'I'd love to work at their place,' Dora said excitedly. 'Imagine waking up in Cyfarthfa Castle! Maybe I'll be sent there instead – that would be heaps better!'

Betsan smiled to herself as she turned away. Dora always wanted to have one up on the rest of them. But at least, for the time being, danger was averted for Enid: she was now out of the firing line.

* * *

Enid was to spend a few weeks in service at 'Hillside House' and then return to the workhouse when it would be assessed whether the Clarkson family might decide to take her on permanently.

'It'll be a great opportunity for me, Master and Matron Aldridge told me. They chose me to go there so that if I gain permanent employment, I can help the rest of my family and maybe Dad can get himself work and they can all live together again!' she said proudly. 'Though I realise I'll be expected to live at the house.'

'I'm pleased for you,' said Betsan. 'Most of the other girls of your sort of age here are not in the same situation. Dora's mother died last year and she never knew who her father was but one day her time will come to be placed somewhere like where you're going.'

'Has she said anything to you then?' Enid's eyes flashed with fear and now Betsan wished she hadn't bothered saying anything at all.

'Er, no, not really. I think one or two are just a little envious, that's all. When we discussed it, Dora said she'd rather work at Cyfarthfa Castle for the Crawshays!'

Enid laughed. It was good to see the girl happy and smiling. 'Only thing is I'm not too happy about my new hairstyle. It's still a bit sprouty here and there!'

'Remove your cap,' instructed Betsan. Enid did as told and Betsan ran her hands over Enid's head. 'It's not too bad. I could borrow a pair of scissors from the sewing room and tidy it up a little for you, if you like?'

Enid nodded eagerly. 'Thank you.'

She reached out and touched her friend's hand.

'In any case, I wouldn't be too worried as they'll make you wear a starched cap at the big house. But your maid's outfit will look a lot smarter than our workhouse uniform – you can bet on it!'

'That's true.' Enid smiled as she looked at her dress. 'This thing is so baggy and shapeless. I look like a sack of potatoes in it!'

* * *

And so, the following day, Betsan kissed her friend goodbye. Enid had been supplied with a serviceable, well-fitting dress, hat and jacket along with a pair of stout leather shoes and two new pairs of woollen stockings. Betsan thought she looked ever so smart.

A thought occurred to her as Enid stood in the dorm, a brown paper parcel of her packaged new clothing under her arm.

'Hang on!' she said and she lifted her pinafore to unpin the white rose brooch she'd been given at Christmas from her auntie. 'Wear this for luck,' she said and pinned it to Enid's jacket.

Enid beamed at her. 'Thank you so much. I promise I'll take care of it and give it back to you when I return in a few weeks.'

Betsan smiled and the pair embraced. Then she watched with tears in her eyes as Enid walked through the dorm towards the door, looking very grown-up indeed.

* * *

Betsan counted down the days until Enid's return. She'd become accustomed to having her around and now she missed her like crazy.

Finally, the Sunday arrived but there was no sign of Enid as expected.

'What's happened to Enid, miss?' Betsan asked the supervisor.

Mrs Parry-Jones's face reddened and then her thin lips appeared to tighten. She paused for a moment. 'Betsan,' she whispered, looking around the corridor to check they were alone, 'you know Enid quite well, don't you?'

'Yes, miss.'

What on earth had happened?

'Come with me then...' She ushered Betsan into her office.

The woman took a seat behind her desk as Betsan stood before her with her hands behind her back.

'What's wrong, miss? Hasn't Enid returned from service?'

'She has, yes, but she tells me an incident occurred while she was at the Clarkson house. Now, I'm entrusting you not to mention any of this to the other girls.'

'No, miss. But what sort of an incident?'

'Before I tell you, I want to ask you if you've ever known the girl to be untrustworthy? Dishonest in any way?'

For a moment, Betsan wondered if Enid had been caught stealing or something of that nature.

'No, miss. Quite the opposite.'

The supervisor huffed out a breath. 'The girl is claiming that the master's son interfered with her while she was working at the house.'

'Interfered, miss?' Betsan frowned.

'You know how babies are made, don't you? What goes on to have a baby?'

'Yes, miss. My mother told me all about that.'

'Well, she's claiming the son of the house did that to her, but I can't establish whether she consented to it or not.'

Betsan shook her head. 'I'm sure Enid wouldn't want to do anything like that, miss. Particularly because of Jimmy...'

'Jimmy? Who is he?'

'He lives with my aunt. Enid is sweet on him. She hopes to marry him someday.'

Mrs Parry-Jones narrowed her gaze. 'Do you think this Jimmy and Enid have already had relations with one another before marriage?'

'Oh no, miss!' Betsan was mortified the supervisor would even think such a thing. 'Jimmy doesn't even know she likes him that much!'

'I see. I've sent her to see the master and matron. It's a strong possibility now that she'll be sent to another workhouse outside the area due to the scandal it might create. The Clarksons won't want this hanging over their heads, particularly if she's now pregnant!'

Betsan gulped. She couldn't believe her ears. Her friend had done no wrong whatsoever and now she was going to be treated like a common criminal.

'But that's not fair, miss. The Clarkson son should be held accountable.'

'How old are you now, Betsan?' The supervisor looked up at her from the desk as if appraising her.

'Thirteen, miss.'

'And have you started your monthly courses as yet?'

'No, miss, but sometimes I notice my breasts seem a bit bigger than they were.'

'Then I'm sure your monthly courses will arrive soon. You must not allow yourself to get into a position where a lad – or a man, come to that – can compromise your morals. Now I'm sure Enid must have got her head turned from a little attention from the Clarksons' son but believe me, she'll have learned a valuable lesson from this, the hard way!'

Tears pricked the backs of Betsan's eyes at the injustice of it all. Swallowing hard, she realised there was nothing she could do.

'What shall I tell the other girls in the dorm, when they ask where she is?'

'Just tell them you've been informed Enid's not returning as she's remaining in service at the house.' With that, Mrs Parry-Jones closed the ledger on the desk firmly, as though she were closing a chapter in Enid's life – and maybe, in a way, she was. They all were.

It was a couple of days later before the supervisor informed Betsan that Enid had been transferred to the Cardiff Workhouse. Life was so unfair, particularly for paupers who got themselves into trouble through no fault of their own.

19

The day had finally arrived when Betsan had to leave the workhouse. Unfortunately, her father, whom Doctor Llewellyn hadn't deemed fit enough to leave, wouldn't be going with her and she was sad about that. Nevertheless, the girls in the dorm had all lined up to see her off, even Dora who appeared to have a tear in her eye. Though maybe her eyes were watering for another reason. Betsan supposed she'd never know which was the case but it pleased her that after being enemies to begin with, she had won the girl over.

For the time being, she'd be staying with Auntie Mags as her aunt and Mrs Jenkins had discussed the matter and both thought it was better that she didn't return home alone to the house.

Dad, though, was making progress and over the time that passed, Betsan was pleased to see him slowly returning to his former self, though his memory had still not fully returned.

She was settled at her aunt's house for a couple of weeks when Florrie called to tell them that Elinor had given birth to a baby girl. Betsan now had a baby sister called Isobelle – 'Izzy' for short – a name that seemed to suit her well. She was thrilled to visit Elinor and the baby at Florrie's place. The infant's dark lashes made her a very bonny baby indeed and Elinor told her she hoped that the birth of their child might finally reunite her and Betsan's father as a couple.

It was now almost a whole year since Betsan had left the workhouse and Mags thought her niece was growing into a fine young lady. Betsan worked afternoons and weekends in the business, which kept the rent going on the Plymouth Street house, and both used the house as the workplace for their thriving sewing business. Soon, on her fourteenth birthday, Betsan would leave school and then she could work full-time. Things were definitely on the up and, best of all, Elgan was being released from prison next week.

Mags stood on the market stall blowing into her gloveless hands. She watched as Mrs O'Connell passed the rose-pink petticoat over to a middle-aged customer for inspection. The woman peered at it closely and tested the seams by gently pulling on them.

'Such fine embroidery on the bodice...' Mrs O'Connell was explaining to the customer.

The woman nodded in agreement. 'It really is a quality piece of work. Where do you get your stock from, Mrs O'Connell?'

Bridget O'Connell hitched her thumb in Maggie's direction. 'This dear lady here – Maggie Hughes.'

Mags nodded towards the woman. 'I can even make things to order,' she offered.

'That's good to hear,' said the customer. 'I'm looking for a few like this for my daughters. They've outgrown their old ones. I love the workmanship; the embroidered flowers are just so pretty. Sets it off a treat.'

Mags smiled. 'That's my niece's handiwork. I made the petticoat itself but she designed it and embroidered the bodice.'

The truth was that Betsan had a flair for that sort of thing but when they worked together they didn't embroider that many items as it was too time-consuming. Sometimes Betsan liked to sketch out some designs for her embroidery and she created her own design for this petticoat that sold well on the market.

'I'll order three of those petticoats for my girls,' said the woman, breaking into Maggie's thoughts. 'I've brought their measurements with me. Here, I've written them on this piece of paper.' She thrust the sheet of paper towards Mags, who took it from her and studied it carefully, nodding as she did so.

'We can get them ready for you by the end of the week,' she said.

'That's fine,' said the woman, then she glanced at Mrs O'Connell. 'Do I pay you a deposit?'

Mrs O'Connell nodded eagerly. 'A tanner will do nicely and you can pay the rest on delivery of the goods.'

Mags grinned to herself. She could almost see the silver coins dancing before Bridget's eyes. She was a good sort as well as being very business-minded. She did not suffer fools gladly. There was no pulling the wool over her eyes!

Satisfied, the woman bade them good day and then went on her way.

Bridget glanced at Mags, a big smile on her face. 'The best thing I ever did was taking you on to help this business, Mags. You and Betsan have been an absolute godsend to me, so you both have!'

'If truth be told, you've helped us too. If you hadn't offered to pay me for work, I'd never have kept things ticking over in Elgan's absence.'

'How do you feel about him coming home next week?'

'I can't wait to see him, of course, but there's something I'm a little concerned about.' She chewed on her bottom lip.

'Oh, yes, now be sure to tell me what that is, as I can't second-guess ye. 'Twill be all right, to be sure.'

But will it though?

She took a composing breath before blurting out, 'I haven't told Elgan that I've got the twins living with us now. I mean, he knows they are his, but he thinks they're still with Betsan's father. How will I cope? Our house isn't really big enough for him when he returns. There's hardly room to swing a cat! It's a squeeze as it is. We could move into Betsan's house of course but that would only be a temporary measure as one day we all hope her father will return from the spike. We need something permanent.'

'Could you not ask Jimmy to move out?'

'Oh, no, he's part of the family is Jimmy. Like a son to me he's been.'

Jimmy had been her favourite out of all the parish lads she'd had boarding with her. He'd earned his keep too – so sending him packing would make no sense whatsoever.

'I've an idea so I have!' said Bridget. 'Now, have a think on this as you'd be doing me a favour. At least you would if you can pay me rent?'

Mags listened, curious and wide-eyed. 'Oh, yes?'

'The house I'm living in is too big for me now my children have flown the nest and my dear Shamus has now gone to be with the Lord. How about I rent you some rooms at the same price you're paying right now? There are two large downstairs sitting rooms, four bedrooms, a nice-size kitchen and utility room and the privy is in the back garden.'

Mags gasped at the woman's generosity. Imagine a house having its own privy that wasn't shared with neighbours in the street! A luxury indeed!

'Oh, thank you! That would solve a lot of my problems! It's so kind of you, Bridget!'

'Also you can run the sewing business from the house. Maybe Elgan can get involved in some way with deliveries on the horse and cart too.'

'Oh!' Mags's hands flew to her face, suddenly remembering something. 'Casper and Jasper! I wasn't thinking about them.'

'Who on earth are they? More parish lads?'

Mags shook her head. 'No, Elgan's horse and donkey.'

Bridget's eyebrows lifted with surprise. 'His donkey?'

'Don't ask.' Mags laughed. 'He loves that old nag. He rescued it from a severe beating and bought it from the owner who is a cruel sort. My Elgan is a real softie.'

Bridget nodded as if she knew that too well. 'I can't see there'll be a real problem. He needs the horse and cart anyhow. My neighbour owns a couple of horses. I can ask if we can pay him to stable both Casper and Jasper in his field.'

All Mags's apprehension and worry dissipated in that moment.

'You're a blessing, Mrs O'Connell,' she said, planting a kiss on the old woman's cheek.

In the year since Betsan had returned from the workhouse, she had not forgotten about Enid and often wondered how she was getting on. There had been no word from the Cardiff workhouse before she had been discharged from the Merthyr one. She hadn't even been able to contact Martha before leaving and now she had no idea where the family was either. At night in bed, she always remembered them all in her prayers.

Someone else who missed Enid was Jimmy. She hadn't told the lad the full details of what occurred at Hillside House but had alluded to an 'unfortunate incident' causing Enid's transfer to Cardiff. Initially, whenever their paths crossed, Jimmy had kept on enquiring after her but eventually, as there was never any news to give him, he stopped asking altogether and Betsan was relieved about that.

Betsan had recently celebrated her fourteenth birthday and finally left school for good. Her teacher, Miss Cartwright, had called her out in assembly to wish her a happy birthday in front of the entire school where she was presented with her very own Bible. She was especially thrilled when her teacher made special mention of how well she'd done at school and that's why she'd been invited to stay on. One of only two female pupils allowed to do so. Miss Cartwright said she thought Betsan would go far in life as she was already working for the clothing stall, designing and sewing garments for it, and the woman wished her all the best for the future.

Betsan thought back to the book of *Mary Jones and Her Bible*. Poor Mary had to save for years and then had to walk to a town miles away to purchase hers. Barefoot at that!

She reassured herself that her own life wasn't as hard as Mary's was. Now, she'd be able to work full-time for Mags and Mrs O'Connell. Sometimes she toiled, sewing away on her mother's treadle machine making petticoats, pinafores, night-dresses, men's shirts and waistcoats and even women's bloomers! On other occasions, she embroidered pretty patterns on garments or else stood on the market stall, selling their wares. Today was one such day.

A well-dressed gentleman appeared as she stood there. He

was young, maybe in his twenties. He wore a silver-grey frock coat, pristine white shirt and silver cravat along with a grey shiny top hat. In his hand he held a gold-tipped walking cane, appearing to peer curiously at the stall, drumming his gloved fingers over his chin as if in contemplation. Auntie had mentioned seeing someone of that description looking at the stall the previous week.

Finally, he began to walk towards her with purpose.

Betsan had just handed over some coins – change for the last customer – and she bid the lady good day as he arrived on the scene.

'Hello, young lady!' He tipped his hat in her direction and then replaced it on his head. 'I'm Joshua Arden,' he said with a big, beaming smile. He was astonishingly handsome with dark, almost black hair and piercing sapphire-blue eyes, which seemed to glint as he spoke to her. 'I'm one of the Arden brothers who run the sewing factory in the town.'

Betsan had heard of that family and their clothing business. They supplied garments to several upmarket shops in the Merthyr area and even to other nearby towns. It was high-quality merchandise.

'Hello.' She smiled and, for a moment, she felt like curtseying, which was ridiculous as this man was hardly nobility.

'I was just wondering, who makes the garments you sell on this stall?'

'I do,' said Betsan, frowning. 'Me and my auntie, that is. Why do you ask? Is there anything wrong with them?'

'Oh, no, no, no!' He chuckled as he waved a gloved hand. 'You mustn't think that. Quite the opposite. They're perfect! I had a look at them last week and examined them in great detail. So, your aunt owns this stall, then, does she?'

'No, sir. It belongs to Mrs Bridget O'Connell.'

'I see.' He picked up a petticoat and inspected it thoroughly, nodding as he did so, as if impressed by the quality of the garment.

A young woman headed towards the stall and after a moment or two of deliberation, she held up a nightdress as if about to ask a question. Betsan excused herself from Mr Arden as she couldn't afford to lose a potential sale. But in the event, the woman explained she was merely browsing but said she would return at the weekend. When customers said that, sometimes it was an excuse because they really didn't want to purchase the item – possibly it was too expensive for their purse. Oftentimes though, they were waiting for their husband to get paid from the pit or the ironworks on a Friday. Or sometimes, they intended to return after borrowing the money or putting something of value in the pawnshop, like a wedding ring. It was a way of paying one debt by incurring another. Lots of people in the area lived that way.

She watched the woman walk away with her shopping basket hooked over her arm. No doubt, going by the expression on her face, she loved what she saw but at the moment it was more important for her to fill her basket with food provisions from the market.

Joshua Arden coughed into his gloved hand as if to catch her attention again. She made her way over to his side and smiled tentatively.

What was his game? Was he after purchasing their stock and selling it on? Or was he looking for ideas? She narrowed her gaze.

'Tell me, young lady, what is your name?'

She felt her face flush. 'Betsan. Betsan Morgan, sir.'

'Now then, Betsan Morgan, is it your intention to carry on

working on this stall and sewing garments for it for the rest of your life?'

Why was he looking at her so intently?

She shrugged. 'I don't know, to be honest, Mr Arden. But what I do know is that I *love* what I do. Maybe not standing here selling things in all weathers, but I enjoy sewing garments and embroidering them too.'

He appeared thoughtful for a moment before saying, 'That's what I love to hear. I need more Betsan Morgans working for me!'

He chuckled before handing her a small white card which read:

Arden Brothers Fashions
Lower High Street
Merthyr Tydfil

She gazed at it for a moment. Why was he giving her his card?

Although he had a serious expression on his face, his eyes were wide and questioning, and appeared to be boring a hole into her soul somehow.

'Think about coming to work for us,' he said softly. 'You already have the skills we need and you won't get wet standing out in all weathers. We treat our workforce very well. All the girls are given adequate breaks throughout the day and the pay is good.'

She stood speechless for a moment. She'd only been helping Auntie and Mrs O'Connell for a few months and she was enjoying the work.

And didn't people refer to those sort of places as 'sweatshops'?

He gazed at her intently. 'I don't expect an answer right now,

Betsan. You'll need to discuss it with your auntie and parents, of course.'

She dragged her gaze from the card to peer at his face.

'My mother is dead, Mr Arden. I really don't know what to think about this. Are you offering my auntie a job too?'

He shook his head. 'No, just yourself. You are the right age to join us with your particular skills. It would be a proper trade for you. I'm looking for someone who will work hard and pay attention to detail. I've just dismissed someone who was lazy and her work was most definitely not up to scratch. The firm can no longer afford to take on slackers and pay them well into the bargain.'

A pang of guilt overtook her. After all Auntie had done for her, if she were to say yes to this man wouldn't she be letting her down? Slowly, she shook her head.

'No, I couldn't possibly, Mr Arden. It wouldn't be right.' She attempted to return the card to him.

'No,' he said, raising his hand to stop her. 'Keep the card in case you change your mind. I know you're young but this might prove a great opportunity for you, if only you could see that.'

She nodded. 'Thank you, Mr Arden.'

He smiled wistfully. 'Then I'll bid you good day and I hope our paths will cross again someday soon, Miss Morgan!'

She watched him walk away in the direction of Lower High Street, no doubt returning to the factory. What a surprise encounter that had been.

20

'He offered you a job there and then!' Jimmy blinked. They were sitting on a bench near the St Tydfil's parish church.

'Yes, I couldn't ruddy well believe it!'

Jimmy chuckled. 'So, you're going to accept his proposal?'

She stared hard at him. 'You make it sound as if he just asked to marry me!'

'Oh no, love. That's not what I meant at all. I meant his job offer.'

'I don't think I can accept. I can't leave my aunt and Mrs O'Connell in the lurch, can I?'

Jimmy blew out a long, hard breath and dipped his hand into his jacket pocket. Producing a poke of peppermints, he offered her one.

She was about to decline with a wave of her hand but then he said, 'When I want to consider something, I suck on one of these.'

Thinking this good advice, she accepted one and popped it into her mouth. It was such a refreshing, cool taste. He also had one and closed his eyes, relishing the flavour. Then he replaced the poke in his pocket.

They sat in companiable silence for some time and then Betsan said, 'I suppose it would be an opportunity for me.'

Jimmy chuckled. 'You've been big-game hunted, my girl!'

Betsan threw back her head and laughed heartily. 'I suppose I have!'

'It's good to see you laughing, love. Look, the factory's only over the way. Why don't you walk over there right now and see if Mr Arden is available to speak to? It wouldn't hurt none for you to ask him a few questions about the job and the place.'

'Oh, I don't know if I could. I'm not suitably dressed.'

'Yes, you are. You look clean and presentable to me!'

She glanced down at her clothing: a serviceable linsey-woolsey overdress with a flowered blouse beneath and a dark grey jacket that fitted her well. She wore a bonnet too, which although not her Sunday best was tidy enough and would do.

'Right! You've inspired me. Take this!' She handed Jimmy her wicker basket and then she crunched on the remainder of the peppermint and swallowed it. 'I'm going there right now!' she said, tightening her bonnet ribbons beneath her chin. Then she stood and began to stride purposely towards the factory.

'That's the spirit, gal!' he shouted after her.

* * *

As Betsan approached the Arden sewing factory, she hesitated for a moment. Her initial reaction was to turn about-face and return to Jimmy's side but his encouraging words were firmly implanted in her mind. So instead, she lifted the door knocker and rapped on it. It looked more like a large house than a factory, with a sign placed to the side of the large door: 'Arden Bros Fashion' emblazoned on a white plaque with black fancy lettering.

Eventually, the door was opened by a lady whose dark salt-and-pepper hair was severely scraped back into a French knot at the back of her small head. Her gold-rimmed half-spectacles gave her a look of intelligence. She wore a high-ruffled-collar blouse, which had navy blue and white stripes and a worsted navy long skirt. A pearl brooch was pinned at the neck of her blouse. She looked smart and business-like, Betsan thought. Younger than Mrs Jenkins though older than Aunt Mags.

'Yes?' the woman enquired, peering over the top of her spectacles.

'Hello, miss,' said Betsan. 'Mr Arden gave me his card a couple of days ago and asked me to call to see him. Is he available right now, please?'

'Which one? Samuel, Joshua or William?'

Betsan consulted the card and then looked up again. 'Joshua, miss.'

'He's in a meeting at the moment, but it should be over soon, if you care to wait?'

'No, sorry. I have a friend waiting for me. I'd better go.' She was about to turn away to leave when Joshua Arden himself appeared behind the woman.

'It's all right, Miss Davies. I'm here now. The meeting has just this moment ended.'

Miss Davies nodded, excusing herself out of the way, now leaving no barrier between her boss and Betsan.

'Miss Morgan!' He beamed at her. 'You're interested in that position I mentioned, I take it?'

Betsan nodded. 'Maybe, Mr Arden. But first I'd like to take a look around and ask you some questions, if I may?'

He chuckled. 'You're the first young lady to request an interview with *me* not the other way around! I admire your nous!'

She didn't understand what the word 'nous' meant but she smiled anyhow as he appeared to approve of her calling in to see him.

'Come inside and I'll show you around and introduce you to some staff members.' He beckoned her with his hand. 'This of course is Miss Davies whom you've already encountered.'

The woman was now sitting behind a wooden desk with a large ledger open in front of her, which appeared to be full of names and figures. Maybe it was the company accounts? She smiled broadly at Betsan as Mr Arden continued to speak.

'Miss Davies has been with us for five years since we started the business in this town.'

'And how did the business begin?' Betsan looked at him.

'My father, Benjamin Arden, began with a market stall in Cardiff. He had a few outworkers sewing garments for him dotted around the area. A little like you and your aunt are doing right now.'

Betsan nodded, feeling impressed the family had started small.

'The stall became very successful and my father employed extra workers and, eventually, he opened a factory in Cardiff.'

'Is it still going?'

'No, my father passed away a few years ago, unfortunately, so my brothers and I made a decision to move production to Merthyr Tydfil as it's such a busy, bustling town.'

'How many people have you working for you at the moment?'

'Fifty full quota. Well, forty-nine, unless you join us?' He shot a smile in her direction. 'Most of those are machinists. The other members of staff are cutters, general workers, administration, delivery men, that sort of thing. Would you care to see the factory floor?'

'Yes, please.' She was beginning to warm to the man. He escorted her down a low-ceilinged corridor towards a small door with a flight of steps behind it, which led to a large basement room that smelled of cotton and wool. The whirring of the machines and chatter echoed around the room. One or two machinists looked up as they entered but most were so engaged with their work that they carried on sewing at their treadle machines.

At the far end of the room were sets of benches with rolls of varying fabrics laid out on them. Chalk was used to mark out the patterns, which were then cut out with large scissors. Two men hefted a big wooden packing crate between them towards the stairs. They acknowledged Mr Arden as they passed.

'Everything going smoothly then, lads?' he enquired.

'Yes, Mr Arden,' the elder of the two replied. 'We're just taking this stock to the cart ready for delivery.'

'Which order is it for?'

'The Bailey order, sir.' The man touched the peak of his flat cap as a mark of respect.

'On your way then. Don't forget to take your break when you return.' Mr Arden smiled.

'So you really do allow your workers breaks?' Betsan enquired.

'Yes, Miss Morgan. My father always maintained to get the best out of his workforce, they needed to be treated well, and he was right, so we do the same here. Now come and meet some of the girls. One or two are around your age.'

She trailed behind him until he paused at a sewing machine where a young girl, not that much older than herself, sat. She stopped what she was doing as Mr Arden addressed her.

'Polly, this is Betsan Morgan. She might be working here someday soon.'

Polly smiled. 'Hello.'

Betsan returned the smile. The girl had lustrous black hair coiled up into a bun at the back of her head. She guessed it was so that her long locks didn't become entangled in the machine.

'Polly has been working here for... how long is it now, Polly?'

The girl paused to think for a moment. 'Eighteen months or thereabouts, Mr Arden.'

'And do you like it here?' Betsan asked, peering at the girl's handiwork. She appeared to be making some kind of lady's blouse.

'Yes, I do.'

Mr Arden turned his back on them for a moment as a middle-aged woman he'd referred to as 'Sal' addressed him from the adjacent machine.

'What do you like about working here?' Betsan asked, making eye contact with Polly, realising the girl would be more likely to tell her the truth when Mr Arden's back was turned rather than to his face.

'I love the way the Arden family take care of their staff. They give us plenty of breaks and treat us fairly. Not like some of those bloomin' factories in the Big Smoke!'

'Wherever's that?' Betsan wrinkled her nose.

'London, of course!'

'Oh, I see!'

'Yes, the boss is very concerned about our safety and welfare here.'

'That's good to hear.' Betsan nodded with satisfaction.

* * *

Betsan hung around to speak to a couple of workers to find out how things worked at the factory. She was shown how the chalk was used to outline a particular pattern and large shears employed. It was all very similar to how she and Auntie worked except for the quantity of clothing produced and the stockists were larger establishments than Mrs O'Connell's market stall. There were some real characters working there. Sal, whom Mr Arden had spoken to earlier, was a salt-of-the-earth, motherly sort, but at the same time she cussed like a London docker. There was no one out of those she encountered who seemed hard to get along with and they were very welcoming. So, she came to the conclusion that the Arden brothers chose their staff carefully.

Afterwards, Mr Arden took her into his office where he asked her how she came to be interested in sewing in the first place. She found herself explaining about her mother's dressmaking business from their home and how, as far back as she remembered, she'd watched her mother at work and sometimes assisted her.

Joshua Arden smiled broadly. 'Well, the position is yours if you want it, Betsan. Have you discussed it with your family as yet?'

Her face grew hot. 'No, Mr Arden. It was only just before I came to see you that I realised I'd like to work here. And especially after meeting the staff and seeing the place for myself.'

He steepled his fingers on the desk, relaxing back into his chair. 'So, what changed your mind, do you think?'

'It was my friend Jimmy. He's a lad who's a year or so older than me. Worldly-wise, my aunt calls him. He lives with her, you see. She took him on as a parish orphan.'

'He must have some persuasive powers, this Jimmy?'

'I suppose. He had an idea how to make money himself by

doing deliveries and drumming up business with a local cobbler.'

'An enterprising sort by the sound of it.'

'Yes, he is.' She smiled. Jimmy really had become a good friend to her lately.

'You'd better have a word with your family sometime soon, if you want this job that is, Betsan,' Mr Arden said, smiling.

Betsan chewed on her bottom lip, deliberating for a moment. There was something she hadn't told Mr Arden as yet. 'My father, Mr Arden.' She paused. 'He's in the workhouse at the moment. I was there with him for a spell. I'll need to have a word with him first.'

'Very well.' He looked at her with questioning eyes. 'Miss Morgan, I don't mean to pry but what were the circumstances of you both going in there?'

'My father suffered a blow to the head and lost his memory. It's slowly returning though. He even remembers marrying my stepmother now. But she left us as she couldn't cope with his violent outbursts at that time.' She looked down at the desk. It was a bad memory for her, but she felt she needed to be honest with someone who was, hopefully, going to employ her. She looked up at him. 'Things are much better now. He no longer gets angry and she goes to visit him. She's had a baby since.'

'So you think they will be reunited in time?'

'Hopefully.' She drew in a composing breath. 'I'll visit my father this evening and ask his permission to work here. When would you like me to start work?'

'Monday morning at six o'clock sharp, Miss Morgan.'

Betsan gulped. Sometimes she'd been on the market stall at eight o'clock and figured that was early enough. Other times she was up at the same time to begin sewing garments with her aunt but never as early as six o'clock! It was practically still night-time in her book.

Seeing the look of dismay on her face, he gazed at her tentatively. 'Don't worry, you'll become accustomed to it. A benefit of beginning work early is that you'll knock off earlier in the day. Your shift will finish at two o'clock so you'll have your afternoons and evenings free unless I ask you to work overtime – if we have a large order to send out. The older women work a little longer than you and the overtime offered is only once in a blue moon.'

She nodded. It all sounded fair enough to her. To be truthful though, it wasn't so much her father's approval she sought, as she felt he'd be agreeable, it was Aunt Maggie's. The woman had been good to her and now she'd be leaving the business they'd both set up together. Would she mind?

* * *

In the event, Aunt Maggie didn't mind. Betsan was going to work at the factory. She viewed it as a great opportunity for her and said she'd be a fool to turn it down.

Maggie, Elgan, Betsan, Jimmy and the twins had now moved into Mrs O'Connell's home. The twins loved it in the big house with its own garden and Bridget enjoyed making a fuss over them, thoroughly spoiling the pair.

Thankfully, Betsan's father was also agreeable to her working at the factory, and he seemed able to cope once again. These days, Elinor had a constant big smile on her face as now she had her own child, Isobelle, to care for.

* * *

'Mags?' Jimmy said when they were sitting in the living room one evening. 'The strangest thing happened today...'

'Oh, yes? What was that? Now, don't tell me you saw a flying pig passing up the high street?' Mags chuckled.

'No,' he said. His voice had a serious tone to it, which caused her to sit up and take note.

'Then what was it?'

'You know Enid ended up getting sent to the Cardiff Workhouse under some cloud or another?'

She did indeed as Betsan had confided the whole sorry tale to her, though told her not to reveal the reason behind it. 'Yes.'

He paused for a moment and then let out a long breath. 'Well, I'm sure I saw her in the marketplace today.'

'She must be back living at home then or maybe allowed out of the Cardiff spike?'

'No.' He shook his head vigorously. 'I'd swear it was her I glimpsed. But she didn't look poor or shabbily dressed. She was toffed up like a real lady. She got out of a fancy carriage an' all.'

'You must be mistaken, lad. It was probably someone who looked just like her. Who was she with?'

'Some gentleman, an older man. He was well dressed an' all.'

Mags frowned. 'That doesn't make any sense to me.'

'Me neither!' Jimmy shrugged.

'Did she see you, Jimmy?'

'Don't think so. Like I said, it was only a glimpse I managed to get; that was all. Have you seen any of her family lately?'

'No. Last thing I heard was they were still in the workhouse. Must have been horrible for them though when Enid shipped off to Cardiff like that.'

Jimmy shook his head. 'That never made any sense to me why she was sent there anyhow. One moment everything was fine and dandy, she got a position as a maid in a big house, the next she's flippin' sent away as if she's done something wrong!'

'Who knows what goes on at those workhouses, lad. Our Betsan put on a brave face when she was in there but even she must have had her own troubles to contend with. Still, that is very puzzling about Enid...'

* * *

Betsan had heard the news about Enid and was equally puzzled. It had been months since the day she'd said farewell to the girl and handed her the brooch. Hadn't brought her much luck, had it? Or were her fortunes now reversed? And if she never saw her again, she'd have lost her mother's brooch forever.

There was no time to dwell on the matter though as work at the factory was keeping her busy. If she wasn't running up seams as fast as she could feed the material through the machine, then she was making cups of tea for the workforce. As the new girl, it seemed to be expected of her and she didn't much mind. The Arden brothers were good bosses to work for. While Joshua was dark and handsome, William had a sandy sort of colouring, sported a beard and had a twinkle in his eyes, while Samuel – the youngest – resembled Joshua but was shorter in stature and far more serious. As the eldest, Joshua took charge while William dealt with retail orders and Samuel with packing and distribution.

Betsan had been working for the firm for around six months when Joshua summoned a work-floor meeting with the staff to inform them soon there would be an 'Arden Fashions' department store opening in Merthyr Tydfil. There were also plans to put into place an option to open similar retail outlets in nearby valley towns including Aberdare, Blackwood, Ebbw Vale and

Pontypridd, but Merthyr would be the flagship store for all of these.

Mr Arden informed them he was seeking suitable people to work in this store.

That's me out then, thought Betsan. *I've been here all of five minutes!*

She absorbed the girls' chatter as they sipped their cups of tea and nibbled on their oatmeal biscuits.

'I'd love to work in a department store!' declared Polly.

'You? You'd be bloomin' hopeless serving folk!' roared Sal, throwing back her head in merriment as she chuckled heartily.

'You wouldn't be much better yourself!' Polly's lips formed into a pout.

Sal ceased laughing. 'Sorry, Pol. I didn't mean no harm by it but they won't want the likes of us working in any of their new stores, gal!'

'Mean, you are, Sally Sugden!' chastised another middle-aged woman known as Maddy who used the sewing machine besides Sal. 'The girl just fancied the position – that's all! Can't she want better for herself?'

'I'm just being realistic...' Sal shook her head as if sorry she'd spoken up in the first place. 'Whoever gets that position will need to be smart and I don't just mean good-looking and well-dressed either, but they'll need to be savvy an' all.'

Their eyes were drawn towards Betsan.

'What are you all staring at?' Her face flamed.

'I reckon,' said Sal, 'you'll be asked to work in the Merthyr store.'

'Me? But why me?' She blinked as she held her hand to her chest.

'Because Mr Arden knows you pick up things fast. You've got a good head on those shoulders of yours, my girl!'

Betsan was astounded by the reaction of the others. She hadn't considered her particular abilities, but maybe they did have a point. Polly was a little unsure of herself to serve successfully behind a counter and Sal, although a confident character, had poor literacy skills, while Maddy and the others wouldn't even consider such a position, preferring to limit their choices in life. The girls and women at the factory for the main part didn't see much of a future for themselves, and she thought that such a shame.

Throughout her school years, Betsan had been ahead of her peers, learning to read and write at a young age, and she'd even been kept on at the school as her teachers had realised she'd do well. She, and just one other female pupil, had been allowed to remain there until they were fourteen whereas the other girls had left school at ten years old – though she'd had a short break from school by being interned at the workhouse.

But today, when the workforce was expecting Mr Arden to make an announcement about who would work at his new fashion store, none was forthcoming. So, Betsan put it firmly out of her mind for the time being.

21

Over the following months, Betsan watched in awe as one of the company designers worked on a series of sketches for an upcoming fashion show to promote the new store, which would be opening on Merthyr High Street.

Francis Bradbury had previously worked in Paris and London. He was a bohemian sort of chap who wore his hair longer than society agreed was a respectable length, but the Arden brothers didn't appear to mind. His auburn moustache was artistically twirled and Betsan guessed he used pomade to keep it like that. His clothing stood out too as his jackets were usually vibrant, coloured in reds, mustards or greens and embroidered at the collars and cuffs.

Betsan watched with interest as a pencil stroke here and there transformed his work into an amazing design.

As if realising he was being watched, he turned from his drawing board slowly, pivoting on the wooden stool to make eye contact with her.

'Interested?' He raised a curious eyebrow.

She nodded and smiled. 'Yes, I am actually. My mother was a

seamstress and sometimes she created her own patterns from sheets of newspaper for a dress or whatever.'

'Really? That is interesting! I didn't start off that way. I went to art college and sort of fell into this designing lark. So, do you have any ideas for designs yourself, Miss er...?'

'Miss Morgan. But call me Betsan, please.'

He nodded. 'I mean, have you ever thought of transforming a particular garment?'

'Oh, I have. My stepmother once bought me a dreadful Bo-Peep dress with frilly pantaloons!' She chuckled. 'I really felt like transforming that one! But to be serious, I have been known to embroider garments, that sort of thing.' She dipped her hand into her skirt pocket and handed him a handkerchief.

He took it from her and inspected it. 'You did this beautiful embroidery?' he said, looking at her.

'Yes. I was taught embroidery skills at the workhouse,' she said proudly. 'Though, as you know, embroidering garments takes up a lot of time.'

He nodded. 'I'm very impressed.' And then, turning back to his drawing board, he carried on with the task in hand.

Viewing it as her cue to leave, she thanked him and returned to her sewing machine.

Betsan was later to discover it was at the House of Worth in Paris where Francis had honed his dressmaking skills. Charles Worth had a flair for design, which he had built into his large business empire, supplying performance costumes to leading actresses and singers of the day. The jewel in his crown though was dressing European royalty. It was an establishment of high repute.

'Worth,' explained Francis, 'elevated his position as a dress-maker to an artist extraordinaire! And do you know when he arrived in Paris as a young man, he had just five pounds in his pocket! He had the foresight to understand how this industry worked, though he did not speak a word of French at the time. He is truly amazing.'

Betsan stood there opened-mouthed for a moment. 'He sounds an exceptional person.'

'Oh, he is. When I was working under him, he even wore a beret and smock to meet with his clients – just like an artist!' He chuckled. 'Though these days he leaves most of the business to his sons.'

'But what's so special about his designs?'

A smile danced upon Francis's lips as though the very thought of the man and his designs brought him pleasure. They were obviously good memories for him.

'I would say it's the use of fabrics. He utilises high-luxury materials like silk and cut velvet. He also uses large designs with motifs like flowers, feathers, butterflies and so on. Now this is where I'd like you to come in to help with the embroidery and fancy appliques and trim. You've got the skill set for it.'

'Oh?' Betsan wrinkled her nose.

'Yes. Charles Worth uses a generous amount of trim with embroidery, beads, fringing, that sort of thing. I think the 'House of Arden' could replicate it. I don't mean exact copies but something similar that would draw the eye and make their pieces stand out from other establishments.'

Betsan smiled. 'Yes?'

'I think we can offer affordable designs at affordable prices. We might be able to offer two ranges: one using expensive materials for the more affluent in society and the other offering a budget range for others on a ready-to-wear basis.'

'The House of Arden,' Betsan whispered. 'It certainly has a ring to it...' Astonished that someone like Francis had asked her to get involved in such a fantastic project, she returned to her sewing machine as though she were walking on air.

* * *

There was a tremendous amount of press and local attention when Arden Fashions Department Store was opened on Merthyr High Street. Colourful bows, ribbons, flags and flowers adorned the façade and fluttered merrily in the breeze.

A newspaper reporter and a sketch artist were despatched to cover the story. A ten-per-cent discount was offered to anyone purchasing an item or placing an order on opening day.

A brass band struck up outside and local music hall star, Lily Thornton, cut the yellow ribbon, declaring the store well and truly open for business.

In the event, a decision was made to employ sales assistants with previous experience to work at the store. Those who had worked for other renowned department stores like James Howell and David Morgan – which shared Betsan's father's name – in Cardiff.

The House of Arden had well and truly arrived in Merthyr Tydfil. Barley sugar twists and Bentley's chocolate drops were handed out to the children and the adults offered refreshments in the form of glasses of brandy or sherry. Betsan realised the brothers were sparing no costs; today, they wanted the world and his wife to try out their store. But tomorrow, their business sense would kick back in.

Betsan and Francis Bradbury watched as customers stormed through the doors and flooded the place. Some settled in the dressmaking department where they stopped to admire his designs. Across the way was another department that sold 'off-the-peg' creations, which proved popular.

All three Arden brothers watched on in sheer delight as a large painting of their father looked down on them in the foyer. They were obviously tremendously proud of him as he'd left behind a legacy of building up his business empire as well as treating his staff well.

'Oh, young man!' A curvaceous lady wearing the silliest hat Betsan had ever seen, which appeared to be a cross between a bird's nest and a thorny hedgerow with feathers projecting out of it from all angles, cornered Francis.

'Yes, madam?' His eyes grew large.

'I was wondering if you could create something for the fuller figure?' She smiled coquettishly like a young girl, causing Betsan to snigger behind the palm of her hand and Francis to blush furiously.

As if pulling himself together, Francis smiled sweetly. 'Of course, madam. I think you'd display our fashions very well, especially with your ample figure!'

Now it was the lady's turn to blush.

Betsan decided to take a scout around and to eavesdrop on what other potential customers were saying.

'I've heard they offer ready-to-wear garments, Mildred!'

'Affordable fashions at affordable prices!' exclaimed another, reciting what she'd read on a bold sign. That saying of Francis was certainly paying off for the firm.

'There's even the opportunity to have a gown made by a Parisian designer!'

Of course this made Francis sound as if he were French, not that he'd spent time working on designs in the fashion capital city of the world. But Betsan didn't correct the woman. The main thing was there was a buzz around the place and if that led to lots of interest and projected into sales, all the better.

* * *

The following day the local newspaper, the *Merthyr Mail*, reported:

ARDEN BROTHERS LAUNCH NEW FASHION STORE ON THE HIGH STREET!

The Arden family name is a renowned name when it comes to fashion and trendsetting. Benjamin Arden began with a market stall in Cardiff, employing homeworkers, but now the business has grown so large that his three sons – Joshua, William and Samuel – have opened a flagship store on Merthyr High Street. Joshua Arden said that in time they hope to open further stores in the South Wales valleys. He added: 'Our father, who died a few years ago, has left behind a long-standing legacy.'

On visiting the store on its opening day, our reporter found crowds amassed outside rushing to be allowed in, a brass band playing merrily, free refreshments for all and ten per cent off a new purchase. Impressive was the ready-to-wear range designed by Francis Bradbury, an upcoming fashion designer, who has worked in Paris under the wing of Charles Worth, who himself established the illustrious 'House of Worth' supplying gowns to European royalty and stage actresses such as Lillie Langtry and Sarah Bernhardt.

Will the new 'House of Arden' make an impression with the folk of Merthyr Tydfil? From what I've seen today, it surely will!

Polly had been reading the local newspaper out to the other machinists on the workshop floor.

'That's well and truly put the House of Arden on the map!' enthused Sal.

Betsan smiled. She was happy about it but would be even happier when her father was home from the workhouse. It didn't make any sense to her why he was still being kept inside. Still, she could take that newspaper with her when she visited him that evening.

'Come on,' said Sal. 'We're due a break. I'm sure the Arden brothers won't mind us all having a cuppa and some Welsh cakes to celebrate!'

* * *

That evening when Betsan entered the workhouse, Mrs Parry-Jones was there stood in the foyer as if waiting to see her. 'Hello, Betsan,' she said. 'I want to see you about something.'

Oh no! Was there something wrong with her father? But then the woman smiled and handed her a white envelope. 'What's that?'

The woman lowered her voice. 'It arrived for you two days ago. I've kept it locked in my desk as I know Matron – she'd open it. I don't know who it's from but I thought it should be given directly to you.'

Betsan smiled tentatively, wondering what it might possibly say. 'Thank you.' The woman was just about to turn to walk away when Betsan added, 'Mrs Parry-Jones, about my father?'

'Yes, dear?' The woman blinked.

'When's he coming home?'

The woman huffed out a breath and she patted Betsan's arm. 'There was a meeting with Master and Matron Aldridge. Doctor

Llewellyn was in attendance along with some other staff members and one or two from the board of governors. The upshot is that the doctor thinks it's in your father's best interests that he remain here for the time being.'

Betsan felt as though the workhouse walls were closing in on her. 'I don't understand. He seems to have made a lot of progress lately.'

'He has but the doctor thinks that although he no longer poses a danger to others, for instance like when his moods were unpredictable towards your stepmother, he does think that he poses a risk to himself.'

She frowned. 'To himself? How?'

The supervisor smiled. 'Please don't go concerning yourself. Your father has been put on some medication that might make him a little drowsy but, in time, should do the trick. Now, go to visit him and try not to worry too much.'

All thoughts of the letter she'd just stuffed absently into her pocket evaporated into the ether as she walked with extreme purpose towards the visiting room.

Her father was seated in a high-backed armchair propped up with a pillow but he smiled as she approached. At least he hadn't forgotten her like he'd forgotten other things in the past. 'Hello, lovely girl,' he said as she stooped to peck his cheek. 'What have you got there in your basket?'

'Oh, some scones Mrs Jenkins baked for you, and I've brought the newspaper as there's an article in about yesterday.'

'Yesterday?' He frowned.

'Yes, the opening of the new Arden store on Merthyr High Street.'

'Yes, of course.'

'Dad, what's going on?'

'How'd you mean?' There was a catch to his voice and his eyes filled with tears.

'The supervisor told me you're on medication?'

'Yes, Doctor Llewellyn examined me the other day and he thinks I have some sort of melancholia going on. Apparently, it's because I didn't grieve properly after your mother's death. To be honest with you, he's right. That whirlwind romance with Elinor just overtook me.'

As she listened to her father she noticed how flat his voice sounded. Now she understood. He'd smothered a salve over an open wound, which had festered with time. She reached out to pat his hard, calloused hand. 'Everything will be all right from now on and one day you'll return home to live with me and Elinor too, if you want her and Baby Isobelle to live with us, that is?'

He nodded. 'I'd like that,' he said as a solitary tear rolled down his cheek. Sniffing, he wiped it away with the back of his hand. Sitting in subdued silence for a moment he added, 'Now how about reading that article out to me?'

It wasn't until Betsan returned home to the privacy of her bedroom that she remembered the letter in her pocket. And when she opened it, she was surprised who it was from and that they wanted to meet with her next week.

22

The following day, Betsan was taking her lunch break from the factory and had promised to meet Jimmy on their favourite bench alongside the parish church. How could she possibly tell him she'd received a letter from Enid? And more importantly, maybe, that the girl wanted to meet up with her next week. It wasn't going to be easy. Enid had informed her in the letter that she didn't want Jimmy to get wind of their meeting and Betsan wondered why. At this point, there were more questions than answers.

He hadn't arrived yet so she seated herself on the bench and just watched the world go on by. In the distance, she could see several of the factory girls leaving the premises, probably popping to one of the tea rooms on the high street for lunch. She didn't tend to leave the factory all that often, preferring instead to take some sandwiches in and make a cup of tea for herself in the restroom. If no one was around, she'd sketch away on her drawing pad.

Then she saw him in the distance, he looked so much taller all of a sudden. Funny she hadn't noticed how broad his shoulders had become either. There was no doubt about it, Jimmy was turning into a man. His voice too sounded deeper, huskier. It was such a shame about him and Enid being parted like that, but she did understand that the girl had something to be embarrassed about. Something that had gone on at Hillside House that somehow brought shame to her. Something that involved the master's son.

'Hello, Betsan!' He shot her a cheeky grin. 'Haven't seen much of you this past week or so, even though we're under the same roof.'

She chuckled as he seated himself beside her. 'I know. It's been madness at the factory since that department store has opened. I've been working so much overtime too.'

He nodded. 'Same here, it's been busy what with helping Elgan and with the shoe business.'

'How are things going with Mr Baxter?' Betsan asked when he'd settled himself beside her.

'Good,' he said, folding his arms. 'He's been giving me more responsibility lately. I've even been running the shop sometimes.'

'Really?' Betsan's eyebrows shot up in surprise at the level of responsibility the lad was being given at such a young age.

'I think the plan is for him to retire and he's hinted that has he has no children, he'd someday like me to take over the business.' There was a tone of regret to his voice, which puzzled Betsan.

'You don't sound very pleased about that?' She hooked her arm in his as in a gesture of support.

'Oh, I am, love. Honest, I am. Most young men in my position would be over the moon to learn a trade as a cobbler's apprentice and then eventually have a shop of their own. It's just that...'

'What?' She turned her face to look up at his.

'It's just I'd have eventually liked someone to share it all with. You know, if Enid hadn't gone like that…'

'I do know,' she said, feeling guilty now for the information she was withholding from him, but she couldn't find it in herself to break Enid's confidence. She paused for a moment to collect her thoughts. 'I think you have to forget about Enid, Jimmy. One day the right girl will come along.'

'Like you, you mean?' He huffed out a breath.

'No, not like me. I think you and I are more like brother and sister to one another, don't you?'

'I suppose so, love. Especially after living in the same house with Mags, Elgan and the twins!'

She laughed and he joined in. It was good to hear his laughter. Whatever happened she only wanted what was best for the lad.

* * *

Following correspondence with Enid who had given her address as some place in Canton, Cardiff, the day had arrived for them to meet in a coffee tavern in Merthyr town. Betsan had taken a half-day off work for the occasion as she was due time in lieu of the hours she had recently worked at the factory. But every time she lifted her head to look up to see who was coming through the door, it wasn't Enid.

The tavern was extremely busy that day and she felt guilty taking up a table as she waited, so she ordered a pot of coffee for herself. The young waitress was smartly attired in a black dress and white frilled apron.

'What can I get for you, miss?'

'I'd like a pot of coffee, please.'

'Which sort?'

Betsan hadn't given it much thought – to her, coffee was just coffee, wasn't it? The waitress tapped a table menu with her pencil, which made Betsan feel like a bit of a fool that she hadn't perused it before now. She'd been that intent on watching the door.

Scanning the menu, which displayed all sorts of coffee from Parisian to Peruvian, she selected Brazilian, having absolutely no idea what it would taste like. As the waitress went to leave with the order, she almost collided into the young woman behind her and then excused herself to get to the counter.

Betsan gasped when she saw who was standing there looking so much taller, elegant too. Well dressed with beautifully coiffured hair into a smart chignon hairstyle. It was whom she'd been waiting for.

'Enid? Is it really you?' She gasped in surprise as she stood to embrace the girl.

'Yes, it's really me,' Enid said with a smile.

'But you look so grown-up and sophisticated too.'

'Thank you,' Enid said, finally breaking away and seating herself opposite Betsan.

'It's so good to see you and catch up. What would you like?'

'Coffee, I suppose.' Enid shrugged. 'Seriously though, I'll have whatever you've ordered.'

'Good, I'll ask the waitress for another cup and saucer as I've ordered a pot of coffee.'

The hour flew by as they chatted with one another like old friends but then Betsan felt she had to say something.

'So what really happened at Hillside House to make them send you away like that?'

'Oh, Betsan.' Enid's bottom lip trembled. 'It was a dreadful experience at the Clarkson house. Their son just made a nuisance of himself trying to corner me at every given opportunity. I had been warned about him by one of the other staff so I was already on guard. But unfortunately...' She bit on her bottom lip as tears filled her eyes and Betsan took her hand in reassurance.

'Take your time,' she whispered as she squeezed her hand.

'One Saturday evening I had some free time so I took a walk around the large grounds. It was dusk and I'd planned to return to the house but it had been such a lovely day and I'd missed most of it. I heard a rustle behind me and then footsteps approaching quickly, and before I even had the chance to turn and glance behind, I was wrestled to the ground. Before I knew what was happening the master's son, Anthony, was on top of me, forcing himself. He had one hand clamped over my mouth and the other dragging away at my drawers. Oh, Betsan, it was horrific! Anyhow...' She swallowed hard 'You can guess what happened next.'

Betsan nodded slowly; of course, she already knew something bad had occurred, but was one of only a handful who did, and she didn't want to hurt Enid any more by telling her.

'He raped you?'

'Yes,' Enid said, her breath becoming ragged from the memory of it all.

'That's awful,' said Betsan, taking Enid's hand.

Enid swallowed hard. 'Anyhow, it turned out that he lied to his parents before I even had a chance to complain. He made out I led him on. Unfortunately, the workhouse master and matron chose to send me to the Cardiff Workhouse to avoid a scandal. I think Anthony's mother paid them off. However, his father took pity on me and tried to make up for things. He'd arrive at the workhouse and take me out for the day, bought me nice clothing when I left and found another house to employ me as a maid.'

'So, that's who Jimmy saw you with recently?'

'Jimmy saw me?' Enid blinked. 'I can't believe it!'

Betsan nodded. 'Yes, getting out of a carriage accompanied by a gentleman in Merthyr town.'

She shook her head sadly. 'To think I never even knew. Yes, I visited here a couple of times at the workhouse to see Mam and Dad and the kids. Eventually though, Mr Clarkson secured employment for my parents at the same house in Cardiff so we could all remain together. We have an apartment there.'

'And your parents? Are they still in good health?'

'Oh, yes. Thank you for asking and the kids too. In a strange sort of way, what happened to me made things easier for them all after going in the workhouse. It was Mr Clarkson who helped us all.'

'But you, what are you doing now? You look so well?'

'Well, I'm happy working at the house. My employer, Mr Darling, is ever so good to me and my parents.'

Betsan asked the question she most dreaded. 'So, can you ever see yourself returning to Merthyr?'

Enid shook her head. 'To be honest with you, no. It's better for me having a fresh start elsewhere. That's why I don't want to make contact with Jimmy though I admit to loving him.' She chewed on her bottom lip as though all of this was difficult for her. Then looking into Betsan's eyes with tears in her own, she whispered, 'You do understand, don't you?'

Betsan nodded. And then she felt something being pressed into the palm of her hand. 'What's this?'

She gazed down to see the white rose brooch there, the one she'd gifted Enid for luck when she had left to work at Hillside House.

'I'm returning it to you as it brought me a lot of luck in the end and I hope it will do the same for you.'

Smiling, Betsan studied the white rose brooch in the palm of her hand. She'd thought she would never see it again. 'Thank you,' she said as she blinked away her tears. 'This brooch means the world to me and I'm so grateful to you for returning it to me.'

'Back where it rightfully belongs,' said Enid.

They remained at the coffee tavern and chatted with one another as they shared another pot of coffee and some fancies. The time flew by and, after borrowing a pencil from the waitress, Betsan scribbled down her home address on a piece of paper to hand to Enid. 'This is my official address,' she said. 'I'm living with my aunt at the moment but still paying the rent until my father comes out of the workhouse. At the moment, my aunt is using my father's house for her sewing business and I pop back and forth there regularly.'

Who knew when or if they'd ever get the chance to meet again? But one thing Betsan knew for certain, she was so glad to have this opportunity to spend time with Enid and treasured every moment in the girl's company.

* * *

Although Betsan missed Enid she now felt bonded to the other girls at the factory, particularly a new one named Jenny. Jenny had started work at Arden Fashions around the same age Betsan herself had been, and so she was able to put herself in the girl's shoes, remembering how things had felt in the beginning for her. Over the upcoming months, she became a mentor to Jenny, demonstrating the best way to feed the material into the machine without it scrunching up, and how to go with the grain of a particular fabric. But one thing that concerned Betsan lately was the way Mr Arden appeared to watch her from his office window from time to time. Was he displeased with her work because she was taking time out to help the new recruits? He didn't appear to watch the rest of the workforce with such intensity.

'I really don't know what it is, Sal,' Betsan confided in the woman one day when both were in the restroom enjoying a well-earned cup of tea. The others had returned to their sewing machines, so Betsan felt able to speak to her workmate without being overheard. 'I'm sure I've done something wrong and Mr Arden is cross with me.'

Sal chuckled. 'I don't see how that can be though. You're the best worker he's got and he knows it too!'

'Do you really think so?' Betsan furrowed her brow. She was beginning to doubt herself and was just about to add something else when Jenny popped her head around the door.

'Sorry to disturb you both but the machine needle is stuck fast and I can't get it out of the material. I was on the last skirt of the day and all. Mr Arden isn't going to be very pleased with me.' She grimaced.

'Please don't fret,' said Betsan, now smiling and forgetting her own problem for the time being. 'The needle in that machine has jammed before. I'll explain that to Mr Arden if he says something about your work. Though I doubt he will. I'll sort out that sewing machine for you and I reckon you'll have time to finish that skirt before home time!'

Sal winked at Betsan as she led the girl away.

Betsan had just sorted the needle problem out and was about to return to finish her cup of tea when Mr Arden appeared by her side. 'Can I see you in my office, Miss Morgan?'

Oh dear! He had such a serious look on his face that it concerned her.

'Yes, Mr Arden. I'll come right away.' That cup of tea would just have to wait. It had probably gone cold by now anyhow.

* * *

'Please close the door behind you and take a seat,' Joshua Arden ordered as Betsan entered his office. She drew out a chair to sit opposite him at his desk.

'Yes, Mr Arden?'

'It's come to my attention that you've taken a few of the new girls under your wing lately?' He stroked his chin.

She nodded. 'Yes. I like helping them. Am I doing something wrong?'

Joshua Arden's eyebrows raised in an amused fashion. 'Good heavens, no! It's quite the opposite. You've impressed me so much that I think you'd make a great supervisor.'

Betsan opened her mouth and closed it again. 'B... but what about the others working here? Sal, for instance? She knows her job well and has been here far longer than I have.'

Mr Arden grinned with an amused glint in his eyes. 'Actually, it was Sal who made the suggestion to me.'

'She did?' Betsan tilted her head to one side in puzzlement. Sal had a large brood back home to contend with; surely she could do with taking the role as supervisor?

'Yes, originally I was going to offer her the position but then she said I should take a look at what you're doing lately with the new girls. That's why I've been keeping my eye on you!'

Betsan smiled. 'To pardon a pun, it appears as if you and Sal have stitched this up between you!'

Mr Arden chuckled. 'Well, what do you say? You're a natural on the shop floor, very approachable and efficient. It would mean a little more pay in your packet for you, too.'

'Oh, Mr Arden! I don't need asking twice. Thank you! I'd love to accept your offer.'

'Right, that's settled then. Go back and join Sal and brew up a fresh cuppa. You've earned it, my girl!'

Betsan beamed as she rose from her chair. If Mr Arden realised Sal was waiting in the restroom for her, she guessed they must have had recent words with one another. Just wait until she told her auntie the good news. But first there was someone she needed to thank: Sal herself. The woman could have accepted that job but she took it about herself to recommend her instead. What a kind and generous gesture to make.

23

Betsan had found her feet and was now confident enough to comment on Francis's design ideas.

One lunchtime, she was walking along Merthyr High Street during her break from work, when she noticed an elegant-looking lady alight from a hansom cab. It was a head-turning moment for her. The lady wore a jade-green damask gown with a short matching jacket with puffed sleeves. This was someone who wanted to catch the eye, but what was so unusual about the lady's gown was that the skirt was more fitted than usual. There was no bustle on the back whatsoever. It made Betsan wonder: what if a gown were created with larger puff sleeves than usual and a more skimming skirt, so fitted that it changed the usual shape of the garment?

Immediately, she decided to return to the factory to sketch out her ideas. Why she was doing this she just didn't know but it was an idea she felt compelled to run with. Francis was out of the office that afternoon, dining at a local restaurant as he was in a meeting with Joshua Arden and a potential buyer from Aberdare.

She removed her jacket and hung it on the coat stand, then took her sketch pad from her drawer and began to work, deep in concentration. This sort of design would prove economical with material too, while at the same time looking stylish and modern.

But what was she thinking? Although she sometimes felt confident enough to suggest ideas to Francis, he was the designer here not her. So for the time being she decided to keep her designs to herself and carefully returned the sketch pad to her desk drawer.

* * *

A few days later, Francis approached Betsan to help him with some garments he was working on. He was a joy to work with and she was able to make several helpful design suggestions. She was pleased about that as she was working with the master – she was the pupil yet he valued her opinion. They both had similar ideas when it came to the use of fabrics: silks, satins and velvet with cheaper options chosen for the budget version of the line. Moire taffeta instead of a more expensive satin and velvet used in moderation on the collars and cuffs for the daywear.

The pair visited an amazing haberdashery store in Cardiff. The store offered all sorts of beading in jet, seed pearls and other touches like feathers and fancy lace imported from France. When they were done with their order, Francis steered Betsan towards a charming coffee shop he knew of where he ordered a pot of coffee for two and some fancies.

Betsan's eyes widened at the spread. She'd never been in such a posh establishment before – the coffee tavern in Merthyr might have fit into a corner of this place with its opulent chandeliers and green potted ferns – nor had she ever been in the company of such a good-looking fellow either. She had noticed that many female eyes were drawn towards her companion as he dressed so differently to everyone else. His mustard long-line brocade jacket fitted his form so well and the velvet collar and cuffs set it off. His black silk cravat was neatly pinned in place and today his auburn moustache appeared expertly twirled. A gold watch chain dangled from the pocket of his black velvet waistcoat, giving him the air of someone who was doing well for himself. He was what her mother would have referred to as a 'dandy' – a fashionable and stylish gentleman.

'So tell me then, Betsan,' he began, taking a sip from his cup of coffee and setting it down again. 'Do you plan on being a sewing machinist for the rest of your life?'

Betsan felt her cheeks flame and she laid down the iced pink fancy she'd been about to consume.

'Oh, I haven't thought quite that far ahead. I mean... I was quite content going my own merry way sewing with my auntie and selling our wares on Mrs O'Connell's market stall, when I got poached by Mr Arden!' She laughed nervously.

'But it didn't just happen though,' he said, now peering intently into her eyes. 'You have something about you that brought you to our attention.'

'Our?' She blinked.

'Yes, mine and Mr Arden's. If you were just like the rest of the workforce, say like Polly or even Sal, for instance, you'd have blended into the background but you didn't – you stood out from it! There's something about you, Betsan, that makes me feel you'll go far in life, my girl.'

She really didn't know what to say and now he was looking at her so intently she was about to say something to fill the space when he carried on speaking.

'Tomorrow all the materials we've ordered should have arrived so I'm hoping you'll stay behind for a few hours when everyone's gone home? We really need to get a handle on my collection as soon as possible.'

She nodded enthusiastically then bit into her fancy. It tasted divine, the sweetness of the pink icing mixed in with the lightness of the sponge and whipped cream – it was absolutely heavenly.

He smiled and then, noticing she had a little cream at the edge of her mouth, he leaned across the table and dabbed at it with his linen napkin in a fatherly fashion. 'Yes, I'm relying on you to help out with the upcoming fashion show, if you don't mind?' he asked, as he laid the napkin down on the table.

'Mind? I'm absolutely delighted!' She beamed.

24

The fashion show was to take place at the Merthyr store. Invitations had been dispensed and the press were ready to record it all. Seated in the audience were Aunt Mags, Elgan and Jimmy, and Mr and Mrs Jenkins. Mrs O'Connell was taking care of the children.

At exactly two o'clock, the performance began where all the guests were treated to a display of day and evening gowns in colours of deep plum and vivid violets, in silks, satins and velvet. Some of the gowns had silk flowers at the neckline that drew the eye, causing the audience to gasp at the boldness of it all. The *pièce de résistance*, at the end of the show, was a tea gown worn by a gracefully tall model from Cardiff. The violet cut velvet on an aquamarine satin taffeta backdrop drew everyone's attention. The pieces of velvet resembled flower petals and the puffed sleeves and high neckline were elegance personified.

At the end of the show, Betsan and Francis were introduced to the guests, who gave them a resounding ripple of applause. And then there was a question-and-answer section before refreshments were served up.

In the distance, Betsan watched Francis talking to a couple of female customers, nodding his head as he answered their questions. His eyes were so alive with passion as he discussed his designs. Charles Worth had issued an invitation for Francis to stay at his home and visit his couture design workshop, so tomorrow he was off to stay in Paris, and he was relying on Betsan to oversee things for him in his absence.

It had been an exciting event and Betsan was thrilled to be a part of it all.

'I'm so proud of you, *cariad*,' said Mrs Jenkins as she walked towards her with arms outstretched to embrace her.

'Thank you, Mrs Jenkins. I'm so glad you were able to make it. But tell me...' Betsan said, looking into the woman's eyes, breaking from her embrace. 'How are you feeling?'

Bronwen huffed out a breath. 'Oh, I get my good days and bad days. Today is a good one. But let me tell you, nothing and no one would have kept me away today! To think you are a part of all of this.' She lightly touched Betsan's arm.

'I know wild horses wouldn't have kept you away. I just wish...'

'I know, you wish your father was able to make it?'

Betsan nodded. 'I did invite Elinor but she declined for the time being. I think it's getting her down now about Dad being stuck inside that place for this long.'

'True enough. But Doctor Llewellyn seems to know what he's doing. He's been our family doctor for years.' Betsan supposed the woman was right. 'Best to leave it to the professionals, I say. Now come on, let's grab a cuppa from that trolley over there before it gets cold.'

It was heart-warming to hear Mrs Jenkins's voice once again. Betsan had been so busy at the factory of late she hadn't much time to pay social visits to people. Guiding the woman by the arm, she whispered, 'We'll have that cup of tea and then I'll take you to meet Francis Bradbury, the designer.'

Mrs Jenkins's eyes lit up as Betsan led her away.

* * *

When Francis returned from Paris, the whole factory was in uproar. So many orders had been taken following the fashion show that everyone wondered how they'd cope with them all. Joshua Arden had reassured them he'd be creating positions for more machinists and there would be other roles available in the factory too. Betsan wondered what those sorts of positions might be. Would they be something her father could apply for if he ever got discharged from the workhouse?

Francis seemed bright and breezy following his overseas trip and he was immediately summoned into a meeting with the Arden brothers first thing on that Monday morning. The factory seemed abuzz with activity and there was a general feeling of expectation in the air.

When Francis left the meeting at midday, he made a beeline for Betsan. 'I need to speak to you,' he whispered in her ear.

'Oh?'

'Yes, not here. I'll meet you in the restroom in ten minutes. It should be empty before lunch then.'

She smiled tentatively, feeling a little uncertain as she watched him head for his office. It seemed the longest ten minutes ever as she worked at her sewing machine watching the hands of the wall-mounted clock slowly shuffle around.

Nervously, at the allotted time, she sat in the restroom clasping and unclasping her hands. Her mouth felt dry. Then the door opened and Francis walked in, closing it behind himself. Taking a seat beside her, he settled down.

'I've brought you here to let you know I've seen some of your designs.'

Betsan's face grew hot. 'You have?' Oh dear. Was he about to get angry with her?

'Yes, they fell out of a desk drawer when the cleaners had been in over the weekend.'

'But how did you know they were mine?' She blinked.

'Because they were signed.'

In amongst her confusion, she hadn't remembered she always put her initials to all her sketches. Just small letters at the corner of the page. 'I see. And you're annoyed?'

'No. Not at all. They're very good. In fact, I'd say you have a flair for design. Maybe one day...'

Maybe one day what? There was a long pause. 'What are you thinking?'

'Just that maybe one day there might be a position here for you as my personal assistant. I knew you were talented but I never realised you were capable of such designs.'

'I used to call them my little scribbles. I've been sketching for years. I'd often draw the gowns Mam made when I was a little girl. It's just something I've carried on with.'

'I could put a good word in with Mr Arden!' said Francis brightly. 'Maybe in a year or so you might come on board as part of the designing team as my official assistant. Would you like that, Betsan?'

Clasping her hands together, she smiled. 'Oh yes, I really would.'

'Then you have my word. For the time being you're doing a great job as a sewing machinist and supervisor to the new girls, as well as helping me, of course. You're young yet, but I'm confident your time will come, my girl.' He stood and then he placed a reassuring hand on her shoulder and whispered in her ear, 'Someday that ship of yours will come in for sure...'

Betsan didn't know where that particular ship was headed at the moment but for the first time she imagined she could see it out there on the horizon.

* * *

Fancy she, Betsan Morgan, was going to be a designer's personal assistant someday! It was far more than she had ever dreamt of. She was floating on air after speaking with Francis and decided to rush home to tell Aunt Mags the good news, but when she made to leave the factory, Jimmy was stood outside and, by the expression on his face, she realised something was badly wrong.

Jimmy walked tentatively towards her and took her hand.

'Whatever it is, please don't tell me. Not today of all days,' Betsan whispered, her bottom lip trembling. 'It's Dad, isn't it?' She began to think about what Mrs Parry-Jones had told her regarding her father's assessment that he 'posed a risk to himself'. Had he finally given up all hope? She bit her lip as she felt the tears begin to flow. It had already been a morning charged with emotion for her and now she knew in her heart her emotions were about to plummet.

'No, Betsan,' he said softly, giving her hand a gentle squeeze. A couple of factory girls brushed past them, glancing in their direction. They must have wondered what was going on. 'Look, let's go over to the bench across the way and I'll explain. But this is nothing whatsoever to do with your father, love. He's safe and well.'

She nodded and in a daze allowed Jimmy to lead her over in the direction of the parish church. Everything around her seemed blurred as her eyes glazed and they sat together on the bench. He dipped into his jacket pocket and handed her a hand-kerchief. 'Blot your eyes, love, you don't want them to look all puffy. I think you may need to take the afternoon off work if they'll allow it.'

She took the handkerchief from him and dabbed at her eyes. 'I don't understand, Jimmy. Is it my auntie?'

'No, love,' he said softly, and he stroked her cheek with tenderness as he looked into her eyes. 'It's Mrs Jenkins...'

Betsan's breath hitched in her throat. 'But what's happened?' Her eyes widened. 'We only saw her at the fashion show about a week ago.'

'She's passed on. I'm sorry to be the one to have to tell you. Mags sent me to see you as soon as she found out.'

Passed on? That could mean anything. She needed to say the words but once she did so, she knew that made them real. 'You mean she's dead?'

Jimmy nodded. 'I'm afraid so. A customer on the market stall told Mags this morning.'

It felt as though someone had socked her in the stomach – it was as if all the air was now being sucked out of her lungs. She drew in a deep breath and let it out again. 'But how? Why?' Betsan felt panicked now. The last time she'd set eyes on the woman she did seemed to have slowed up a little but seemed all right otherwise.

'Her husband told the woman she'd had a weak heart for a long time. I suppose it's a wonder she lasted as long as she did.'

'That's true. I remember how her lips would turn blue some-times and she seemed out of breath, yet at the fashion show last week she seemed so full of life.'

'That's because she was so happy for you and to see all that you've achieved, Betsan. She was so very proud of you.'

A tear trickled down Betsan's face and she dabbed away at it. 'I've just thought of something, Jimmy...'

'What's that, love?'

'Mrs Jenkins will never know now what good news I had today. I'd love to have told her. Francis Bradbury, the designer you all saw at the show last week, found my designs and he really likes them and thinks someday I might have some sort of future in the fashion industry. He said he'd eventually like me to join the design team as his personal assistant when I'm a little older. I think when the time is right he'll approach Mr Arden about it.'

'That's brilliant news!' Jimmy's eyes lit up. 'I'm so pleased for you. But how did all that come about?'

She let out a composing breath. 'It seems some of my designs were discovered having fallen out of a desk drawer when the cleaners were in at the weekend, and Francis was very impressed with them.'

'That's wonderful. I always knew you were hiding your light under a bushel somewhere.' He chuckled, and then as if realising maybe this wasn't the time for such merriment added, 'Come on, let's take you back over to the factory and you can explain to Mr Arden about receiving such shocking news and ask for time off.'

She nodded, reminding herself of that line from *A Tale of Two Cities*: 'It was the best of times, it was the worst of times...' It certainly felt that way today.

* * *

The day of the funeral was dark and dismal, reminding Betsan of when her mother had died. Although that had been a few years ago and she'd been little more than a child at that time, being twelve years old. Now she was considered a young woman, yet today, in her mind, she was that young girl once again.

She and Mags had offered to help at Mrs Jenkins's house cutting sandwiches and greeting the guests. All told, there were only a few neighbours and friends there, but someone who showed up that would have amused Bronwen herself was Elinor. Even she, given time, had grown fond of the woman and Bronwen of her.

As they were buttering bread in the scullery, Mags turned to Betsan. 'How are you feeling today, love?' she whispered.

'Oh, I'll cope, Auntie Mags,' Betsan said stoically.

'That's good. I know it's a difficult time for you as Bronwen was like another mother to you, darling. I've had a thought. Now stop me if you think I'm going too far, but have you considered moving back in next door for a while? I'm not trying to get rid of you or anything and you won't be there all alone, as most days I'll be popping back and forth to work on the sewing machine as I always do.'

No, in truth, Betsan hadn't even considered that, even though she was making the rent payments on the property. 'I suppose if I did, I could always keep an eye on Bert. He looks like he could do with some feeding up since…'

'I know what you mean. He's missing her dreadfully and she was always so kind to you and the twins.' Mags laid down her butter knife on the counter as if in quiet reflection for a moment as Betsan began to arrange the buttered slices of bread on a large serving plate.

'Not just to you, but Mrs Jenkins was kind to everyone.' Their heads turned to see Elinor stood there in the doorway with tears in her eyes. 'I wish I'd appreciated her more when she was alive.'

'Come in and sit yourself down,' said Mags. 'I think we're all upset today.'

Elinor rubbed her eyes and then took a seat at the scrubbed pine table. 'It's just that I was so offhand with her when I first met her.'

Betsan remembered it well. Sparks seemed to fly in every direction when those two were in the same room to begin with. Mrs Jenkins had even refused to enter the house when Elinor was in it at one point. She laid a hand of reassurance on Elinor's shoulder. 'She wouldn't want you to reprimand yourself today of all days. Mrs Jenkins had a very forgiving nature.'

Elinor nodded and smiled through her tears. 'Yes, she did. Now then, can I be of any help?'

Mags beamed. 'That's the spirit – come and pitch in with us. We don't do things as well as Mrs Jenkins did but I think she'll forgive us on this occasion!' Mags chuckled. 'One thing you can do, Elinor, is keep Reverend Glanmor Griffiths well topped up.'

'With tea?' Elinor raised a brow.

'No, brandy!' Betsan laughed, telling her what he'd been like at her mother's funeral. The man was quite elderly now and his services not quite as booming as they'd been, but she knew he'd appreciate a glass or two before he gave a short service at the house.

In the event, the day of Bronwen Jenkins's funeral was not as sad as Betsan had imagined it to be. It was heart-warming to hear so many testimonies of all the good things she'd done for folk and all the wonderful things they had to say about her. Betsan took comfort from the fact that Mrs Jenkins and her mother were going to have a good natter with one another up in heaven just like they did when mam had said she was 'popping next door' and Dad had raised his eyebrows, realising she'd be gone for quite some time.

I hope you're both chatting your heads off up there, thought Betsan with a smile as she placed her key in the lock of her house next door.

25

The following few months were difficult for Betsan as she came to terms with Mrs Jenkins's death. She didn't feel too alone in the house though as Mags was there sewing in the daytime so she'd see her sometimes when she'd return home from the factory. Other times, Jimmy would call for a chat and she'd often pop in next door to check on Bert. Work at the pit was saving Bert's sanity. He was a quiet man who didn't say a lot about things but she guessed he must be feeling a large part of himself was now missing.

Betsan managed to visit her father a few times a week at the workhouse. He was keeping up his spirits though she feared he'd get upset to learn of Mrs Jenkins's death and she was going to keep it from him, but Mrs Parry-Jones had reassured her that the truth was best, telling her that learning about it unexpectedly might set back his progress, especially as he and her mother had been so close to the woman. It was Bronwen who had helped them get their first proper home and Bronwen who had cared for the children. She'd always been there for them all and now her absence created a big gulf in their lives.

Betsan's new role as the personal assistant to Francis Bradbury kept her busy and from dwelling too much on things. There were lots of tasks to organise including another upcoming fashion show for the new designs they'd been working on together. Extra machinists and cutters had been employed especially at the company. Joshua Arden had been busy drumming up business by meeting with buyers from various department stores in the area, even as far away as Cardiff. The plans to open new stores were also in force. All in all, life was on the up at the factory, but although Betsan's professional life was going extremely well, something or someone was missing. There was a void that needed to be filled.

* * *

Elinor had asked Betsan if she might take care of Isobelle one afternoon, which was unusual, but she had some hours owing to her so she agreed. The little girl was like a smaller version of her mother, very pretty with dark hair and thick fringed eyelashes. Betsan had baked some cakes especially for her. She loved jam tarts and iced sponge fingers so Betsan had set around making those in time for her arrival. Then she intended to allow the little girl to spoon on the icing mix herself as she enjoyed helping out.

They'd had a wonderful time together playing upstairs with Betsan's old dolls, then they'd iced the sponge fingers and Betsan spent the rest of the time with Isobelle curled up on the couch as she read her fairy stories from a book the child had brought with her. She was getting sleepy and her mother still hadn't arrived. It was most unusual. Betsan glanced at the mantel clock and sighed. It was now seven o'clock and her half-sister had been with her for almost five hours. Where on earth was Elinor? Had something happened to her?

Betsan was considering wrapping Isobelle up in her shawl and calling to Florrie's place to see if Elinor was there when she heard the front door opening. It had been left on the latch. But then she heard voices coming down the passageway, an unmistakable male voice!

The living room door burst open and Betsan gently removed herself from Isobelle's side as she went hurtling towards the door. 'Dad!' she shouted as she ran into his arms and he embraced her for the longest time as Elinor sat beside her daughter.

'Oh, Betsan!' he said as he wiped her tear-stained cheeks with the pads of his thumbs. 'It's so good to be here at long last! I never thought I'd be allowed home!'

Betsan swallowed hard, her eyes wide and questioning. 'So, you're home for good?'

'You'd better believe it!' He wiped away his own tears with the back of his hand.

Betsan turned to glance at her stepmother. 'So, does that mean that...?'

'That we're back here living together as husband and wife so we can be a family again?' Elinor nodded. 'Yes, we intend to give it a go!'

Betsan could hardly believe it. Tears of joy coursed down her cheeks. 'That's wonderful!'

Elinor rose from the couch to join the embrace. 'I'm so pleased for us all to be together again. We must celebrate our reunion but before we do anything, and your father and I have discussed this,' she said, breaking away from them, 'there's something that needs putting right first.'

'Oh?' said Betsan, wondering what on earth Elinor was referring to.

'Yes.' Her father nodded. 'I'll go and fetch it right away. I know it was put back after you left the workhouse...'

Betsan was trying to fathom what was going on here. What was put back? Nothing was making sense. Then she watched as her father left the room and she heard his boots on the stairs as he ascended them. All the while Elinor had a little smile on her face. She moved over to the couch and lifted a sleepy Isobelle into her arms. 'I want Izzy to see this too,' she said.

'But what?'

'You'll just have to wait and see.'

It was a couple more minutes until Betsan heard her father's footsteps descend the stairs and there was the sound of him moving around in the passageway. 'You can come out and see now!' he announced.

Tentatively, Betsan went through the living room door and stepped into the passageway. Dad had hung some sort of gilt-edged painting on the wall. It wasn't until she had turned properly to view it that she realised just what he'd done.

Elinor was now stood behind her with Izzy in her arms and she felt the woman's free hand on her shoulder. 'It's where it should be, for all to see,' she whispered. 'Not left in the attic.'

Izzy stirred herself to gaze at the painting. 'Who's that pretty lady?' She pointed at the portrait.

'That's my mother,' said Betsan as she smiled at her father and she blinked away the tears. These were tears of happiness. Mrs Jenkins had kindly taken care of that painting when they'd been at the workhouse for fear they'd lose the house. Elinor must have asked Mr and Mrs Jenkins to return it to the attic at some point.

'Come on,' said Elinor softly. 'I'll just put this one to bed and then I'll make us something to eat.'

Betsan and her father looked at one another as Elinor took Izzy up the stairs to bed.

'Your mother would be so proud of you,' he said as he kissed her cheek. 'And so am I.' She watched her father head off towards the living room, probably to seek out his favourite armchair.

As she gazed a final time at her mother's portrait, she thought she heard her whisper, *All will be well from now on, Betsan my love, all will be well...*

ACKNOWLEDGMENTS

I was delighted to find myself working with Emily Yau once again. Emily has the ability as an editor to weave her magic by making my stories sparkle and shine. Thank you, Emily, for your guidance and insight with this book. Also many thanks to all the team at Boldwood. It's been a pleasure working with each and every one of you.

ABOUT THE AUTHOR

Lynette Rees is the bestselling author of several historical fiction titles and lives in Wales.

Sign up to Lynette Rees' mailing list here for news, competitions and updates on future books.

Visit Lynette's website: www.lynetterees.wordpress.com

Follow Lynette on social media:

facebook.com/authorlynetterees

x.com/LynetteRees0

instagram.com/booksbylynetterees7

bookbub.com/authors/lynette-rees

Sixpence Stories

Introducing Sixpence Stories!

Discover page-turning
historical novels from your
favourite authors, meet new
friends and be transported
back in time.

Join our book club
Facebook group

https://bit.ly/SixpenceGroup

Sign up to our
newsletter

https://bit.ly/SixpenceNews

Boldwood

Boldwood Books is an award-winning fiction publishing company seeking out the best stories from around the world.

Find out more at www.boldwoodbooks.com

Join our reader community for brilliant books, competitions and offers!

Follow us
@BoldwoodBooks
@TheBoldBookClub

Sign up to our weekly deals newsletter

https://bit.ly/BoldwoodBNewsletter

Printed in Great Britain
by Amazon

37070954R00169